Create your own
'Done for you'
Short Sale System

Monica Adams

Ryan,
You are the greatest
partner! Keep Believing,
stay Positive & Never
give up.
monica Adams

Important Notice and Disclaimer

Pink Short Sale Mentor

Monica Adams

Copyright © 2011 Monica Adams, MBS
Published by
New Covenant Publishing
www.newcovenantpublishing.com

Contact information for Monica Adams
2760 N Academy Blvd., Suite 201
Colorado Springs, CO 80917
Telephone (719) 471-PINK (7465)
www.PinkShortSaleMentor.com

Contents

Acknowledgements

I would like to first and foremost thank my mentor Deborah. Without you, I don't think I would be where I am today. You took me under your wing and showed me everything about the short sale business. You didn't have to do what you did, but you did, and I don't have words to express how much I value and honor you. I would also like to thank Jeff. For eight years you told me real estate was the only way to true wealth. If you hadn't engrained that into my head, I would probably be working for the FBI right now, risking my life. You were also the one who introduced me to books regarding your mind and the power we all have within. These books and the theories contained in them changed my life.

I would like to thank my mom, dad and brother for always supporting and believing in me. I want to give special thanks to my partner Russ for always looking out for both of us by making sure we complied with the laws and sought legal advice when we needed it most. I'm so thrilled we share the same interests. There is no better match for me. We both have the same drive and love for real estate, and I'm blessed to be able to share that with you. I also want to thank my entire team for always working so hard and taking pride in helping homeowners. I know your work can be stressful; I just wanted you to know how much I value and appreciate each and every one of you. I love you all so much!

I would also like to thank Dr. Joseph Murphy for his teachings. Although he passed only a few days after I was born, the information in his books contributed greatly to my success. He taught me the power of my own beliefs and how I could achieve anything I wanted as long as I believed. I know that applying his teachings to my life helped me achieve all my goals. After reading his books and making his lessons a true part of my life, I have always been able to get what I asked for. This is because I believed I would! He taught me the power of positive thinking, and I believe that applying positive thinking in all aspects of my life is the primary reason I never lost any money or made a bad decision that affected my life negatively.

Introduction

Short sales are my favorite strategy for acquiring a good deal. As an investor, it seems like every deal out there is a short sale. This is primarily because no one has equity in their homes anymore. The MLS has no deals listed. The truth is, I always get outbid and learn there are several other offers on the table within an hour after a good deal is published in the MLS. Who wants that kind of competition? I certainly don't! As a result, I like to create and be in full control of my deals. I use short sale deals to find my fix-and-flip deals, or I use short sales to sell immediately to a retail buyer for a quick profit.

In the years I have been selling and working short sale deals, I have definitely learned the "ins and outs" of the industry and know all the "what to do's" and the "what not to do's." When I first started, I handled every aspect of every deal because I wanted to be in full control. I would:

- Take and answer all the calls
- Meet with the homeowners
- Negotiate the short sale
- Sell to my end buyer

It wasn't long before I was absolutely overwhelmed and going nuts. Before I knew it, my partner and I were both working 100 hours per week—a combined 200 hours of work every week! I was feeling like I was working at a high-stressed, high-paying job. But I didn't want the high stress. I quickly learned I had to put a system into place that would streamline everything so we were working smarter and not harder.

Accomplishing that, today I have my system so everything is completely done for me; the system is on autopilot. All I do now is manage my system. In this book, I will show you how to create your own system, and I will let you know how you can partner with me so you don't have to go through the headaches that I went through. I will show you how to create your system with little or no money up front. I will do this by showing you all of the aspects of the business, which you will need before you can put your system into place. Then I will show you my "Done for You Short Sale System."

Overview

Short sales are a great way to make money. They have always been around, but today, with the decline in the real estate market, short sales are a popular item, and their popularity is expected to remain for at least the next five years or more. During this time, you have the opportunity to rake in the big bucks! This enormous opportunity is available to both real estate agents and investors. You can make very good money working short sales, and you can help homeowners avoid foreclosure at the same time.

You may have heard negative things about short sales on the street. Things like, "They don't work," "They take too long," or "They don't pay much." These are myths. Once you learn more about short sales and how to negotiate them, you will see that these comments aren't true. When you have a good system in place, short sales are an easy way to make an additional $10K per month. Depending on your motivation and determination, your earning potential is unlimited. Should you move into luxury home investing, you have the opportunity to earn up to $100K per deal!

Don't get me wrong, short sales take time and effort, but if you have a streamlined system in place, most of the work is done for you, and you get to reap the financial rewards. A key component for being successful in the short sale business is learning all you can about the industry, the process and successful negotiating. Another key component for success is building your pipeline and setting up your system so the work can be outsourced. Once you have the knowledge and experience, you will see how easy it is. After reading this book, you will have the knowledge and tools you need to become a short sale expert.

Each month approximately 250,000 homes go into foreclosure nationally. This means there is a steady stream of deals coming into the marketplace to allow enough deals for everyone. While this is a good time for you to make money, it is also an opportunity to help communities and homeowners alike. Being successful in the short sale business allows you to help homeowners avoid foreclosure and keep neighborhoods from losing more market value. You will become the homeowner's savior. They will be grateful when you save their house from foreclosure. Their appreciation will bring you a continuous stream of referrals!

Earning Potential

To give you an idea of what your earning potential is working this program, here is just a small example of what you can earn:

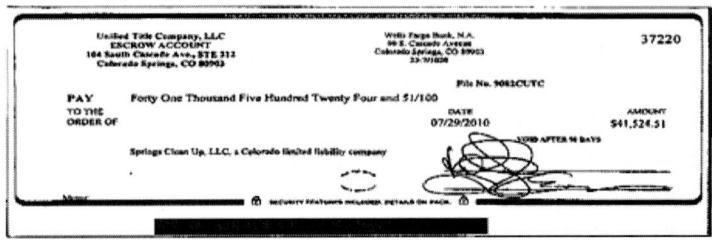

Unified Title Company, LLC
ESCROW ACCOUNT
104 South Cascade Ave., STE 212
Colorado Springs, CO 80903

Wells Fargo Bank, N.A.
90 S. Cascade Avenue
Colorado Springs, CO 80903
23-7/1020

37220

File No. 9082CUTC

PAY TO THE ORDER OF Forty One Thousand Five Hundred Twenty Four and 51/100

DATE 07/29/2010   AMOUNT $41,524.51

Springs Clean Up, LLC, a Colorado limited liability company

VOID AFTER 90 DAYS

SECURITY FEATURES INCLUDED. DETAILS ON BACK.

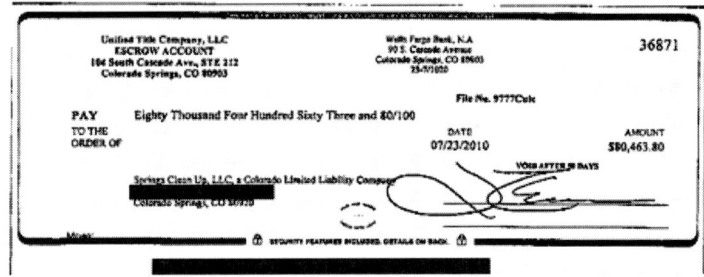

Unified Title Company, LLC
ESCROW ACCOUNT
104 South Cascade Ave., STE 212
Colorado Springs, CO 80903

Wells Fargo Bank, N.A.
90 S. Cascade Avenue
Colorado Springs, CO 80903
23-7/1020

36871

File No. 9777Cutc

PAY TO THE ORDER OF Eighty Thousand Four Hundred Sixty Three and 80/100

DATE 07/23/2010   AMOUNT $80,463.80

Springs Clean Up, LLC, a Colorado Limited Liability Company
Colorado Springs, CO 80920

VOID AFTER 90 DAYS

SECURITY FEATURES INCLUDED. DETAILS ON BACK.

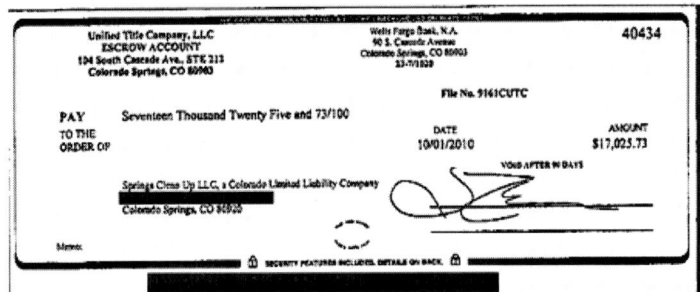

Unified Title Company, LLC
ESCROW ACCOUNT
104 South Cascade Ave., STE 212
Colorado Springs, CO 80903

Wells Fargo Bank, N.A.
90 S. Cascade Avenue
Colorado Springs, CO 80903
23-7/1020

40434

File No. 9161CUTC

PAY TO THE ORDER OF Seventeen Thousand Twenty Five and 73/100

DATE 10/01/2010   AMOUNT $17,025.73

Springs Clean Up LLC, a Colorado Limited Liability Company
Colorado Springs, CO 80920

VOID AFTER 90 DAYS

SECURITY FEATURES INCLUDED. DETAILS ON BACK.

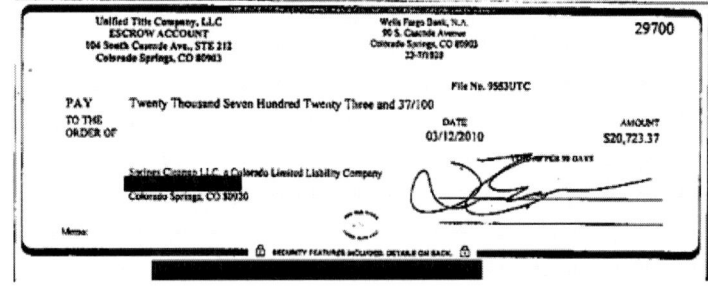

Unified Title Company, LLC
ESCROW ACCOUNT
104 South Cascade Ave., STE 212
Colorado Springs, CO 80903

Wells Fargo Bank, N.A.
90 S. Cascade Avenue
Colorado Springs, CO 80903
23-7/1020

29700

File No. 9583UTC

PAY TO THE ORDER OF Twenty Thousand Seven Hundred Twenty Three and 37/100

DATE 03/12/2010   AMOUNT $20,723.37

Springs Cleanup LLC, a Colorado Limited Liability Company
Colorado Springs, CO 80920

VOID AFTER 90 DAYS

SECURITY FEATURES INCLUDED. DETAILS ON BACK.

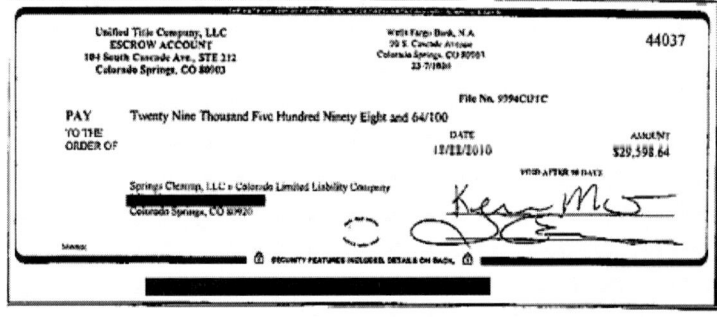

Unified Title Company, LLC
ESCROW ACCOUNT
104 South Cascade Ave., STE 212
Colorado Springs, CO 80903

Wells Fargo Bank, N.A.
90 S. Cascade Avenue
Colorado Springs, CO 80903
23-7/1020

44037

File No. 9094CUTC

PAY TO THE ORDER OF Twenty Nine Thousand Five Hundred Ninety Eight and 64/100

DATE 12/13/2010   AMOUNT $29,598.64

Springs Cleanup, LLC a Colorado Limited Liability Company
Colorado Springs, CO 80920

VOID AFTER 90 DAYS

SECURITY FEATURES INCLUDED. DETAILS ON BACK.

Create your own *Done for you* Short Sale System

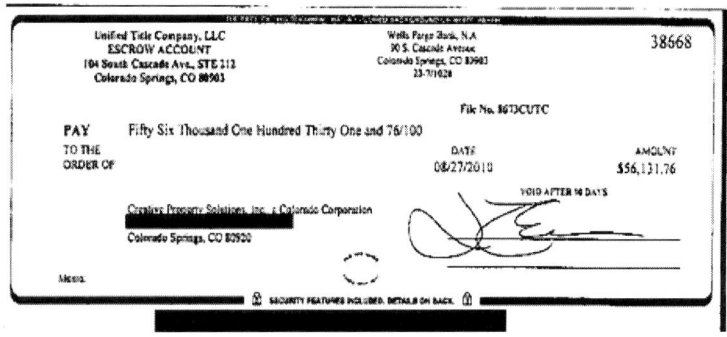

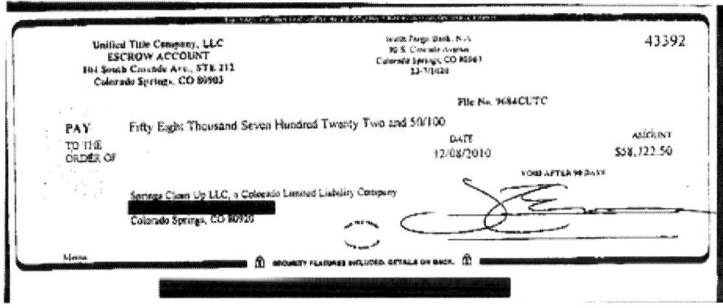

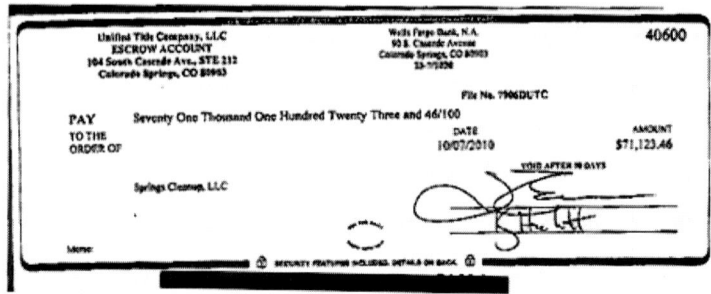

Unified Title Company, LLC
ESCROW ACCOUNT
104 South Cascade Ave., STE 212
Colorado Springs, CO 80903

Wells Fargo Bank, N.A.
90 S. Cascade Avenue
Colorado Springs, CO 80903
23-7/1220

40600

File No. 7906DUTC

PAY
TO THE
ORDER OF

Seventy One Thousand One Hundred Twenty Three and 46/100

DATE
10/07/2010

AMOUNT
$71,123.46

VOID AFTER 90 DAYS

Springs Cleanup, LLC

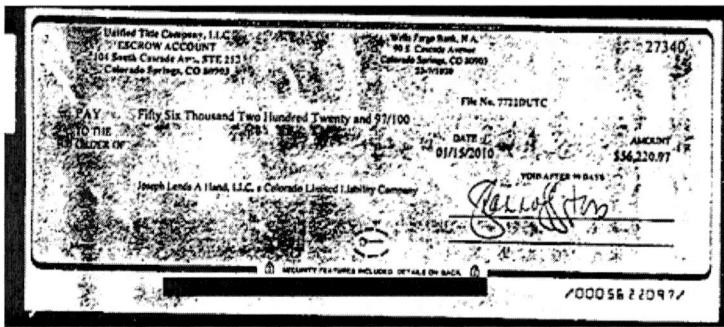

Unified Title Company, LLC
ESCROW ACCOUNT
104 South Cascade Ave., STE 212
Colorado Springs, CO 80903

Wells Fargo Bank, N.A.
90 S. Cascade Avenue
Colorado Springs, CO 80903
23-7/1220

27340

File No. 7721DUTC

PAY
TO THE
ORDER OF

Fifty Six Thousand Two Hundred Twenty and 97/100

DATE
01/15/2010

AMOUNT
$56,220.97

VOID AFTER 90 DAYS

Joseph Lends A Hand, LLC, a Colorado Limited Liability Company

/000 56 220 97/

Your Secret Weapon—"Believe in Yourself!"

This program is so easy anyone can do it! I have many students who come to my one-day seminars and my three-day boot camps to learn my system. Now I am giving you the opportunity to learn my system by reading my book. If you are wondering why I am so willing to share all my knowledge and information, it's because I want you to be successful like me! And you can. We all have the ability to be successful. But the truth about success is that it starts from within you. It starts by changing your internal thoughts about how you feel. Once you do that, the world is in your hands. You literally have the ability to have anything you want as long as your internal thoughts truly reflect what you want in your life and what you believe you can achieve.

If you don't believe this, I am here to let you know that my success today is a direct result of changing my own belief system. I was 25 years old when I started. My brother, who stutters over his words when he gets nervous or talks too fast, was able to do this. He was only 19 years old when he bought his first house. If you are still a skeptic, keep reading. I will show you just how easy this is. I will prove to you that you too can do this.

If after reading my book you still feel lost or unsure, don't worry. You can attend one of my boot camp classes, or you can purchase my home study course. I am here for you, and I will be your coach. In addition to my classes and home study courses, I offer one-on-one mentoring to help you with any trouble spots you may encounter.

When I got started, I had a personal coach who took my hand and taught me everything I needed to know. I wanted to learn as much as I could, so I attended as many boot camp classes and purchased as many home study courses as I could. I took advantage of every opportunity I could find to learn everything about the industry. Between my attitude, motivation and determination, I achieved the success I knew I wanted and deserved.

Monica Adams

How I got started: My own inspiring story as a 25-year-old Police Department Fingerprint Girl with absolutely no money!

Before I started my career in real estate, my dream was to become a crime scene investigator. I went to school and received my bachelor's degree in criminology and my master's degree in forensic science. I began working at the police department as a finger printer in hopes of working my way up to be a crime scene investigator. I wanted this so much that I did an internship in the crime lab in between my hours working as a finger printer.

I really thought this was what I wanted to do with my life until I realized the program CSI on TV did not depict the real life of a crime scene investigator! I quickly realized I would be on call 24 hours a day. I learned most crimes happen over the weekends and holidays, so if I pursued this career, I would never have time to spend with my family and friends. After working at the police department, I also realized I would not be qualified for a position in the crime lab until I gained real street life experience. This meant I had to become a police officer first. I didn't want to be a police officer and risk my life!

It didn't take long for me to realize this was NOT what I wanted to do with my life, so I began looking at other career options. This is when I started seriously looking into real estate investment. I knew real estate was a way to true wealth, so in March 2007 I purchased several books and home study courses and got started. The books and classes weren't enough for me, so I started attending local investment club meetings and found mentorship programs that provided more information. I attended several "boot camp" programs and monthly support meetings. The programs were incredibly valuable and offered a wealth of information. However, after completing them, I realized I still needed more help. I met Deb, a short sale expert, at one of the boot camp programs I attended. She took me under her wing and became my mentor. She taught me how to put short sale packages together, and she let me listen in on conversations with the banks so I could learn the various negotiation techniques. I went on several appointments with her to get more hands-on experience. Once I felt comfortable enough, I began helping Deb negotiate her short sales for more experience. I worked for Deb several hours a day. If I had questions, she was there to help me. Eventually I became comfortable enough to start doing my own deals and negotiating them by myself.

I continued working the midnight shift at the police department. After my shift, I would go home and work my real estate deals for a few hours and then get some sleep.

I knew I had to work hard if I was going to meet my goals and realize my dreams.

When I ventured out on my own, I knew the most important thing would be getting leads into a system and filling up my pipeline. I started with one simple ad in the paper to start generating leads and I became a local affiliate for a lead generating website, www.cashhomebuyers.com. I had no money in the bank when I started this venture, but I believed I could make real estate investment work for me, so I charged all the education costs and beginning marketing costs to my credit card.

I signed up my first deal in the summer of 2007 and before I knew it, I had 20 active short sales. Between the police department and working these deals, I lived on only a few hours of sleep a night. When I got home from work at 7 a.m., I would begin calling banks and negotiating my short sales. Then I would sleep for a few hours before I would get up and go on appointments to meet with homeowners who needed my help.

In October 2007 I closed my first deal and had 40 more in my pipeline. I only made $3,000 on that first deal, but I was very excited. That $3,000 income was twice as much as what I made working at the police department. This was only my first deal, but as I learned more, I knew my profits would get larger, and I would get to where I would have one or more closings per week. Even if I only made $3,000 per closing and had four closings per month, I would be financially set. But I aspired to make more money I wanted to become a millionaire!

Eventually all of my short sale deals started to close one after another, and I was making money hand over fist. In April 2008, I was able to quit my job at the police department. I was beginning to realize my dream only one year after I got started . . . and I was still learning.

It was only six months from my first closing when I had enough money in the bank to support myself for two years, which was my safety net in case something didn't go right with my short sale business. Today, I am my own boss, I set my own schedule, I have time for my family and friends, I can go on vacation when I want and I am experiencing the financial freedom I dreamed of.

I absolutely love real estate and what it has done for me personally and financially. I make a ton of money doing what I love to do, and I am always happy. My significant other and I met through real estate meetings and became partners. We now work together every day, and this is the greatest feeling in the world.

Anyone who is an action taker can do what I did. I was 25 years old when I got started and had absolutely no money in the bank. It just takes a little training, confidence and a positive attitude to be successful in this business. Some people will be able to read through this book and begin working on their short sale business immediately. Others may need a little extra guidance and coaching like I did. I had my mentor who was my one-on-one coach to teach and guide me every step of the way, and I am so grateful for her help. I don't think I would be where I am today if it weren't for her help. Today, I can be your mentor if you need that extra help!

Mentorship Program and Home Study Course

We offer many different mentorship options; however,

the primary mentorship program includes a "Boot Camp" course that teaches you everything you need to know about short sales. This course includes live negotiations with banks and email and fax negotiations. Many times, you don't have to pick up the phone to call a negotiator as a lot of deals are negotiated online.

After the boot camp course is finished, I meet with students once a month to go over new changes in the short sale business and offer additional training. Additionally, my students are free to call me with any questions. They are also welcome to email me or come to my office whenever they need help. I want you to be successful like me, and I am here to help you!

If you are not completely satisfied with this program, we offer a 100% money back guarantee.

Please go to **www.PinkShortSaleMentor.com** to sign up or send me an email at **Monica@PinkShortSaleMentor. com.**

Pink Real Estate and Pink Realty Available for Franchise

Pink Real Estate and Pink Realty are now being offered as franchise businesses for other investors who want to use my proven marketing, branding and investing strategies. All marketing and phone numbers are in PINK, and we are a local sponsor for the Susan G. Komen Foundation. Our branding theme is very unique and gets a lot of attention because it stands out from the others, and people love and respect our sponsorship.

Having a Pink Realty franchise along with a Pink Real Estate franchise allows for a higher level of cash flow because you can hire agents to work for you, and you receive income from all of their closings. Even if you don't do anything, you will get paid as long as the agents are producing closings! Or, you can set up monthly desk fees where agents pay you, whether they have closings or not.

If you would like more information about franchise opportunities, please go to the website:

www.PinkShortSaleMentor.com/PinkBusiness

or you can call us directly at (719) 471-PINK or email me at

Monica@PinkShortSaleMentor.com.

Customer Testimonials

Dear Monica,

Arely and I can't express in words how grateful we are for you buying our home while under foreclosure, so all we will simply say is thank you. As you know, I am on disability and after just two years in the home, I could no longer go up the stairs to the bedroom. We could no longer afford the mortgage. All we could do is let the house go. We entered into foreclosure. We had lots of offers to sell the home but you were the only one offering to buy the home and in addition get a $1000.00 check. I didn't believe you until you knocked on the door and still decided to take the mortgage off my hands with nothing being owed on the house.

I am now a believer because we closed and I received a $1000.00 check free and clear. I will recommend you to anyone that is in the same situation I was in.

So please accept our gratitude.

Sincerely,

Chiwon and Arely

My husband & I were on the verge of loosing our home to foreclosure. I met w/ Veronica & 2 days later our home was listed on the market. The whole Pink Realty team was awesome. They took ALL of the stress off myself & my husband. They worked very hard on our behalf! I would recommend Pink Realty to anyone! Pink Realty saved us from foreclosure and we were able to successfully sell our home!

Thank you to the whole Pink Realty Team!!

Jennifer & Raymond King

Hi Monica,

I ran across your flyer today with my family pic and story and it brought me back to when you helped us so much. I never got a real chance to thank you. To be 100% honest I was very skeptical until I received the letter from our finance company that we were free and clear with a 0 balance. I was so worried the remaining balance wouldn't be cleared and that we would have yet another worry but that wasn't the case, I was amazed! Thank you again so much. You truly are honest and amazing!

Christina, Scott, and kids

Hi Monica:

To say that Monica Adam's Short Sale Training is comprehensive is an understatement. I have been a full time real estate investor since 2004, and have specialized in Short Sales since 2005. This industry is ever changing and can be difficult to navigate at times due to constant rule and timeline changes. Monica takes a step by step approach to investing in short sales and breaks everything down into manageable pieces. Her wealth of knowledge is incredible, and she has put together a very thorough training program that will get you started down the right path immediately.

—Ryan

March 29, 2011

Pink Realty

Attention: Veronica Gurule

Dear Veronica, and the rest of the Pink Realty Team,

It is with our deepest gratitude that Sharon and I write this letter to you today. We want the City of Colorado Springs to know how happy we are with the professional courtesy, honesty, and sincerity in which you conduct your business. First I will begin by telling our story.

On February 18, 2010 my family and I moved back from South Dakota, having previously leased out our home here in Colorado Springs, CO. We came back home excited to be home again. As the current housing market here in Colorado was very gloomy we had no intention of selling our beautiful home.

While being home just one week later I, learned my mother had been put in the hospital, she was diagnosed with terminal cancer. She passed away on March 28, 2010 close to 40 days after we had been home. My family came to me and asked to help with the proceeds with her funeral.

At the time I had no job and was unemployed. Being of great faith, we juggled around some of our bills and did not make our April house payment to help out. However during the next few months I returned to work in April going to Kansas for three short weeks. I work for a pipeline and spend a lot of time on the road without per-diem so my hotel expenses get pretty expensive. Well I was sent to Utah, during which time I had to use my normal income again to get from point A to B. We fell another house payment behind.

During the months of May through September I continued to work and support the family making most of my house payments on time, still two payments behind. Well Labor Day rolled around and I decided to come back from Utah to visit the family. It was while I was on the plane home I got sick on 5 September 2010 and had to go to the hospital.

I was diagnosed with Diabetes Type II. I was unable to return to work, so in September I could not make our house payment of $1911.00 because we had a 7.6 percent loan rate. Well we were three months behind in our payments so we were getting nervous as any other American is in today's market.

Facing foreclosure and nowhere to turn my wife seen a Pink Realty sign on a bus stop chair. We called the number and met with Veronica Gurule; she sat down and explained how easy the process would be to sell our home in 90 days. Well to make a long story short and to thank everyone at Pink Realty we sold our home today exactly one year after all our troubles started. Most of all we are truly blessed to have placed our faith and situation in your hands.

Thank you truly from the bottom our hearts.
Paul & Sharon

Chapter 1
Changing Your State of Mind

Before you begin any new endeavor, you need to get yourself psyched up for the challenge. To be successful in any part of your life, you need to be in the right state of mind. I chose to start my book with this in mind, because before you get started in investing, you do need to be in the right state of mind. You may get nervous or scared when you are about to try anything new. You may be scared about getting started in this real estate investment endeavor.

Being scared is OK, but not having a positive attitude isn't. The most important thing is to always think positively about the outcome and believe in yourself! If you aren't quite sure that you believe in yourself, this is something you can change. With proper training and with a mentor or coach who can show you what you need to do, your confidence will blossom, your belief in yourself will grow and you will be successful.

Before I started investing in real estate, I came across a very powerful book titled, The Power of Your Subconscious Mind, by Dr. Joseph Murphy. The principles in his books changed my thoughts, my beliefs and my life. There are also other books and movies like The Secret by Rhonda Byrne that can help you change your belief system as well. I recommend these books to everyone. Read them before you get started. Read them while you are learning. Read them again when you have doubts. They can change your life too. A good part of my success today came from applying the principles in these books to my everyday life.

Dear Monica,
I just wanted you to know how much I enjoyed your one day short sale class. I learned a lot, and I already had some knowledge. It was worth the time and money. The best part was the amazing organization you created; so very inspiring. You truly amaze me "". Thanks again! Lisa Robe.

The Power of Your Subconscious Mind

"Your subconscious mind is principle and works according to the law of belief. The law of your mind is the law of belief."[1] What you believe in your mind brings you results from your thoughts. The reactions of your subconscious mind correspond directly with the nature of your thoughts. If you truly believe you are successful and believe you will succeed with this business, you will.

The Power of Suggestion

Your subconscious mind reacts to impressions given by your conscious mind. Most people are surrounded by negativity. It's all around us, and we encounter it wherever we go. It's even more prevalent today with the state of the economy, unemployment, the real estate market, the rate of foreclosures and people losing their homes. You will find that oftentimes the purpose of other people's negative suggestions is to get you to think, feel and act the way they

1 self-improvement-ebooks.com/books/tpoysm.php

do. Misery loves company, and people use their negative attitudes to their advantage. You can't always avoid negative people, but you can counter their negativity by giving your subconscious mind constructive autosuggestion when you are faced with having to deal with other people's negative attitudes.

For example, my mom was my biggest disbeliever. She always had something negative to say, whether it was a negative comment about me quitting my job to do real estate or that she thought I was making the wrong decision and I was going to lose a lot of money. I let her speak her mind, but I never let her negative suggestions stick in my mind or overpower my thoughts and beliefs. I blocked them out, and I would begin giving myself positive suggestions and affirmations. These are the thoughts I allowed to stay in my mind.

I would continuously tell myself, "I can do this, I will quit my job, I will be successful, and I will live the life I have always dreamed about."

3-12-11

After many years of investing and rehaba I decided to expand into the "scary field" of Short sales! Monica's Class has put it into a very easy to follow and understandable system. I would recommend her class or seminar to anyone interested in expanding their knowledge in this area.

Do the things you fear the most and the death of fear is certain

Thank you monica!

Cheryl Utback
Colorado Springs, Colorado

Law of Control

The Law of Control states that we only feel as good about ourselves to the degree in which we feel we are in control of our own lives. When we are physically, mentally and emotionally controlling the changes in our lives, then this naturally leads to greater achievement, emotional satisfaction and a sense of fulfillment.

Law of Cause and Effect

With every cause there is an effect, and with every effect there is a cause. Simply put, "Your thoughts, behaviors and actions create specific **EFFECTS** that manifest and create your life as you know it. If you are not happy with the **EFFECTS** you have created, then you must change the **CAUSES** that created them in the first place... Change Your Actions and you Change your life . . . Transform your thoughts and you will create a brand new destiny." [2]

Law of Expectation

Simply stated, the Law of Expectation tells us that whatever one expects, with confidence, becomes a self-fulfilling prophecy. When one expects with confidence that good things will happen, good things usually happen. If, on the other hand, one expects a negative outcome to a situation, then the outcome is usually negative.

Law of Correspondence

"The Law of Correspondence tells us that our outer world is nothing more than a reflection of our inner world—as within, so without. This is an extraordinary principle and really says that our current reality is a mirror of what is going on inside us. If our outer reality is unhappy, chaotic or unfulfilling it is a direct result of what is happening inside us. If we have low self-esteem, feel badly about ourselves or constantly feel anger, hatred or loathing, then our outer world will be a place of turmoil." [3]

Law of Belief

"The Law of Belief states that whatever you believe with feeling and conviction becomes your reality. It is not until you change your beliefs that you can begin to change your reality and your performance." I believe in myself.[4] I believe I will always be successful, I will always get what I want, I believe that my business will be successful, I believe I will help a lot of people save their homes from foreclosure. I never believe anything bad will happen to me or that I will lose money on a deal.

Law of Attraction

The Law of Attraction states: I attract to myself, whatever I give my focus, attention, or energy to; whether wanted or unwanted. If you focus thoughts about being unsuccessful, broke or lonely, guess what? That is exactly where you will end up . . . unsuccessful, broke and lonely. If, on the other hand, your focus your thoughts on success, prosperity and happiness, this is where you will end up... successful, prosperous and happy. You attract into your life what you believe. This Law applies to your life and every other person's life. Like all laws, it is impartial and impersonal, which means it works when you want it to and

3 ezinearticles.com/?Universal-Law-Series---Law-of-Correspondence&id=111639
4 ezinearticles.com/?Universal-Law-Series---the-Law-of-Belief&id=70997

when you don't want it to.

Everything comes to us through the most elemental laws of physics—The Law of Attraction is simply "like attracts like"! It is absolute and has nothing to do with your personality, your religious beliefs, being a "good" or a "bad" person or anything else. No one lives beyond this law. It is an unquestionable law of the universe.

Imagine starting to believe in yourself and your infinite possibilities. Imagine believing you deserve everything you want out of life. Imagine getting everything you want out of life. The Law of Attraction simply says that you attract into your life whatever you think about. Your dominant thoughts will find a way to manifest themselves. [5]

There are several other character traits that contribute to success, and they all have a "state of mind" attitude in common. Your attitude is a key component to your success.

Visualization

If you continually visualize your dream, you can create the reality of your dream. Visualization is picturing in your mind, with all details attached, that which you want. Visualization creates thought, and thought manifests reality. If you continually visualize defeat, defeat will reign. If you continually visualize your success, success will manifest itself. Through visualization, you have the power to make your dreams come true. When you are visualizing, it should be like having a daydream. For at least 10 minutes a day, visualize what you want. Create a vision board that you can look at every day with everything you want.

5 applying-the-law-of-attraction.com/

Be Positive

I think positive thoughts, and I try to surround myself with positive people. I don't think negative thoughts about myself or my business. I always expect the best for myself and expect increasing success for my business. There are times when you just can't avoid negative people. When I encounter them, I counter their negativity with positive thoughts and just let their attitude go. I never take it personally, and I don't let their thoughts stick in my mind. Your thoughts reflect what happens in your world. If you constantly think positive thoughts, positive things happen. If you constantly think negative thoughts, negative things happen. Just like the law of attraction. Like attracts like!

Be Confident

I am a very confident person, and I portray myself to others as being a confident person. I don't show others any personal insecurity in myself. While it is easier to show confidence when you are an expert in the field, you can still portray confidence in yourself while you are learning. Don't let others see your insecurities. Confidence always sells the deal.

Be a "Go Getter"

It is much easier to move forward and just go for it once you have changed your state of mind. But you can't go anywhere unless you start somewhere, so just get out there and get started! There is nothing wrong with learning as you go. I did! Part of this program is being able to ask questions and get help when you need it. When I had questions, I went to my mentor. I knew what I wanted, and I knew I could ask questions if I got stuck, so I jumped right in head first and got started. So, what are you waiting for?

Don't Give Up!

I don't give up on anything! I fight to the very end no matter how many setbacks I may have. Even if you fail, don't give up! With each failure, you are only one step away from victory. Failure allows us to learn, so while you may encounter failure, use the experience positively and believe in your success.

Set Goals and Stick to Them!

Goals should be realistic, so be sure to set reasonable goals for yourself, your business and your personal life. My first year's goals were goals to get me started. As I evaluated the goals I had accomplished, I began setting more aggressive goals for myself. Each year, as I evaluated past goals, I was realizing I was accomplishing more than I had set out to accomplish. Setting goals and evaluating your progress keeps you focused, keeps your career growing and gives you the added confidence boost when you realize you have exceeded your own goals!

Don't Doubt Yourself

Doubting yourself can be the biggest factor in holding yourself back. If you don't believe in yourself and send messages to yourself that you can't do this, or you will never be able to do this, you won't be successful. If you carry this attitude with you, then no, you won't be successful. Change your thinking! Change is not always easy, but once you change your thinking from negative to positive, your doubts begin to go away and you begin to manifest the positive. Don't doubt yourself!

You Can't Fail

Your only failure is to give up and stop trying. With each failure you are one step closer to your ultimate success. Most investors fail because they give up or they never really put forth the effort. If you put out the effort, stay in the right state of mind and follow my program, you will succeed!

Take Massive Action

When there is something I want or something I want to do, I always take massive action. I want to be the best I can be in everything I do. Therefore, I have a can-do attitude and put my best foot forward all the time. Now is your time for taking Massive Action.

I started back in real estate investing shortly after Monica did, actually going through one of the same educational courses that she went through, I came out of that program trying numerous different things where she came out with one focus and she has literally created a monopoly on the short sale market in our area. I am very honored to both say that I know her and to have gone through her Short Sale class. Her information that she provides is not only up to date and very thorough but there is no question as to whether she is just copying material or actually doing it. The proof is in the pudding with her! And not only that but she understands something that many (most) don't— and that is—"The power of the mind" and she is very clear to teach that without that understanding, there is no use wasting your time. No matter where you are at currently your future is based off what you believe of yourself—you will attract what you think about and what you believe! There is no question about it—whether you want to believe it or not the "Law of Attraction" is real and it is always working. And she understands that truth. Which is very evident within her successes. If you are looking for no hype—down to earth—up-to-date material and support I strongly suggest Pink Real Estate whether you are wanting to blow up on your own or have it handled for you, Monica and her Conglomerate are the ones for you!!!

Craig Dillion
CEO of ATP Property Solutions Inc. & 550-FAST~
Craig Dillion, C.E.O

Chapter 2
Foreclosure vs. Short Sale

A short sale happens when a property is sold and the lender agrees to accept a discounted payoff. The lender is willing to release the lien for less money than is actually owed on the property.

A short sale is presented to a lender for several different reasons. One reason can be because the homeowner is "upside down" on their mortgage, meaning they owe more on their mortgage than the current market value of their home. Another reason may be because the homeowner is behind on their payment because of a financial hardship.

If the homeowner is far enough behind on their payments, they may be facing foreclosure. A homeowner who is behind on payments because of a hardship simply can't afford to sell their house for less than what they owe on their mortgage. If they don't have the cash to make their payments or bring their mortgage current, they certainly don't have the cash to pay the difference between the sale price and the mortgage balance.

In order to "short" a mortgage loan, an offer to buy the property needs to be made to the homeowner and presented to the lender. The homeowner can accept the offer; however, the closing can't take place on the property until the offer is formally approved by the lender in writing. If there is more than one mortgage on the property, all lien holders must agree to the short sale and short payoffs.

Qualifications for a Short Sale

The homeowner can be either current or behind on their payments to do a short sale, with the exception of FHA Loans. If the homeowner has an FHA loan, they must be at least 31 days behind on their mortgage to do a short sale. Additionally, to qualify for a short sale, the homeowner must be experiencing a financial hardship.

If the homeowner is current on their mortgage, they must have a good reason for the bank to accept a short sale and take a substantial loss on the note. The homeowner must have a valid reason that threatens their ability to stay current on their mortgage or proves they will fall behind on the mortgage. This hardship needs to be presented to the lender.

Types of Hardships

There are many different types of hardships homeowners face, and nearly every reason for delinquency can be turned into a hardship. Below are several examples of homeowner hardships:
- Divorce
- Death in family
- Medical issues and medical bills
- Loss in pay or loss of a job
- Having to relocate because of work
- Being incarcerated
- New baby in the family
- An increase in living expenses
- An increase in their mortgage payment amount because of an increase in interest rate due to an

Adjustable Rate Mortgage (ARM)

- An increase in their mortgage payment amount because of an increase in property taxes or insurance
- Crime in a neighborhood causing the homeowners to leave their home
- Home is a rental and the owners can't find a tenant
- Tenants destroying the house and owners can't afford the repairs

The homeowner must be experiencing a valid financial hardship to qualify for a short sale. A homeowner will not qualify to sell their home as a short sale simply because they want a new house, a bigger house or a home in a different neighborhood. A bank will not take a loss on their asset because of a homeowner's personal preference!

Different Types of Short Sales

In order to be successful with short sales, you must be familiar with each different type of loan you may encounter and know how to best negotiate not only each loan type, but also how to negotiate when there is more than one loan on the property and/or additional liens. The type of loan the homeowner has will let you know what type of short sale you will be doing.

There are three different types of loans: FHA loans, VA loans and conventional loans. Then there are conventional loans that qualify for HAFA (Home Affordable Foreclosure Alternatives). We will briefly go over all four of the different types of loans.

FHA Short Sales

The FHA short sale program is called the Pre-Foreclosure

Sale Program. The Pre-Foreclosure Sale Program allows a mortgagor in default to sell his or her home and use the sales proceeds to satisfy the mortgage debt, even if the proceeds are less than the amount owed.

Pre-Foreclosure Sale Program Requirements:

• The homeowner can't abandon the property! They must be living in the home. If the homeowner has moved out, they must have vacated the property because of an "unstoppable" reason such as a job transfer or they couldn't afford the utilities any longer.

• The homeowner must be at least 31 days behind on their mortgage payments.

• The homeowner must be able to show a reduction in income or an increase in living expenses.

FHA Testimonial

9/25/09

My children, wife, and I were on our way to foreclosure and Monica surprised my at my front door one morning and a month and a half later we were out of foreclosure and living in a much more comfortable situation with my family.

THANX for everything

John McCain

Christoraff Westerman

FHA Short Sale Benefits:

• The lender will always do a full settlement on the property. They can't pursue collection of the loan deficiency from the homeowner.

- The lender will pay a $750–$1,000 incentive to the seller when the house sells.
- The foreclosure sale will be postponed for four to six months to allow the homeowner time to sell their house under the program.

VA Short Sales

- The homeowner can be either current or behind on their mortgage to do a short sale.
- If the homeowner has a security clearance, doing a short sale will most likely not challenge their security clearance.
- The veteran will be able to keep their VA eligibility if they do a short sale; however, the amount of their eligibility will be reduced by the deficiency amount.
- The lender will always do a full settlement on the property. They can't pursue collection of the loan deficiency from the homeowner.
- Homeowners get a $1,500 incentive to help with moving expenses.

Conventional Loan Short Sales

- Any homeowner can sell their home as a short sale as long as they are experiencing a financial hardship.
- The homeowner can either be current or behind on their mortgage payments.
- There are no seller incentives on a conventional short sale, unless the homeowner qualifies for the HAFA program. If they qualify, they can receive an incentive of $3,000 for moving expenses.

- Some individual banks may offer their own incentives. For instance, some offer a moving expense incentive of $1,000 to $3,000. You need to check with the individual banks to see if they offer any incentives.

HAFA Conventional Loan Short Sales (Home Affordable Foreclosure Alternative)

HAFA Requirements:

- The home must be the homeowner's primary residence.
- The loan must have been originated prior to January 1, 2009.
- The homeowner is currently delinquent on their mortgage or they have a financial hardship that deems delinquency will be inevitable.
- The unpaid principal balance on the mortgage must be less than $729,750.

HAFA Benefits:

- Homeowner can receive up to $3,000 in seller incentives for relocation expenses.
- The foreclosure sale will be postponed for four months to allow the homeowner time to sell their house.
- The lender will fully release the homeowner from future liability of the debt.
- Lender pays all servicing fees.
- Homeowners have no out-of-pocket expenses.

To: Pink Real Estate Team (Veronica & Monica)

Hi, I like to say thanks to all your Pink team, they are great people and hard worker who fight for the customers. I was worry that I have to foreclose my home before, but Pink team helps our family to avoid foreclose.

I will recommend all the people whose are in trouble with their home, whatever the reason. Give a simple call to the Pink, than you will list get help or advice from personal. I call and my house avoid foreclose and had closing on September 17, 2010. I also got my $3,000.00 from HAFA program and Pink team also helps start to the end to get approval from the bank.

Again I like to say thank you for all your hard work.

Sincerely

9. 22 .10

Kyu Hwang

HAFA Testimonial

Why Are Short Sales Popular?

Short sales are currently a very popular opportunity for both investors and realtors. The housing market has been steadily declining and the number of foreclosures continues to rise. These two trends are happening at an alarming rate. As a result, the retail housing market is slow because so many of the properties listed for sale are either short sale properties or bank owned properties (Real Estate Owned or REO).

It is very difficult in today's real estate market for a real estate agent to sell a house for a retail price that nets enough proceeds to pay off the existing mortgage in full.

Both retail buyers and investors are fighting for the

best deals, and these deals are the shorts sales and REO properties. Additionally, many investors are getting outbid by investors who have lower rehabilitation costs, those who want to buy and hold on to a property, those that have access to cheaper money and investors who are taking higher risks by offering more money for a property.

This means there is a lot of competition out there right now for the good deals. However, investors can create their own deals and be in full and complete control of the transaction from start to finish without having to compete with everyone else!

Why Short Sales Work and Why Banks Do Short Sales

A bank will do a short sale because they will usually net more from a short sale than they will if they take the house back as a REO and then sell it. Even a low-ball offer generally nets the bank more money than they would receive reselling the property themselves. Banks are not in the business of holding properties or selling them. They are in the business of issuing loans and making a return on the loans.

Statistically, a bank will lose 20% more money by letting a house go to foreclosure. Once a property becomes a REO property, the value of the home drops drastically. If we lose a file to foreclosure, I check back to see if the house sold and what it sold for, and it always sells for less than the short sale offer we were trying to negotiate.

Banks are motivated to get their money. They would rather take the loss now than incur more costs and take a bigger loss trying to resell the property later. The faster the bank can get their money, the faster they can re-lend that money

Create your own *'Done for you'* Short Sale System for a better return.

Short Sale vs. Foreclosure

The following table gives a brief overview and comparison of the homeowner consequences when they sell their home as a short sale and when they allow their home to be foreclosed on. You will see by these consequences, foreclosure is rarely the better option.

Issue	Foreclosure	Short Sale
Security Clearances	Foreclosure is the most challenging issue against a security clearance outside of a conviction of a felony or serious misdemeanor. If a homeowner is a police officer, in the military or CIA, or has another position that requires security clearance, in most cases, their security clearance will be revoked and their position terminated.	A Short Sale on its own does not challenge most security clearances.
Current Employment	Employers have the right to regularly check the credit of all their employees who are in sensitive positions. A foreclosure in many cases is grounds for immediate reassignment or termination.	A short sale is not reported on a credit report and is therefore not a challenge to employment
Future Employment	Many employers require credit checks on all job applicants. A foreclosure is one of the most detrimental credit items an applicant can have and in most cases will challenge employment.	A short sale is not reported on a credit report and is therefore not a challenge to employment
Deficiency Judgment	In 100% of foreclosures (except in those states where there is no deficiency) the bank has the right to pursue a deficiency judgment.	In some successful short sales it is possible to convince the lender to give up the right to pursue a deficiency judgment against the homeowner.

Issue	Foreclosure	Short Sale
Deficiency Judgment Amount	In a foreclosure the home will have to go through an REO process if it does not sell at auction. In most cases this will result in a lower sales price and longer time to sale in a declining market. This will result in a higher possible deficiency judgment.	In a properly managed short sale the home is sold at a price that should be close to market value and in almost all cases will be better than an REO sale resulting in a lower deficiency.
Future Fannie Mae Loan—Primary Residence	A homeowner who loses a home to foreclosure is ineligible for a Fannie Mae backed mortgage for a period of 7 years.	A homeowner who successfully negotiates and closes a short sale will be eligible for a Fannie Mae backed mortgage after only 2 years.
Future Fannie Mae Loan—Non Primary	An investor who allows a property to go to foreclosure is ineligible for a Fannie Mae backed investment mortgage for a period of 7 years.	An investor who successfully negotiates and closes a short sale will be eligible for a Fannie Mae backed investment mortgage after only two years.
Future Loan with any Mortgage Company	On any future 1003 application, a prospective borrower will have to answer YES to question C in Section VIII of the standard 1003 that asks, "Have you had property foreclosed upon or given title or deed in lieu thereof in the last 7 years?" This will affect future rates.	There is no similar declaration or question regarding a short sale.
Credit Score	Score may be lowered anywhere from 250 to over 300 points. Typically will affect score for over 3 years.	Only late payments on mortgage will show and after sale mortgage will be reported as paid or negotiated. This will lower the score as little as 50 points if all other payments are being made. A short sale's affect can be as brief as 12 to 18 months.
Credit History	Foreclosure will remain as a public record on a person's credit history for 10 years or more.	Short sale is not reported on a credit history. There is no specific reporting item for short sale. The loan is typically reported "Paid in full, settled."

Mortgage Forgiveness Debt Relief Act

When the bank forgives all or part of a mortgage debt, they must report the amount of the loss to the IRS. The IRS, in turn, sends a 1099 to the homeowner. This 1099 reflects the bank's loss as income to the homeowner, and they must report this income to the IRS on their taxes. For example, if the homeowners made $50K in income from their job and the loss to the bank was $50K and they received a 1099 from the IRS in the amount of $50K, the homeowner must report $100K in income for that year.

President Bush passed an act on December 20, 2007, to help homeowners who lost their home to foreclosure or had to sell their home on a short sale. The act helped qualify homeowners so they would not have to pay taxes on this. Homeowners would qualify if the home was their primary residence and they never refinanced their mortgage. If a homeowner doesn't qualify for this, they may have to pay the taxes.

While this is better than having to repay the full mortgage amount or the deficiency to the bank, it may still bring hardship to the homeowner at tax time. Oftentimes, a CPA may be able to work numbers so the homeowner doesn't have to pay the taxes, or the CPA may be able to determine a homeowner insolvent. If they are insolvent, they don't have to pay taxes.

NOTE: NEVER GIVE TAX ADVICE! Always tell homeowners they need to consult a tax accountant or CPA for any tax advice or have them look up the act online at the IRS website to see if they qualify (www.irs.gov/individuals/article/0,,id=179414,00.html).

What Is a Deficiency?

A deficiency is the amount left unpaid on the mortgage after a foreclosure or short sale transaction. The deficiency on a short sale is the difference between what was owed on the property and the net proceeds the bank received at closing. The deficiency on a foreclosure is the difference between the amount owed on the house and the amount the home sold for at auction.

Deficiency After Short Sale or Foreclosure?

If there is a deficiency on the mortgage after a short sale transaction or the foreclosure auction, the action taken by the bank will depend on whether the property is in a deficiency state or a non-deficiency state. If the property is in a non-deficiency state, the homeowner does not have to worry about the deficiency. The bank cannot come after the homeowner for the difference.

If the homeowner is in a deficiency state, the bank does have the right to pursue the deficiency from the homeowner. The bank has up to six years to pursue a deficiency judgment. However, depending on what type of loan the homeowner had, the loan may not have a deficiency. For example, if the homeowner had an FHA, VA or conventional HAFA short sale, they will not have a deficiency. If they had a regular conventional loan that was not HAFA approved, then the bank can pursue the deficiency. However, you can work with the banks to try and have them waive the deficiency amount. If they will do this, they accept the short sale net proceeds as a full satisfaction of debt and will not pursue the deficiency.

The only types of loans that may have a deficiency are conventional loans that are not in a program where the deficiency is waived. When the bank is doing a short sale, one of the reasons why they want to review a homeowner's financials is to see if they have any valuable assets for the bank to pursue in a deficiency judgment. They will even run your credit to see if you own any assets. However, most people doing a short sale don't have available cash or assets for the bank to pursue. They are low- to middle-income families who have lost most of their assets. In most cases, the banks don't see these cases as worth pursuing the deficiency judgment, so they write the deficiency as a loss and issue a 1099 to the homeowner.

There is a small subset of the population doing short sales where the banks deem it favorable to pursue a deficiency judgment. These people are those who own a house with equity or own several investment properties with equity. There are also people who may show an increase in income when a house sells on a short sale. For example, we had a doctor who owned a four-plex. He stopped making his payments on the four-plex because he was losing money on it. Once the four-plex was to sell, the doctor would have an extra $2,000 in income per month. As a result, the bank would only approve the short sale if the homeowner was willing to sign a promissory note for the deficiency.

What happens when the Bank Pursues a Deficiency Judgment?

If the bank chooses to pursue a deficiency, they file a judgment against the homeowner and sue them for the deficiency amount. If this happens, homeowners need to be aware that this judgment will attached itself to any home they currently own or attempt to own in the future. Before a homeowner can purchase any other property, they must satisfy this deficiency judgment. This can be very detrimental to the homeowner, so you want to do everything you can to get the bank to issue a deficiency waiver on a short sale. The bank can also garnish wages and their bank accounts.

Deficiency and Non Deficiency States[6]

In a non-recourse mortgage state, borrowers are not held personally liable for more than the home's value at the time the loan is repaid. The lender may recoup some of its loss through foreclosure. However, the lender may not sue the borrower for additional funds. If the foreclosure sale does not generate enough money to satisfy the loan, the lender must accept the loss.

Each non-recourse state has its own anti-deficiency statutes that prohibit lenders from seeking deficiency judgments. In a few cases, anti-deficiency statues do allow lenders to collect a limited amount of money from the borrower, such as the difference between the mortgage debt and the fair market value of the property.

Note that in some states, such as California, non-recourse laws apply only to "purchase money" loans (i.e., original home loans that are used to purchase property). Almost all HELOCs (home equity line of credit) and home equity loans are considered recourse loans, and lenders for these loans may sue borrowers to recoup loss. There are, however, some exceptions (i.e., where the second mortgage

6 www.helocbasics.com/list-of-non-recourse-mortgage-states-and-anti-deficiency-statutes/

lender forces the foreclosure). There has been some speculation that mortgage refinances do not constitute "purchase money" loans. However, there have been no cases to determine this issue one way or the other.

In some states, lenders are only permitted a single lawsuit to collect mortgage debt. This plays out differently depending on the state's laws. In New York, for example, a lender must choose between the actions of foreclosing on the property or suing to collect the debt. States with such laws are one-action states.

The table below lists those states that are anti-deficiency/non-recourse states and those that are one-action states.

Anti-Deficiency/ Non-Recourse States	One Action States
Alaska	California
Arizona	Idaho
California	Montana
Connecticut	Nevada
Florida	New York
Idaho	Utah
Minnesota	
North Carolina	
North Dakota	
Texas	
Utah	
Washington	

Short Sale Time Frame

The length of time it takes to do a short sale from contract close depends on several factors, including the bank you are dealing with and the type of loan the homeowner has. Each bank follows its own short sale process, with some banks moving short sales more quickly than others. It also depends on whether there is a first and second mortgage on the property and if these mortgages are with the same bank or different banks.

If you are dealing with two different banks, it can take longer. If there are judgments added to the property, this also can delay the short sale. If the homeowner has filed bankruptcy, you can easily add two months to the process length. A bankruptcy can completely stop the short sale as well, as there are extra steps that need to take place first. So you cannot put an actual duration on a short sale. It is hard to say how long it will take.

The quickest short sale I have done took two weeks from start to finish, but this isn't typical. The longest short sale I did took over one year to complete, but this is because it went through several offers and counter-offers between the bank and the end buyer. This is not typical either. On the average, a short sale takes between two and three months from submitting the short sale package and the offer to receiving bank approval. Then it takes approximately another month to prepare for closing and close the deal. If you plan on buying the house as a cash deal and you don't need to wait for an end buyer, you can close as soon as you receive approval from the lender.

Chapter 3
Foreclosure Laws

Foreclosure Process [7]

The foreclosure laws vary from state to state, and these laws lay down the terms and conditions that apply for the foreclosure processes in a particular state. The process of foreclosure can be initiated through a judicial system (court) or a non-judicial system.

There are some states that allow both judicial and non-judicial foreclosure processes, while other states allow one or the other. Usually after three to four months of missed payments, the mortgage company will begin the foreclosure process.

In states where the foreclosure laws allow both types of foreclosure processes, the type of mortgage loan document is the determining factor for which process will be used. Based on the clauses mentioned in the mortgage loan document, the foreclosure process is followed either judicially or non-judicially.

If there is a deed of trust involved, then the foreclosure process will be non-judicial; however, if there is a mortgage involved, the foreclosure will be judicial. There are some mortgages that have a clause that allows the lender to sell the foreclosed property non-judicially.

According to foreclosure laws, a judicial foreclosure

7 www.bankforeclosuressale.com/foreclosure-laws.php

an take place only when the lender files the required court action against the homeowner who has defaulted on the loan. This form of filing is known as a *lis pendens* or pending lawsuit. If the owner loses the lawsuit, then the court will initiate the process of public auction to sell the homeowner's property.

According to foreclosure laws, in the case of a non-judicial foreclosure, the trustee whose name is on the deed of trust needs to file a public notice of default. The recording or filing of this notice initiates the non-judicial foreclosure process.

In such a case there is a grace period, and if the homeowner is unable to pay off the loan within the grace period, then the trustee will go ahead and schedule a public auction of the homeowner's property.

Judicial vs. Non-Judicial Foreclosures[8]

The primary difference between judicial and non-judicial foreclosures is that judicial foreclosures are processed through the courts, much like civil law suits, while non-judicial foreclosures are without court intervention and the requirements for the foreclosure are established by the various state statutes.

With judicial foreclosures, the lender begins the process by filing a complaint (filing a *lis pendens* as stated above). After the homeowner receives the notice of complaint, they have an opportunity to be heard by the court. If the court finds the default valid, the court issues a judgment for the amount that is owed, plus foreclosure costs. The property is then put up for auction or put up for sale through a sheriff's

8 realestateandwomen.net/2011/03/08/judicial-vs-non-judicial-foreclosure/

sale, and the property is sold to the highest bidder.

In cases where the foreclosure sale doesn't satisfy the amount owed on the mortgage, a deficiency judgment can be ordered under state laws and tax codes, which becomes a lien against the borrower, making them responsible for paying the difference between what was owed and what the property sold for. This is one of the biggest differences between judicial and non-judicial foreclosures.

In the case of non-judicial foreclosures, each state follows different procedures based on its own state statutes. Therefore, it is important to understand the laws in the state where the property is. In a non-judicial state, the homeowner will receive a letter upon default. A Notice of Default (NOD) is typically filed at the same time, and this is posted on the tax records (which are public records). The home owner will then have a certain time period to cure the default or pay the money owed. If the homeowner does not cure the default within the required time frame, the lender will schedule an auction in order to sell the property.

State to State

The following table lists the judicial and non-judicial states and provides information such as whether a state is a deficiency or non-deficiency state, the length of the foreclosure process and the redemption period.

Please note that each state's foreclosure laws continually change; therefore, this chart may not be 100% accurate. You are responsible for doing your own due diligence to make sure you verify individual state laws and regulations for the states you are doing business in. To get current, up-to-date state foreclosure law information, go to www.realtytrac.com.

	Judicial	Non-Judicial	Comments	Anti-Deficiency	Process Period (Days)	Sale Publication (Days)	Redemption Period (Days)	Sale/NTS
Alabama	•	•	Judicial not common		49-74	21	365	Trustee
Alaska	•	•	Judicial as last alternative	•	105	65	365 (Judicial O	Trustee
Arizona	•	•	Judicial not common	•	90+	41	30–180 (Judici	Trustee
Arkansas	•	•	Both are used equally		70	30	365 (Judicial O	Trustee
California		•		•	117	21	365 (Judicial O	Trustee
Colorado		•			145	60	None	Trustee
Connecticut	•			•	62	NA	Court Decides	Court
Delaware	•				170-210	60-90	None	Sheriff
District of Columbia		•	Trustee sale only		47	18	None	Trustee
Florida	•			•	135	NA	None	Court
Georgia		•			37	32	None	Trustee
Hawaii		•			220	60	None	Trustee
Idaho		•		•	150	45	365	Trustee
Illinois	•				300	NA	90	Court
Indiana	•				261	120	None	Sheriff
Iowa	•				160	30	20	Sheriff
Kansas	•				130	21	365	Sheriff
Kentucky	•				147	NA	365	Court
Louisiana	•				180	NA	None	Sheriff
Maine		•			240	30	90	Court
Maryland	•				46	30	Court Decides	Court
Mass.		•			75	41	None	Court
Michigan		•			60	30	30–365	Sheriff
Minnesota		•		•	90-100	7	180–365	Sheriff
Mississippi		•			90	30	None	Trustee

State	Judicial	Non-Judicial	Comments	Anti-Deficiency	Process Period (Days)	Sale Publication (Days)	Redemption Period (Days)	Sale/NTS
Missouri	•	•	Non-Judicial More Common		60	10	365	Trustee
Montana	•				150	50	None	Trustee
Nebraska	•				142	NA	None	Sheriff
Nevada		•			116	80	None	Trustee
New Hampshire		•			59	24	None	Trustee
New Jersey	•				270	NA	10	Sheriff
New Mexico	•				180	NA	30–270	Court
New York	•				445	NA	None	Court
North Carolina		•		•	110	25	None	Sheriff
North Dakota	•			•	150	NA	180–365	Sheriff
Ohio	•				217	NA	None	Sheriff
Oklahoma	•				186	NA	None	Sheriff
Oregon		•			150	30	180	Trustee
Pennsylvania	•				270	NA	None	Sheriff
South Dakota	•	•	Judicial more common		150	23	30–365	Sheriff
Tennessee		•			40-45	20-25	730	Trustee
Texas		•		•	27	NA	None	Trustee
Utah	•			•	142	NA	Court Decides	Trustee
Vermont	•				95	NA	180–365	Court
Virginia		•			45	14-28	None	Trustee
Washington	•	•	Trustee sale more common	•	135	90	None	Trustee
West Virginia		•			60-90	30-60	None	Trustee
Wisconsin	•				290	NA	365	Sheriff
Wyoming		•			60	25	90–365	Sheriff

Second Mortgage Foreclosure

There are very few times you will see a second mortgage lender file for foreclosure. Sometimes, both lenders will file for foreclosure. These foreclosures are handled in the same manner as if a first mortgage was foreclosing. If a second forecloses, they must foreclose with the first mortgage intact. The first mortgage does not get wiped off at foreclosure like second mortgages get wiped off. The second mortgage will have to either pay off the first mortgage, or they can make payments to the first mortgage and bring the loan current while they are marketing the property to get it sold.

The only time a second mortgage would foreclose is if there is equity after they bought out the first. You very rarely see this happen. If there is no equity, it is usually a mistake.

I've seen a third mortgage take their loan position into foreclosure. The lender believed they were in first position; however the chain of title listed the lender in third position. We were actually doing the short sale on this property, so we notified the attorney handling the foreclosure of the chain of title discrepancies.

As a result, the attorney has been extending the foreclosure sale. Apparently the third mortgage lender had documentation proving it should have been in first position, but something went wrong. So before the lender can foreclose, the chain of title must to be corrected. To date, this process has taken six months, and we are still trying to do a short sale on this property.

Colorado Foreclosure Process

Usually after three to four months of missed payments,

the mortgage company begins the foreclosure process. The bank will hire a foreclosure attorney in Colorado to initiate the foreclosure. The foreclosure attorney then notifies the public trustee in the county where the house is in of the foreclosure.

The public trustee is the official in each county who holds the foreclosure auction. Depending on how big the county is, the public trustee's office usually has a website that shows all the active foreclosures in the county, as well as their status.

Whenever a foreclosure needs to be postponed, the attorney must notify the public trustee. The public trustee then immediately updates their website of the postponement. Once a house is officially in foreclosure, the foreclosure process lasts four months, and it ranges from 110 to 125 days from the start date. This time frame gives the homeowner the opportunity to dispute the foreclosure, to try and bring the loan current, negotiate a short sale or sell the property. If nothing happens by the time the foreclosure sale date is set, the house will foreclose.

There is a court hearing usually one month before the foreclosure sale, which gives the homeowner an opportunity to be heard in court. If they are wrongfully in foreclosure, this gives them the opportunity to dispute the foreclosure. The homeowner is not required to go to this hearing.

A house can only be in foreclosure for one year from the initial scheduled sale date. If a foreclosure sale gets postponed for one day past the one year mark, the public trustee has to withdraw the foreclosure and the foreclosure has to be re-initiated. The only time a foreclosure can be postponed past one year is if the homeowner is in Chapter

13 bankruptcy. I've seen several properties get withdrawn from foreclosure because the foreclosure sale went past the one year mark. This was because the homeowner was doing a loan modification or a short sale and it caused the foreclosure sale to exceed one year.

The attorney must submit an initial bid amount, referred to as a bid figure, by noon at least two business days before the foreclosure sale. So, in El Paso County, the bid figures must be submitted by noon on Monday because the foreclosure sales are at 10 a.m. on Wednesdays. If there are no bid figures, the foreclosure sale is automatically postponed for one week. Without bid figures there can be no foreclosure sale as they don't have an amount to begin the foreclosure auction.

If the foreclosing lender is the highest bidder at the sale, the lender has an opportunity to rescind the public trustee sale, in certain narrow circumstances, within eight business days after the foreclosure sale. This means that if you have an offer on the property and the bank was expecting to sell it at the auction, they may want to rescind the sale, which means reversing the foreclosure to entertain that offer.

Colorado Foreclosure Time Table[8]

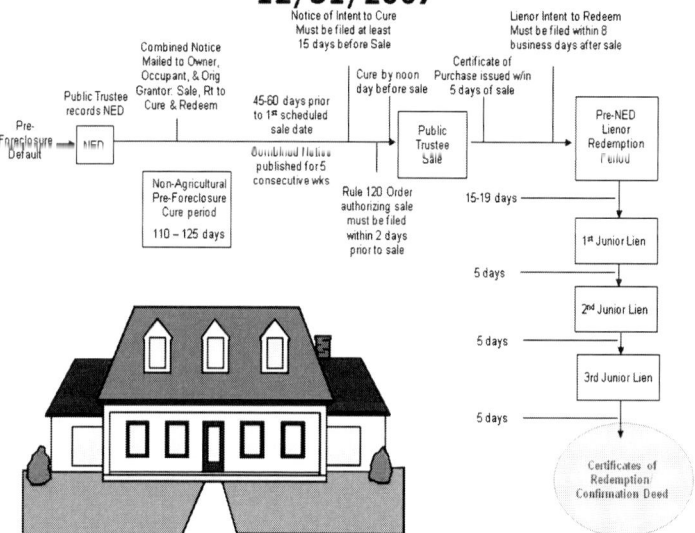

RENAV Your source for distressed property information

info@renav.com   (303) 731-3334   www.RENAV.com

Foreclosure Timeline for NED's Filed AFTER 12/31/2007

Redemption

The homeowner cannot redeem the property after the foreclosure sale. Redemption rights are only available to the holders of liens that are junior in priority to the lien foreclosed. A junior lien is a Deed of Trust or other lien/ encumbrance subordinate to the Deed of Trust or other lien being foreclosed. To prevent misuse of the redemption process, the junior lien must be recorded prior to the Notice of Election and Demand.

The junior lien must file the intent to redeem within eight business days after the sale. Once the public trustee receives the intent to redeem, they then request a statement from the holder of the certificate of purchase or their attorney. This signed statement must be submitted back to the public trustee's office within thirteen business days after the sale.

Redemption dates are set nine business days after the sale date. The most senior junior lienor may redeem 15 to 19 business days after the sale but no later than noon of the final day. Each subsequent junior lienor has an additional five business days and must redeem by noon of the final day. Redemption periods are not shortened if someone redeems early.

There can be no partial redemptions. A lienor holding a lien on less than all of, or a partial interest, in the property sold at sale must redeem the entire property. Short redemptions are allowed. The public trustee may accept less than a full redemption amount with written authorization from the certificate of purchase holder, the certificate of redemption holder, or their attorney. An agreement to accept less than the full sum required for redemption by the certificate of purchase holder does not affect the amount of the deficiency bid at sale. Any redemption constitutes a full redemption of all sums that the certificate of purchase holder is entitled to. Once the payment has been made, a certificate of redemption is recorded by the public trustee.

A Homeowner's Association (HOA) can also redeem a property, but they must provide additional documentation.[9]

A Homeowners' Association (HOA), or its assignee, has the right to redeem in the most-senior junior position to the first Deed of Trust if all of the following are true:

- The first Deed of Trust was recorded after the Declaration of Covenants for the HOA.
- Either the Deed of Trust or the Declaration of Covenants was recorded after 6/30/1992.
- There is a positive balance remaining after doing the following:
- Take the amount of unpaid assessments, with interest, due through the end of the first redemption period.
- Subtract an amount equal to the assessments due (paid or unpaid) in the six months immediately prior to the recording of the NED.

For more information, visit the El Paso County Public Trustee website:

www.elpasopublictrustee.com/HOALiens.aspx.

The following information was obtained from the El Paso County Public Trustee's website and pertains to HOA liens

---

[9] www.elpasopublictrustee.com/HOALiens.aspx

Monica Adams

in Colorado.

Colorado Foreclosure Protection Act (FPA)

If you are in the pre-foreclosure business, you should already know about the huge changes to the Colorado Foreclosure Protection Act (FPA) that took effect on January 1, 2011. Please note I am not an attorney, and the information contained in this book is for educational purposes only. Do not take any of the information presented here as legal advice. The consequences of violating the FPA can be fines up to $25,000, imprisonment up to a year or both! Always consult the advice of your attorney.

Definitions: Equity Purchaser and Subsequent Purchaser

Equity Purchaser: [10]Equity purchaser means a person who, in the course of the person's business, vocation, or occupation, acquires title to a property that is thirty days behind on payments. Equity purchaser does not include a person who acquires such title:

(1) For the purpose of using such property as his or her personal residence for at least one year;

(2) By a deed in lieu of foreclosure to the holder of an evidence of debt, or an associate of the holder of an evidence of debt, of a consensual lien or encumbrance of record, if such consensual lien or encumbrance is recorded in the register of deeds office of the county where the residence in foreclosure is located prior to a foreclosure sale;

(3) By a deed from any trustee, sheriff, or other person appointed by a court as a result of a foreclosure sale;

10 www.coloradoattorneygeneral.gov/sites/default/files/uploads/COLORADO%20FORECLOSURE%20PROTECTION%20ACT.pdf

56

(4) At a sale of property authorized by statute;

(5) By order or judgment of any court;

(6) From the person's spouse, relative, or relative of a spouse, by the half or whole blood or by adoption, or from a guardian, conservator or personal representative of such person.

In other words, an Equity Purchaser is a person who acquires title to a property that is at least thirty days behind on payments, but does not intend to occupy the property as his or her personal residence.

Subsequent Purchaser: A person who buys a property from an investor (AKA the C in an A–B, B–C transaction), and it must be sold under 14 days and be under contract prior to the short sale approval.

When Does the Foreclosure Protection Act (FPA) Apply for an Investor?

The foreclosure protection act now only applies when the property is not a short sale and the home has equity and the homeowner is at least one month behind on payments. The old law said the FPA applied to all properties, whether a short sale or not. If the FPA applies to your transaction, you must follow the law.

Are You Considered an Equity Purchaser? What You Must Do!

If you are considered an Equity Purchaser, you must abide by the new laws. The following is a list of what you must do if you are an Equity Purchaser:

- Use the Colorado Foreclosure Protection Act Contract. Include the Notice of Cancellation, and Seller Warning. Use the state-approved forms found at:

www.dora.state.co.us/real-estate/contracts/contracts2011.htm

• Clear and conspicuous disclosure of any financial or legal obligations of the home owner that will be assumed by the equity purchaser. If the equity purchaser will not be assuming any financing or legal obligations of the homeowner, the equity purchaser shall provide the homeowner with a separate written disclosure that substantially complies with the Equity Skimming or Real Property statute.

• The total consideration to be paid by the equity purchaser including the terms of payment and any services to be provided to the home owner either before or after the sale.

• The date and time possession is to be transferred to the equity purchaser.

• The contract shall be written in English, and if the equity purchaser has actual of constructive knowledge that the homeowner's principal language is other than English, the homeowner shall be provided with a fairly short notice in the homeowner's principal language.

Who Is Exempt from Being an Equity Purchaser?

• The transaction will be a short sale transaction.

• Must use the approved Colorado Real Estate Commission Short Sale Addendum as part of the contract.

• The transaction complies with the new Double Closing section of the FPA.

What Is Required by the New Double Closing Section of the FPA?

If the equity purchaser in a short sale transaction intends to resell the property in foreclosure to a subsequent purchaser, the equity purchaser shall provide full disclosure to the homeowner and all holders of evidence of debt on the residence in foreclosure (or such holder's representative) of the terms of the agreement with the subsequent purchaser including but not limited to the purchase price within one business day of identifying the subsequent purchaser and not later than the closing of the short sale transaction. This is only if you plan on reselling the property within fourteen days.

My suggestion is to not resell the property to a buyer until after day fifteen. Get a hard money loan or transactional funding, and then resell the property.

If you plan to resell the property within 14 days, you must:

• Provide full disclosure to the subsequent purchaser, subsequent purchaser's lender (or such lender's representative), homeowner and short sale bank of the terms of the agreement with the homeowner, including but not limited to the purchase price within one business day of identifying the subsequent purchaser and not later than the closing of the short sale transaction.

• Comply with all rules adopted by the Colorado Real Estate Commission with regard to short sales.

• Comply with all good funds laws.

California Home Equity Sales Contract Law [11]

Pre-foreclosure Sale Requirements

A mistake that real estate investors make when

---

11 www.forecloseddreams.com/california-home-equity-sales-contract-law

purchasing residential property in California is not following the requirements if a notice of default has been recorded by the lender.

California has a detailed set of statutes setting out requirements for contracts for residential pre-foreclosure sales. (Civil Code §§1695-1695.17.) These statutes apply to any residential real property consisting of one- to four-family dwelling units, one of which the owner occupies as his or her principal place of residence, and against which there is an outstanding notice of default. These statutes require, among other things, that the contract:

- Spell out all terms of the agreement (including, for example, buyback rights).
- Contain certain notices that meet certain size and bolding requirements.
- Allow the seller to cancel, usually up until midnight of the 5th business day after signing.
- Be accompanied by a Notice of Cancellation form in duplicate.
- Also, until the cancellation period ends, the buyer cannot:
- Have the seller sign a deed or deed of trust.
- Record any deed or deed of trust regarding the property.
- Transfer any interest in the property to a third party.
- Pay the seller any money or other consideration.

In addition, the purchaser cannot make any untrue or misleading statements regarding the value of the residence in foreclosure, the amount of proceeds the seller will receive after a foreclosure sale, or any other untrue or misleading statement concerning the sale of the residence.

Moreover, purchasers are forbidden from taking "unconscionable advantage" of the seller. This applies if the seller is incompetent or does not understand the transaction (for example, if the seller is not fluent enough in English) and may apply in other situations as well. If "unconscionable advantage" is taken, the transaction may be rescinded at any time within two years of the date of the recordation of the conveyance of the residential property.

If any of these provisions is violated, the seller may not only be able to rescind the agreement but also recover actual damages, attorneys' fees and costs and exemplary damages in an amount equal to the greater of three times the actual damages or $2,500. Fraud or deceit may additionally be punished by a fine of $25,000, by imprisonment in the county jail or in state prison for not more than one year or by both for each violation. Other remedies may apply as well.

Any provision of a contract that attempts or purports to limit the liability of the purchaser is void and, at the option of the seller, renders the purchase contract void.

Use caution! If you are going to be purchasing pre-foreclosure residential property in California, you should have a real estate attorney review your forms. Or just use the California approved real estate commission contracts.

Illinois Mortgage Rescue Fraud Act[12]

Pre-foreclosure Sale Requirements

Similar to the state of California, Illinois has a detailed set of statutes that must be followed for contracts for residential pre-foreclosure sales (Public Act 094-0822).

12 www.ilga.gov/legislation/publicacts/fulltext.asp?name=094-0822

Illinois defines distressed properties as those consisting of one- to six-family dwelling units that are in foreclosure, at risk of loss due to nonpayment of taxes, or whose owner is more than 90 days delinquent on any loan that is secured by the property.

Additionally, the Illinois Mortgage Rescue Fraud Act specifically defines distressed property consultants and the contractual responsibilities of these consultants as well as the homeowner's rights and right to cancel. Illinois, like California, has a five-business-day right of rescission period.

For more information and to review the entire Public Act, visit:

www.ilga.gov/legislation/publicacts/fulltext.asp?name=094-0822.

Maryland SB 761 – Real Property – Foreclosure – Protection of Homeowners [13] [14]

Pre-foreclosure Sale Requirements

Senate Bill SB 761 changed many of the existing laws regarding investing in residences in foreclosure. As a result it is recommended that you make sure you have a legal opinion from a Maryland attorney who specializes in Maryland real estate law. Should you not have a clear understanding of the law and inadvertently break the law, the penalties are severe. You could be subject to three years in jail and/or $10,000 fine for each violation. In addition to this, the State of Maryland can obtain a judgment against you for the cost of prosecution, and the homeowner can sue for damages as well.

---

13   www.realfinancialsolutions.com/realfinancialsolutions/index.php?option=com_c
ontent&view=article&id=2:investors-corner-sb-761-2005&catid=13:information-for-
investors&Itemid=164
14   mlis.state.md.us/2005rs/fnotes/bil_0001/sb0761.pdf

On the next page is a summary of SB 761 for the state of Maryland:

In addition to any other right under law to cancel or rescind a contract, the bill grants a homeowner the right to:

- Rescind a foreclosure consulting contract at any time.
- Rescind a foreclosure reconveyance at any time before midnight on the third business day after any conveyance or transfer of legal or equitable title to a residence in foreclosure. Rescission occurs when the homeowner gives written notice to the foreclosure consultant as prescribed under the bill. The notice is effective if it indicates the intention of the homeowner to rescind the foreclosure consulting contract or foreclosure reconveyance.

The bill specifies the required contents of a foreclosure consulting contract, including information about the services to be provided and the foreclosure consultant's compensation and a notice about the right to rescind the contract. The bill requires that the foreclosure consultant provide the homeowner a signed and dated copy of the contract, along with the notice, upon execution. The bill limits the amount a foreclosure consultant may charge the homeowner to 8% a year of the amount of any loan that the consultant makes to the homeowner. The consultant may not receive any consideration from a third party in connection with foreclosure consulting services provided to a homeowner unless the consideration is first fully disclosed to the homeowner.

A foreclosure consultant may not demand payment

until after having performed all the services promised under the contract. The consultant may not accept a power of attorney from the homeowner for any purpose except to inspect documents. If a foreclosure reconveyance is included in a foreclosure consulting contract or arranged after the execution of the contract, the foreclosure purchaser must provide the homeowner with a document entitled "Notice of Transfer of Deed or Title." The document must contain the entire agreement between the parties; describe the terms of any foreclosure reconveyance, and other specified information required under the bill.

The foreclosure purchaser must also provide the homeowner with a document entitled "Notice of Right to Cancel Transfer of Deed or Title." The document must include specified information, including the right to rescind within three days after transfer, and must be provided to the homeowner immediately on execution of any document that includes a foreclosure reconveyance. If the homeowner rescinds the agreement, the homeowner must repay any money spent on the homeowner's behalf by the purchaser within 60 days, along with 8% annual interest.

A foreclosure purchaser may not enter into, or attempt to enter into, a foreclosure reconveyance with a homeowner unless the purchaser verifies and can demonstrate that the homeowner has or will have a reasonable ability to pay for the subsequent reconveyance of the property back to the homeowner on completion of the terms of the conveyance. Until the homeowner's right to rescind or cancel the transaction has expired, the purchaser may not: (1) record any document signed by the homeowner; or (2) transfer or encumber or purport to transfer or encumber any interest in the residence in foreclosure to a third party. The bill establishes a rebuttable presumption that: (1) a homeowner has a reasonable ability to pay for a subsequent reconveyance if the homeowner's payments for primary housing expenses and regular principal and interest on other personal debt, on a monthly basis, are not more than 60% of the homeowner's monthly gross income; and (2) that the purchaser has not verified reasonable payment ability if the purchaser has not obtained documents other than a statement by the homeowner about the homeowner's assets, liabilities and income.

The foreclosure purchaser must make a detailed accounting of the basis for the amount of a payment made to the homeowner of a property resold within 18 months after entering into an agreement and must ensure that the homeowner receives at least 82% of the net proceeds of any resale of the property.

A foreclosure surplus acquisition must be in the form of a written contract. The contract must contain specified information about the transaction, including the total consideration to be given to the foreclosure surplus purchaser and a description of any services the purchaser will perform for the homeowner. The contract must be accompanied by a notice of homeowner's right to rescind the contract within 10 days after the auditor states the account of the foreclosure sale. A homeowner who rescinds a contract must repay any consideration received, along with 8% annual interest.

A person may not induce or attempt to induce a homeowner to waive the homeowner's rights under the bill. Any such waiver is void and unenforceable. The Attorney

General may seek an injunction to prohibit a person who has violated or is violating the bill from continuing to do so. A court may enter any order or judgment necessary to:

- Prevent the use of any prohibited practice.
- Restore any money or property acquired from a person by means of any prohibited practice.
- Appoint a receiver in case of a willful violation of the bill. In an action brought by the Attorney General, the Attorney General is entitled to recover the costs of the action for the State's use.

A homeowner may also bring an action for damages incurred as the result of a violation of the bill, including reasonable attorney's fees. If the court finds that the defendant willfully or knowingly violated the bill, the court may award three times the amount of actual damages.

Violation of the bill is a misdemeanor, with maximum penalties of three years' imprisonment and/or a $10,000 fine.

The Consumer Protection Division is required to maintain a list of nonprofit organizations that

- Solely offer counseling or advice to homeowners in foreclosure or loan default; and
- Are not related to and do not contract for services with for-profit lenders or foreclosure purchasers. The division must provide the name and telephone number of an organization on the list to a homeowner who contacts the division.

Under the bill, a "foreclosure consultant" is a person who makes a solicitation, representation, or offer to a homeowner at risk of foreclosure to perform, or who performs, one of a number of specified services that the person represents will help the homeowner. A "foreclosure purchaser" is a person who acquires title or possession of a deed or other document to a residence in foreclosure as a result of a foreclosure reconveyance. A "foreclosure surplus purchaser" is a person who acts as the acquirer by assignment, purchase, grant or conveyance of the surplus resulting from a foreclosure sale.

The bill does not apply to (1) a Maryland attorney while performing an activity related to the attorney's regular practice of law in the State; (2) a person who holds or is owed an obligation secured by a lien on a residence in foreclosure while providing services in connection with the obligation or lien; (3) banks, trust companies, savings and loan associations, credit unions or insurance companies; (4) judgment creditors of a homeowner; (5) title insurers; (6) title insurance producers; (7) a licensed mortgage broker or mortgage lender acting while under the license; (8) a licensed real estate broker, associate real estate broker or real estate salesperson while acting within the scope of the license; or (9) a nonprofit organization that solely offers counseling or advice to homeowners in foreclosure or loan default, if the organization is not directly or indirectly related to and does not contract for services with for-profit lenders or foreclosure purchasers.

The bill also establishes that the entry of an order for resale on default by a purchaser at a foreclosure sale does not affect the prior ratification of the sale and does not restore any right or remedy that was extinguished by the prior sale and extinguishes all interest of the defaulting purchaser.

Current Law: In addition to any other required notice,

the person authorized to make a sale in an action to foreclose a mortgage or deed of trust must give written notice of the proposed sale to the record owner of the property to be sold.

Foreclosure consulting services, foreclosure purchasers, and foreclosure surplus purchasers are not specifically regulated by statute.

Based on the above three states, it becomes more clear to make sure that you fully understand the laws in the states with which you do business. Always check with a real estate attorney versed in the state laws where you are investing.

Homeowner's Rights in Foreclosure

Many times when a homeowner receives a letter in the mail from the bank or the public trustee that states the bank is beginning foreclosure, they get scared. They assume once the bank starts the foreclosure process, that is the end, and they have to move out of their home. Most homeowners don't realize that once they are in foreclosure, the process takes four months. While a homeowner is in the foreclosure process, they still own their house and they cannot be forced to leave their house prior to the foreclosure sale date. Make sure your homeowners understand this process. They will be so happy you took the time to explain this to them.

Additionally, if homeowners are working on a loan modification with their bank, the foreclosure sale date usually gets extended. The public trustee does not need to notify a homeowner of every extension. It is the homeowner's responsibility to follow up on the current foreclosure sale date of the house. If the bank says they don't have a foreclosure sale on file, that doesn't mean that the foreclosure was withdrawn. It generally means the bank didn't schedule the next foreclosure sale date. Always check the foreclosure website for the current sale date information or call the foreclosure attorney.

Can a Foreclosure Be Better for a Homeowner?

In some rare cases a foreclosure can be better for a homeowner. If the beginning bid at the time of the auction is the same amount as the amount owed to the bank and it says zero deficiency, it means the bank is foreclosing without a deficiency, and they cannot pursue the homeowners for that deficiency.

In this situation, the foreclosure may be more beneficial for the homeowner. But beware! The information on the public trustee's website is only for the lender that is foreclosing. If there is a second mortgage on the property, that entire balance is still outstanding. In this situation, a short sale is definitely the better option because oftentimes, you can get a full settlement approval letter on the second mortgage. When a full settlement is negotiated, the lender cannot come after the homeowner for the deficiency.

The safer choice is to pursue a short sale because you will not know until it's too late whether a foreclosure or short sale would have been the better solution. Bid figures don't get posted until two days before the foreclosure sale. By that time, it is too late for the homeowner to decide whether they should do a short sale or foreclosure. In almost all cases, it is better for the homeowner to do a short sale.

After Foreclosure—When Should the Homeowner Move Out?

The homeowner should make arrangements to move out of the house as soon as the house has been foreclosed. There are certain laws and eviction processes, but many times the banks are knocking on the doors asking the homeowners to leave as soon as possible. Some banks start the eviction process two days after the foreclosure sale. This varies depending on the state and on whether there are redemption laws or not. Banks are usually trying to avoid an eviction process, and they offer the homeowner cash for keys as long as they leave the house in good condition and clean it for them.

Can the Banks Change the Locks and Winterize the House?

Homeowners and real estate agents frequently ask me if the bank has the right to change the locks on a property that they don't own. Yes, banks do have the right to change locks to secure the property if it has been abandoned and payments are not being made. There is a paragraph/clause in the note and deed of trust that was signed that says if you fall behind on payments, the bank will start foreclosure proceedings, and they will do everything they need to do to secure their asset. So the bank will change locks to keep people from breaking in and vandalizing their asset. They will also winterize the property to keep pipes from freezing in the winter.

If you have never experienced a frozen pipe issue, be thankful! It is horrible and the damage can be devastating. Oftentimes people think if they shut off their water, their pipes won't freeze. This is not true. Water stays in the pipes until they are drained. If you don't have heat in the house, the pipes will freeze during freezing temperatures. The pipes burst while they are frozen. When the ice thaws, the water inside the pipes start spewing everywhere. The water damage can cost thousands.

We've had two houses where pipes froze during a cold Colorado winter. The homeowners didn't winterize the property and had the utilities shut off. Both houses had water damage costing $50K each. In one house, the water went all the way to the basement and the entire ceiling caved in from the water damage. So yes, the banks can change locks to protect their asset!

What Is Equity Skimming?

This is where an investor buys the property subject to the existing loan and doesn't pay the mortgage. The investor basically takes the deed to the property and is now the owner. The mortgage stays in place on the property. The investor then rents the house out in less than six months and does not make the payments. The investor basically pockets the payments. The only way it's not equity skimming is if you disclose to the homeowner that you won't pay the mortgage and they agree. Whatever you do, don't do this. This is serious, and you could go to prison for fraud.

Are There Renter Laws to Be Aware Of?[15]

Before May 2009 there were no renter laws to protect renters who were living in a house that is foreclosing. There is a new law called the Federal Protecting Tenants at

---

[15] www.frascona.com/resource/war110_protecting_tenants_foreclosure_act_eviction.htm

Foreclosure Act. This act seems to be very ambiguous and may be left for the court system to sort out.

The lease must be written before the home is put into foreclosure and must have the following:

- The tenant is not a child, spouse or parent of the debtor.
- The lease or tenancy was formed in an arm's length transaction.
- The lease or tenancy provides for rent that is not substantially less than fair market value.

If there is a tenant living in the property, the recipient of a PT Deed cannot start an eviction for a minimum of 90 days. The Act will likely be interpreted to allow for this minimum 90-day notice to quit a property in only the following three situations:

- The recipient of the PT Deed intends to occupy the property as a primary residence;
- The recipient of the PT Deed provides the required 90-day notice and then sells the property to someone who intends to occupy the property as a primary residence; or
- The tenant or occupant is without a lease or with a lease which can terminate in a shorter period of time under state law.

So, if the property is going to be utilized as a primary residence, or if the tenant has a weekly or monthly rental or a lease set to expire sooner than 90 days, a tenant complying with the terms of a lease must receive a minimum 90-day notice to quit before an eviction action can be filed in court.

Of perhaps greater significance to the foreclosure

investor is that if the above minimum 90-day notice criteria do not apply, the Act provides that the recipient of the PT Deed takes the property subject to the lease and the tenant gets to occupy the property for the remainder of the outstanding lease term. There is no language in the Act limiting this duration of time. So, if a tenant has a four-year lease on a property and one year has passed as of the date of the foreclosure sale, unless one of the 90-day exceptions apply, the Act seems to provide that the tenant can remain in the property for the remaining three years of the lease.

While not explicit, the Act will likely be interpreted to permit eviction if a tenant fails to comply with the terms of the existing lease post-foreclosure. So, if a tenant fails to pay rent or fails to comply with any other covenant in a written lease, the recipient of the PT Deed can likely initiate the eviction process under Colorado law sooner than the time frames set out in the Act. The Act is also likely to be interpreted to permit any tenant to waive its rights and vacate the property after the foreclosure sale without any further obligations to the recipient of the PT Deed.

For foreclosure investors looking to take possession of a residential property occupied by a bona fide tenant in less than 90 days, "Cash for Keys" is an option to consider.

The Act expires on December 31, 2012, unless Congress takes action to extend its effective date.

Chapter 4
Homeowner Foreclosure Avoidance Options, Scams to Avoid and MARS

A lot of emotions surround a homeowner when their home has been put into foreclosure, so once I'm involved with the homeowner on a short sale, the first thing I offer them is the option to back out at any time. They want to explore and try every option before they consider selling their home. Their situation is very sensitive and emotional, and selling their home is usually their last resort. If you were in their situation, you would want the same option. Therefore, always allow the homeowner to pursue other avenues for keeping their house while you are working the short sale. Selling their home on a short sale is a back-up plan for them if their other options don't work.

This approach keeps you from being the "bad guy" and getting a bad name. You want to keep your reputation so you can be rewarded with many great future referrals.

In order to make the homeowner feel safe and to ensure them you are providing a great service, you should always use the commission approved forms. These forms include many "outs" for the homeowner. We also add additional "outs" in the additional provisions section of the contract. This assures the homeowner that they can back out at any time without consequence.

Foreclosure is one of the most devastating financial challenges a family can face, but it is also something that many times can be avoided. Homeowners have several options to avoid foreclosure. You should be familiar with all these options so you can share them with the homeowner.

The following gives a brief explanation of the many options and solutions a homeowner has to avoid foreclosure.

Downloadable Form

Reinstatement

A reinstatement is the simplest solution to a foreclosure; however, it is often the most difficult for the homeowner faced with foreclosure. The homeowner simply requests the total amount owed to the mortgage company to date and pays it. This solution does not require the lender's approval and will "reinstate" a mortgage up to the day before the final foreclosure sale.

Forbearance or Repayment Plan

A forbearance or repayment plan is when the homeowner works with the lender to negotiate a repayment plan to pay back past due payments over time. In the case of forbearance, the homeowner typically makes their current mortgage payment in addition to a portion of the back payments they owe for an agreed-upon period of time until the back payments are paid. This is great for homeowners whose hardship situation was just temporary.

Mortgage Modification

A loan modification is a process where the homeowner tries to change the terms of their loan in order to make their mortgage more affordable. A mortgage modification involves modifying the interest rate on the loan, the principal balance of the loan, the term of the loan or a combination of these.

Unfortunately many loan modifications are unsuccessful. If loan modifications actually resulted in lower payments that were truly affordable to the homeowner in their situation, they would be successful. However, the reality is, most banks approve loan modifications with mortgage payments higher than the original payment so the bank can recoup their losses in the short term.

These modifications only work for homeowners who were in a short-term, temporary financial struggle. Most homeowners are suffering from a long-term or permanent hardship, so higher payments certainly can't be afforded.

Most loan modifications across the country are not working. Currently, the success rate for loan modifications is less than 20%. When a loan modification is approved, the homeowner is put on a six-month trial payment period. Unfortunately, nearly 40% of the homeowners do not make it through the trial period.

Rent the Property

If a homeowner's mortgage payment is low enough for the rental market in their area, they can convert their property to a rental property and use the rental income to pay the mortgage.

Deed in Lieu of Foreclosure

A Deed in Lieu (DIL) is also known as a "friendly foreclosure," as it allows the homeowner to return the property to the lender instead of having to go through the entire foreclosure process. Some banks will actually offer homeowners cash in return for their keys as long as they surrender the house in good condition. Lender approval is required for this option, and, if accepted, the homeowner must vacate the property. This is not a good option for the homeowner because they not only have to vacate the property quickly, but a DIL also shows up on their credit report as a foreclosure. A short sale is the better option.

Bankruptcy

Bankruptcy is oftentimes marketed as being a "foreclosure solution"; however, this is true only in some states and in certain situations. If the homeowner has non-mortgage debts that hinder or prohibit their ability to repay their mortgage and a personal bankruptcy will eliminate these debts, this may be a viable solution for them. However, if they file bankruptcy and include their home in the bankruptcy, their home will be foreclosed on, and the foreclosure will show on their credit report in addition to the bankruptcy.

With a bankruptcy, the homeowner does not have to worry about paying a deficiency. Doing a short sale and a bankruptcy together is much better than doing a bankruptcy and allowing the home to foreclose because of the credit implications. A foreclosure has a much more detrimental effect on a credit report than a bankruptcy does. You will soon realize many bankruptcy attorneys advise the homeowners to walk away from their houses after a bankruptcy. The bankruptcy attorney wants his life to be as easy as possible.

The truth is, if there is a foreclosure on a homeowner's credit report, they won't be able to buy a house for another seven years. If there is just a bankruptcy on their credit report, they can buy another house within three years. If there is a short sale on their credit and no bankruptcy, they can buy another house in two years. So from a credit standpoint, it is much better not having a foreclosure on their credit. If you are working with a homeowner in bankruptcy, you can explain the credit benefits of doing a short sale after bankruptcy, as opposed to allowing the home to foreclose. A foreclosure is far more detrimental than doing a short sale.

Make sure you work with a bankruptcy attorney who will do an Order of Abandonment. If the homeowner happens to already have a bankruptcy attorney and they won't cooperate by doing an Order of Abandonment, you will need to find another attorney willing to handle this portion of the bankruptcy. Doing an Order of Abandonment normally costs around $500–$750, depending on the homeowner's situation.

Refinance

If a homeowner has sufficient equity in their property and their credit is still in good standing, they may be able to refinance their mortgage.

Servicemembers Civil Relief Act (Military Personnel Only)

If a member of the military is experiencing financial distress due to deployment, and that person can show that their debt was entered into prior to deployment, they may qualify for relief under the Servicemembers Civil Relief Act. The American Bar Association has a network of attorneys who work with service members in relation to qualifying

Create your own *'Done for you'* Short Sale System for this relief.

Sell the Property

If the homeowner is in foreclosure but has sufficient equity in their home, they can list their property with a qualified agent in their area who understands the foreclosure process.

Short Sale

If a homeowner owes more on their mortgage than their property is currently worth, then they can hire a qualified real estate agent to market and sell their property through the negotiation of a short sale with their lender. This typically requires the property to be on the market, and the homeowner must have a financial hardship to qualify.

Hardship can be defined as a material change in the financial stability of the homeowner between the date the home was purchased and the date of the short sale negotiation. Acceptable hardships, as explained in Chapter 2, include, but are not limited to, an increase in mortgage payments due to a rise in their interest rate (ARM) or an increase in their taxes or insurance, or it can be from the loss of a job, divorce, death of a spouse, excessive debt, health issues and medical bills or a forced or unplanned relocation.

Foreclosure Scams

Advise homeowners to be aware of the many different foreclosure scams. Fraudulent foreclosure "rescue" professionals use half truths and outright lies to sell services that promise relief, but fail to deliver. Their goal is to make a quick profit through fees or mortgage payments they collect from the homeowner, but they do not pass the payments on to the lender.

Sometimes they assume ownership of your property by deceiving the homeowner. Then, when it's too late to save your home, they take the property or siphon off the equity. You've lost your home to foreclosure despite your best intentions. [16]

Foreclosure "Rescue" and Refinance Fraud

The scam artist offers to act as an intermediary between you and your lender to negotiate a repayment plan or loan modification and may even "guarantee" to save your home from foreclosure. You may be told to make mortgage payments to the scammer directly—along with significant, upfront fees—and be told that the scammer will forward the payments to your lender.

In reality, the scammer may pocket your money and leave you in worse shape on your loan. The scam artist also may tell you to stop making payments or stop communicating with your lender. Don't follow that advice. Remember that your mortgage lender should be the starting point for finding options to avoid foreclosure. You also should consider contacting qualified and approved credit counselors. [17]

Fake "Government" Modification Programs

Unscrupulous people may claim to be affiliated with, or approved by, the government or may ask you to pay high up-front fees to qualify for government mortgage modification

16 www.ftc.gov/bcp/edu/pubs/consumer/credit/cre42.pdf
17 www.occ.gov/news-issuances/consumer-advisories/2009/consumer-advisory-2009-1.html

programs. While government supported mortgage modification and refinancing initiatives are legitimate, the scam artist's claims are not. Keep in mind that you do not have to pay to benefit from these government programs. All you need to do is contact your lender or loan servicer.

The scam artist's name or website may be very similar to those of government agencies. The scam artist may use such terms as "Federal," "TARP," or other words or acronyms related to official U.S. government programs. These tactics are designed to fool you into thinking the scam artist is somehow approved by, or affiliated with, the government.

The government is taking actions to stop this fraud, but you also need to protect yourself. So be wary of claims offering "government-approved" or "official government" loan modifications. Your lender will be able to tell you whether you qualify for any government initiatives to prevent foreclosure. You do not have to pay anyone to benefit from them. [18]

Leaseback/Rent-to-Own Schemes

In this type of scam, you are asked to transfer the title to your home to the scammer, who will supposedly obtain new and better financing and/or allow you to remain in the home as a renter and eventually buy it back. If you do not comply with the terms of the rent-to-buy agreement, you will lose your money and face eviction.

The agreement may be very hard to comply with, because it may require high upfront and monthly payments that you can't afford. In fact, the scammers may have no intention of ever selling the home back to you. They simply

[18] www.occ.gov/news-issuances/consumer-advisories/2009/consumer-advisory-2009-1.html

want your home and your money.

Remember that transferring your title does not change your payment obligations—you will still owe your mortgage debt. The difference will be that you will no longer own your home. If payments are not made on the mortgage, your lender has the right to foreclose, and the foreclosure and any other problems will appear on your credit report.[19]

Bankruptcy Scams

You may have heard that filing bankruptcy will stop a foreclosure. This is true—but only temporarily. Filing bankruptcy brings an "automatic stay" into effect that stops any collection and foreclosure while the bankruptcy court administers the case. Eventually, you must start paying your mortgage lender, or the lender will be able to foreclose. Bankruptcy is rarely, if ever, a permanent solution for preventing foreclosure. In addition, bankruptcy will negatively impact your credit score and will remain on your credit report for 10 years. [20]

Debt-Elimination Schemes

Scammers may claim to be able to "eliminate" your debt by making illegitimate legal arguments that you are not obligated to pay back your mortgage. These scammers will provide you with inaccurate claims about applicable laws and finance, such as that "secret laws" can be used to eliminate debt or that banks do not have the authority to lend money. Do not stop making payments on your mortgage based on their claims.[21]

19 www.occ.gov/news-issuances/consumer-advisories/2009/consumer-advisory-2009-1.html
20 www.occ.gov/news-issuances/consumer-advisories/2009/consumer-advisory-2009-1.html
21 www.occ.gov/news-issuances/consumer-advisories/2009/consumer-advisory-2009-1.html

Where to Find Legitimate Help

If the homeowner is having trouble paying their mortgage or they have gotten a foreclosure notice, they need to contact their lender. They may be able to negotiate a new repayment schedule. Remember that lenders generally don't want to foreclose; it costs them money.

The homeowner can also contact a credit counselor through the Homeownership Preservation Foundation (HPF), a nonprofit organization that operates the national 24/7 toll-free hotline (1.888.995.HOPE) with free, bilingual, personalized assistance to help at-risk homeowners avoid foreclosure. HPF is a member of the HOPE NOW Alliance of mortgage servicers, mortgage market participants and counselors. More information about HOPE NOW is at www.995hope.org. [22]

Red Flags

If you're looking for foreclosure prevention help, you need to be aware that there are a lot of scams out there. Be sure to avoid any business that does the following:

- Guarantee to stop the foreclosure process—no matter what your circumstances.
- Instruct you not to contact your lender, lawyer or credit or housing counselor.
- Collect a fee before providing you with any services.
- Accept payment only by cashier's check or wire transfer.
- Encourage you to lease your home so you can buy it back over time.
- Tell you to make your mortgage payments directly

[22] www.ftc.gov/bcp/edu/pubs/consumer/credit/cre42.pdf

to the business instead of your mortgage company.

- Tell you to transfer your property deed or title to the business.
- Offer to buy your house for cash at a fixed price that is not set by the housing market at the time of sale.
- Offer to fill out paperwork for you.
- Pressure you to sign paperwork you haven't had a chance to read thoroughly or that you don't understand.[23]

Report Fraud

If you think you've been a victim of foreclosure fraud, contact the following agencies:

- Federal Trade Commission (FTC)
- Your state Attorney General
- Your local Better Business Bureau

More Information

To learn more about mortgages and other credit-related issues, visit www.ftc.gov/credit and www.mymoney.gov, the U.S. government's portal to financial education. The FTC works for the consumer to prevent fraudulent, deceptive and unfair business practices in the marketplace and to provide information to help consumers spot, stop and avoid them.

The following contact information is available if you need to file a complaint or get free information on consumer issues. Visit www.ftc.gov/ or call toll-free: 1-877-FTC-HELP (1-877-382-4357); TTY. 1-866-653-4261.[24]

---

23   www.ftc.gov/bcp/edu/pubs/consumer/credit/cre42.pdf
24   www.ftc.gov/bcp/edu/pubs/consumer/credit/cre42.pdf

Be an Ethical Investor

If you are going to be in the short sale business, you need to act in an ethical manner at all times. Ensure you always get everything in writing. Do not give verbal commitments to homeowners. It will come back to haunt you. Make sure everything is documented and every email is tracked. Put the property address in the subject line of every email. The new FTC regulations for MARS require you to keep all documentation with homeowners, whether you were able to help them or not.

If you are an investor who does not conduct business in an ethical manner, you will get caught! Many agencies are looking for unethical investors or investors committing fraud. Since I started investing, I have run across several unethical investors. I simply choose not to ever do business with them.

Even if you do everything legally and ethically, there is always a chance that you could get called to the real estate commission or attorney general, or get a complaint filed with the Better Business Bureau. Even when you don't do something wrong, homeowners will get upset, especially if their houses foreclose and they feel they need to blame someone. So work with the highest integrity, be honest and ethical and always make sure you have your ducks in a row.

(MARS) Mortgage Assistance Relief Services

The purpose of the MARS rule is to protect struggling homeowners who are facing foreclosure from unscrupulous service providers who take their money and provide little or no services and in some cases actually harm the homeowner. Realtors are now exempt from the MARS ruling effective July 15th, 2011, as long as their license is in good standing and they are giving accurate claims in their marketing.

If you market to homeowners to help them "avoid foreclosure" or other similar services such as loan modifications, this new rule will apply to you. If you are just marketing "we buy houses" or are just offering to list the house without mentioning "Avoid Foreclosure," then this new rule does not affect your business.

This new rule outlaws advanced fees from sellers, regulates claims made in marketing and requires specific disclosures.

This new federal rule applies to all types of mortgage relief assistance services, including anything having to do with short sales, loan modifications and/or deed-in-lieu settlements. It's a rule you don't want to break: penalties for non-compliance with the Federal Trade Commission's new MARS rule are up to $10,000 PER VIOLATION.

> **This new rule outlaws advanced fees from sellers, regulates claims made in marketing and requires specific disclosures.**

So, what should you do? SEEK LEGAL ADVICE. Even if after reading the entire MARS rule you think you are in compliance with it, you should have a qualified real estate attorney/firm look over ALL of your correspondence, marketing and forms. Make sure you comply. NO this new law won't shut us down, so please don't get scared, just change up your marketing, don't charge an upfront fee and for goodness sake don't make a claim you can't back up.

Here is an outline of the major changes taken from www.ftc.gov/opa/2011/02/pdf/110210mars_business.pdf.

•It's illegal to charge upfront fees

> As an, investor, short sale negotiation company or mortgage modification company, you can no longer charge an upfront fee to the homeowner.

> You cannot try to rename the fee and charge, for example, a "marketing fee," "co-list fee" or "negotiation fee" in advance for the short sale.

> You cannot charge an upfront fee from a customer until you've met the three requirements:

a. You get an offer of mortgage relief from your customer's lender or servicer. You must have persuaded your customer's lender or servicer to reduce, modify or otherwise change the terms of the customer's mortgage loan.

b. You give your customer the written offer. You must provide your customer with a written agreement from the lender or servicer to reduce, modify or otherwise change the terms of the customer's mortgage loan.

c. Your customer accepts the written offer. The customer's acceptance must be in the form of an executed written agreement with the lender or servicer that incorporates the changes to the terms of his or her mortgage loan.

•You must clearly and prominently disclose certain information before you sign people up for your

services.

> You must tell them upfront key information about your services, including:

a. The total cost

b. That they can stop using your services at any time

c. That you're not associated with the government or their lender

d. That their lender may not agree to change the terms of their mortgage

•**If you advise someone not to pay his or her mortgage, you must clearly and prominently disclose the negative consequences that could result.**

> You must warn customers that failure to pay could result in the loss of their home or damage to their credit rating.

•**Don't advise customers to stop communicating with their lender or servicer.**

> Under the Rule, it's illegal to tell people they shouldn't communicate with their lender or servicer.

•**You must disclose key information to your customer if you forward an offer of mortgage relief from a lender or servicer.**

> You must give your customer a written notice from the lender or servicer describing all material differences between the terms of the offer and the customer's current loan. You also have to tell your customer that if the lender or servicer's offer isn't acceptable to them, they don't have to pay your fee.

•**Don't misrepresent your services.**

> Under the Rule, it's illegal to make claims that are false,

misleading or unsubstantiated.

a. The likelihood of negotiating, getting or arranging a specific form of mortgage relief

b. How long it will take to get the advertised mortgage relief

c. An affiliation with the government, public programs or lenders or servicers

d. The terms and conditions of homeowners' mortgages, including how much they currently have to pay

e. Your refund and cancellation policies

f. Whether homeowners will be getting legal services

g. The benefits and costs of using alternatives to for-profit MARS providers

h. The amount homeowners may save if they use your service

i. The total cost of your service

j. The terms, conditions or limitations of a lender or servicer's offer of mortgage relief, including the amount of time the homeowner has to accept the offer

•**Disclosures you must make in ads meant for a general audience:**

> The Rule requires certain disclosures in what it calls "general commercial communications"—that is, advertising meant for a general audience, like ads on TV, radio or the Internet. In those ads, you must clearly and prominently disclose two key facts, in these words:

a. "[Name of your company] is not associated with the government, and our service is not approved by the government or your lender"; and

b. "Even if you accept this offer and use our service,

your lender may not agree to change your loan."

> The two disclosures must be presented together. The Rule has specific requirements for presenting them.

•Disclosures you must make in communications with prospective customers:

> The Rule requires additional disclosures in any "consumer specific commercial communication"—that is, a letter, phone call, email, text or the like, directed at a specific person you're soliciting for your service. In every communication you have with prospective customers, the Rule requires that you clearly and prominently disclose three key facts, in these words; they must be preceded with IMPORTANT NOTICE in Bold; and it must be two font sizes bigger than the statement below:

a."You may stop doing business with us at any time. You may accept or reject the offer of mortgage assistance we obtain from your lender [or servicer]. If you reject the offer, you do not have to pay us. If you accept the offer, you will have to pay us [insert amount or method for calculating the amount] for our services."

b. "[Name of your company] is not associated with the government, and our service is not approved by the government or your lender;" and

c."Even if you accept this offer and use our service, your lender may not agree to change your loan."

> The three disclosures must be presented together. The Rule has specific requirements for presenting these disclosures to prospective customers.

•You must keep your records for at least two years
> You must keep records for at least two years from the

date you create, generate or receive documents

> You must keep a copy of each substantially different advertisement, brochure, telemarketing script, website, training document or other material related to the advertising or marketing of your service. You don't have to keep separate copies of documents that have minor, immaterial differences.

> You have to keep records showing the name, last known address and telephone number of each of your customers; the services they bought from you; and how much they paid you. You need to maintain records relating only to customers who agree to use your services. You don't have to keep records relating to people who asked about your services, but didn't sign up.

> You must keep copies of all written communications between you and customers that occurred before they agreed to use your service.

> You must keep copies of all contracts or other agreements between you and your customer.

> It is the business owner's responsibility to make sure all employees or independent contractors within the business are complying with the new law.

For more information about this new law, please refer to the following links:

www.ftc.gov/opa/2011/02/pdf/110210mars_business.pdf
www.ftc.gov/os/2010/11/R911003mars.pdf
www.ftc.gov/opa/2010/11/mars.shtm

Chapter 5
Finding Short Sale Leads

Marketing—Starting Small

When you are ready to pursue marketing, I recommend you start out small and expand a little at a time. When I first started, I put a monthly ad in the local thrifty nickel paper for $50 per month, and I paid $65 per month to use a lead generating website. These were two effective advertising sources I engaged in that cost me just over $100 a month. I did this for about a year and was very happy with the number of leads I received from doing this. As I grew, I expanded my marketing by establishing a website for my company. The cost to do this was about $1500 for the design and programming. I used a local computer expert who had previously done websites for other investors, so he already had most of the programming I needed available. He just needed to customize it for my business.

As my earnings began to come in, I added bandit signs to my marketing mix. When I first started, I did it myself with the help of my partner. Then I hired someone to build them and put them out for $1 per sign. We also started mailing weekly letters to the homeowners on the foreclosure list in El Paso County. Our letters were personal and explained how we could help them avoid foreclosure. We mailed letters to the homeowners weekly until they either called us to help them or called us to remove them from our mailing list or until the house foreclosed. We used revenues to continue expanding our advertising and marketing. If you start out small and simple, your start-up costs and advertising costs are minimal. As you grow, build your advertising. You will find you get a great return on your investment.

Finding the Pre-Foreclosures

There are several ways to find homeowners in distress; in this chapter we will discuss several of them, giving strong emphasis on the ways we know work best. A homeowner does not need to be in foreclosure to do a short sale. In fact, depending on the homeowner's loan type, they can be current and still do a short sale. Simple marketing techniques can make any distressed homeowner call you for help. You can use a software system to pull up pre-foreclosure information. In Colorado, there is a website called www.RENAV.com that provides a service that will instantly notify you of new pre-foreclosures. It also notifies you when the foreclosure sale dates get postponed and when the banks post bid figures. I use this system every day to bring me instant leads.

 www.Renav.com

If you want a 10% discount on your first month, type the discount code "Pink."

Downloadable Form

Door Knocking the Foreclosure List

Other than the gas you spend driving from house to house, door knocking is absolutely free! Each county has its own foreclosure list, so do an online search to pull up the website that lists all the active foreclosures in your area. In El Paso County, Colorado, you can look at people who are in active foreclosure by going to the El Paso County Public Trustee's website: www.elpasopublictrustee. com. Or you can use Renav.com to instantly pull up the pre-foreclosures. In Colorado, once a homeowner is put into foreclosure status, they have four months before their house forecloses.

There are several ways you can search on the foreclosure list, so if you want to target a specific neighborhood, do a search on that particular subdivision. If you want to target a certain zip code, search by zip code. Being able to search in many ways lets you organize your time and leg work!

When you go door knocking on homeowner's doors, you will get many different types of reactions. A common reaction is rejection. Some people will simply slam the door in your face! No one likes rejection, but you will get a lot of it, so it is good to prepare yourself. You don't need to be afraid of it. Their rejection is not personal; it has absolutely nothing to do with you. It has to do with their ability to deal with their situation.

Homeowner objections are another common "door knocking" scenario. They will come up with one objection after another. So be prepared to use your knowledge so you can professionally combat each objection they throw at you. The more you face and deal with these two common issues, the more comfortable you'll feel and the more experience you'll gain. And before long, you will be confident and completely prepared for any type of person that may be on the other side of that door.

The good news about door knocking is you won't have a

lot of competition. Most people don't want to do it because they don't like rejection. The more you do it and the more you experience people's different reactions, the better you will get at it and the better prepared you will be to handle them. You will experience a variety of negative reactions, but you will also get people who are relieved when they find out you can help them.

The biggest key to successful door knocking is being knowledgeable about the foreclosure process, the short sale process and all the homeowner benefits. You need to present yourself as an expert in the field. You will stand out if you are confident, know what you are talking about and can handle any objection. Balance your knowledge with your compassion. Be smart enough to answer all their questions and compassionate enough to let them know that the benefits of what you are doing go to them. What you do is help homeowners! Going through my program will help you become the expert you want to be.

Some suggestions I can make from my own personal experience include dressing casually so you don't appear intimidating. You don't want to scare the homeowner by making them think you're an official there to evict them or the bank demanding their payment. You want to go to their door dressed in jeans and a nice shirt or business casual—khaki pants with a polo shirt that has your company name on it.

Be confident! Have a big smile on your face when you knock on their door. Confidence in yourself and being very knowledgeable about short sales definitely helps you sell yourself to the homeowners. Don't be pushy. Be nice, be professional and explain how you can help them. Let them know you are there to help them save their house from foreclosure. Ask them if they are working on a solution, such as a loan modification, to save their home. If they are, explain the benefits of not relying on one avenue in the event their solution does not work. Explain that you can help them at the same time they are working their loan modification and that they can cancel or back out at any time.

Who Should Door Knock?

You can either go door knocking yourself, or you can hire a birddog to go door knocking for you. I find that the best door knockers to hire are birddogs who are good sales people. You want to target people who are either currently working in sales or those who have previous sales experience who are also accustomed to being paid on commission, as this is how you will pay them.

In my experience, younger people who have an adorable face are the ones that give homeowners a warm and fuzzy feeling when they are at the door, because they don't look intimidating. It is OK to have men be door knockers, but I have had the best success when I've used a young adult, a female, or a couple. I do not recommend having two older men do your door knocking together. Oftentimes, using a couple to do your door knocking can bring about great results. There are times when you may encounter women who don't respond well to men, or you may find men who would prefer talking to another man. So having both sexes at the door is sometimes quite beneficial.

I don't recommend hiring someone who wants to be an investor, as you will end up training someone who will be your future competition. It is best stick with motivated and experienced sales people who are good with people and who are used to selling things door-to-door.

Step 1: Creating a List

The first thing you need to do is create a list of leads and organize them by area. It works best for saving time and gas when you knock on doors in one specific area at a time. The El Paso County Public Trustee's website will allow you to pull up homes on the foreclosure list by area. You can build your list on an Excel spreadsheet, or you can print out the assessor's information and foreclosure information from the website. If you build an Excel spreadsheet, you should include the following information:

- Homeowner's names
- Property address of the house being foreclosed
- Homeowner's address if it is different from the property address
- Name of the foreclosing bank
- Type of mortgage
- Principal balance and mortgage amount owed
- Foreclosure sale date

You may want to do some extra research before you begin your drive to neighborhoods. Try to verify if the homeowners live at the property. Sometimes there is no way to know if they have moved until you go to the house, but you can check the assessor's website to see if the mailing address is different from the property address. Also, the El Paso County Public Trustee's foreclosure site has a tab for mailings. You can see the address where notifications were mailed and know if it is the same as the property address.

hese extra steps can save you time and money.

Another step you can do is search by name and address by going to www.phonenumber.com. You can search by name and address. This can give you their current address and home phone number. If you can obtain a phone number, it is helpful so you can cold call them after you have been to their house and knocked on their door. I have found that many times the phone number listed has been disconnected, but it is still worth the effort. You can also do a reverse address search. You may find the name listed is not the owner. This is a good indication that the house is currently rented. Renters generally know how to contact the homeowner. If a property manager is managing the property, they generally know how to reach the homeowner.

Step 2: Create a Package

The next step is to create a credibility package, so you can provide the homeowner with quality information about how they can save their house from foreclosure. Below are some suggestions for putting a package together and what information should be included:

*(Downloadable Sample Door-knocking Package)

•Create a book with foreclosure and short sale information that also includes homeowner options for avoiding foreclosure. You want to include all of your contact information, testimonials, etc. You can get them printed and bound at Kinko's or other office supply stores.

•Create a professional folder with your company information on it and include the information on foreclosures, short sales and homeowner options for avoiding foreclosure.

•Have a testimonial page printed so the homeowners can see the past clients you have helped and their positive responses.

•Include a list of services that your business provides as well as the benefits you can offer them if they work with you.

•Include a business card that has your name on it and contains all your contact information.

•Include a refrigerator magnet! People love magnets, and when they are ready they will call you

•Feel free to include anything else you think will motivate the seller to call you.

Step 3: Plan Your Route

Plan and organize your door-knocking route by grouping together houses in the same neighborhood. This will save you a lot of time. If you have a GPS system in your car, that helps organize your route even more. If you don't, it is helpful to print out driving directions and maps from one house to another.

Step 4: Understand Different Types of Homeowners

Before you begin knocking on doors, it is a good idea

to understand the different types of homeowners you will encounter.

Seller in Denial

Sellers in denial are homeowners who haven't admitted to themselves that their home is really in foreclosure. They have not yet accepted this fact. This type of homeowner generally ignores bank letters and public trustee notifications because they have not yet grasped the fact that they are losing their home. When you confront a person in denial, they may tell you they are not in foreclosure or they have already taken care of the problem.

Angry Seller

An angry seller is a homeowner who is very upset and generally looks to blame someone else for their current situation. They usually blame the bank that is foreclosing and say how they won't help them or how they are wrongfully foreclosing on their house. The angry seller may slam the door in your face. It is best not to be confrontational with this type of person as they may become verbally abusive and get very angry. If you are able to get this type of person to open up, it is best to agree with them. You can make comments such as, "I can't believe the bank would do that to you," or "I heard a similar story from another person trying to do the same thing with that bank and it seems like they just want to screw you." Just agree with them and be on their side.

The Sad Seller

The sad seller has begun to accept responsibility for

their situation and what caused them to get to the point of foreclosure. They have stopped blaming others for their financial situation. This leaves the homeowner very emotional about their situation, but they are in a mental state where they are much easier to talk to. They are more willing to accept help, and you can usually sell them a deal when they are in this stage.

The Acceptance Seller

When a homeowner has finally reached the point of acceptance, it is the best and easiest time to contact them. If you have already contacted the homeowner prior to this point, this is the time when they are most likely to contact you. They have finally accepted the fact that they are losing their home and need help. Unfortunately, many homeowners do not reach the acceptance stage until right before the foreclosure date. You will get more deals from desperate homeowners at this stage; however, it is best to try to have them sign a deal prior to this time so there is time to postpone the foreclosure.

Step 5: Opening Lines

There are many different things you can say to a homeowner when they open the door.

- •Hi, my Name is Monica with Pink Real Estate. I'm here to possibly offer some help regarding your foreclosure. What have you tried to do so far to save your house from foreclosure and has it been working for you?
- •Hi, my Name is Monica with Pink Real Estate. Have you received any help yet regarding your foreclosure?
- •Hi, my name is Monica with Pink Real Estate. I

wanted to help you avoid foreclosure and possibly give you $3k in moving expenses.

• Hi, my name is Monica with Pink Real Estate, have you heard about the new government short sale programs? You may be eligible to receive up to $3k in moving money.

Step 6: Selling the Deal

Tell the homeowner how a short sale can help them save their home from foreclosure. Briefly tell them about the particular program they may be in. If they are already working on a solution, explain the advantage of having a backup plan ready in case their solution doesn't work out. Tell them that when they are dealing with a foreclosure, they only have one shot to save their house, and if they only focus on one alternative and find it doesn't work, they could risk losing their house to foreclosure. It's best to work on several alternatives at the same time. This is a risk-free solution because if they are able to keep their home, they can cancel. There is special verbiage in the contracts that protect homeowners so they can cancel at any time.

While you are telling the homeowner how you can help them, it is very important that you also get them to open up about how they got into this situation. Let them vent and talk about everything they have done so far. Listen to them and show them your sympathy for having to go through this tough situation. Once you have them sold, schedule a time when you can have a real estate agent meet with them.

Step 7: Follow Up

If the homeowner isn't completely sold on doing a

short sale, hand them your package of information and ask if you can follow up with them. If their plan doesn't work out, you want to be able to help them when they are ready. Ask for their phone number and email address. Make sure you follow up with them every two weeks to see how they are doing.

Step 8: When No One Is Home

If the house is vacant or the homeowners aren't home, don't just walk away. Put a note on their door with your information packet. On your note write, "Hi Jessica, I wanted to help you save your house from foreclosure. I'm very interested in buying your house. Please call me. Monica 123-5555."

Then you want to knock on the doors of every house around that house. Ask the neighbors if they know how to reach the homeowners. Tell them you are interested in buying their house to help them avoid foreclosure and to help clean up the neighborhood by fixing the house up. If the neighbors know how to reach them, they may give you their information. Ask if they know where they moved, their phone number, where they work or what their email address is, or for any information they may have that will help you contact them. If neighbors are not home, leave notes on their doors as well, asking them to call if they know how to reach the homeowner, because you want to help them avoid foreclosure.

Here is a sample note you can leave on a homeowner's door:

Hello Sam,

I am very interested in buying your house and keeping it out of foreclosure. Please call me to talk about it.

Monica
(719) 471- Pink
(7465)

Here is a sample note you can leave on a neighbor's door:

> 1/1/11
>
> Hi,
>
> I am very interested in buying the house across the street at 123 Main St. They are facing foreclosure and I really want to help them. Do you know how I can contact them?
>
> Monica
> (719) 471-PINK
> (7465)

Mailing People on the Foreclosure List

If you don't feel comfortable door knocking, you can also contact homeowners in default via a marketing campaign by sending out a series of letters and postcards. When the homeowners are ready, they will call you. The best approach is to be professional and compassionate with the mailings. Please don't be rude or say anything harsh in your letters or postcards. You typically get a much better response when you show the homeowners in your letters that you actually care about them and want to help.

Letters

The letters you send to homeowners shouldn't be all about you and your company. They shouldn't be impersonal, pushy or threatening. The letters need to be very personal and compassionate, and they need to specifically explain to the homeowners how you can help them avoid foreclosure.

Handwritten letters are very effective. You don't need to handwrite all of them. You can handwrite one letter, scan the letter into your computer and save it as a file. Then print it out. It will look like you handwrote that letter to the homeowner.

I like to also send out a professional letter. When I send out a professional letter, like the example below, I include a handwritten note on the letter. It completely personalizes the letter, and I have seen a lot of very positive responses from doing this.

Hi Jennifer,   1/28/11

    I am very interested in ~~by~~ buying your house at
123 Main St and keeping it from foreclosure. My company
Specializes in helping people avoid Foreclosure. Even if
you have no equity in your house and are completely
upside down, I can help.
    There is a process that we can buy your house called
a short sale. A short sale is where you sell your house
for less than what you owe on the house. Your lender
will negotiate a price with me to buy your house.
    I see that you have an FHA loan. There is actually
a special government short sale program for homeowners
with this loan. It's called the Pre-foreclosure
Sale Program. When you sell this house under
the program, You will receive $1,000 for moving
expenses!
    If you are interested in hearing more about
this program, please give me a call, I would love
to help.

    Sincerely,

    Monica Adams
    (719) 471-PINK
         (7465)

Handwritten letter

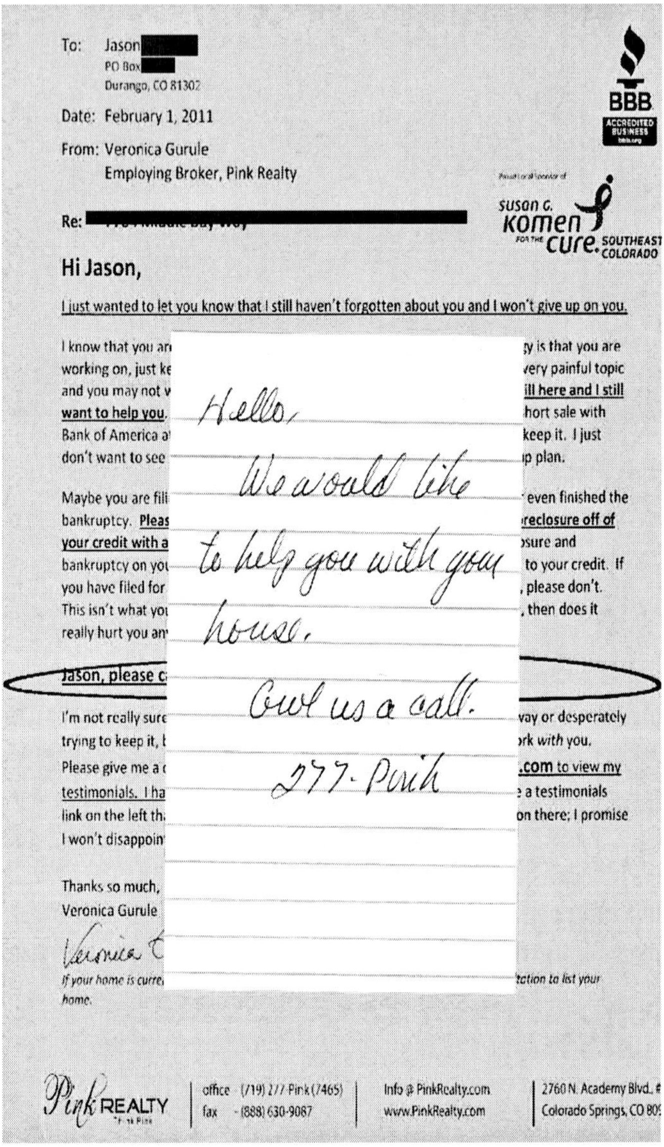

To: Jason ▓▓▓
PO Box ▓
Durango, CO 81302

Date: February 1, 2011

From: Veronica Gurule
Employing Broker, Pink Realty

Re: ▇▇▇▇▇▇▇▇▇▇

BBB
ACCREDITED
BUSINESS
bbb.org

Proud Local Sponsor of
SUSAN G.
KOMEN
FOR THE CURE. SOUTHEAST COLORADO

Hi Jason,

I just wanted to let you know that I still haven't forgotten about you and I won't give up on you.

I know that you ar... ...y is that you are working on, just ke... ...very painful topic and you may not v... ...ill here and I still **want to help you.** ...hort sale with Bank of America a... ...keep it. I just don't want to see ... ...p plan.

Maybe you are fili... ...even finished the bankruptcy. **Pleas...** ...reclosure off of **your credit with a...** ...osure and bankruptcy on you... ...to your credit. If you have filed for... ...please don't. This isn't what yo... ...then does it really hurt you an...

Jason, please c...

I'm not really sure... ...vay or desperately trying to keep it, b... ...rk with you. Please give me a c... **...com** to view my testimonials. I ha... ...e a testimonials link on the left tha... ...on there; I promise I won't disappoin...

Thanks so much,
Veronica Gurule

Veronica G

If your home is curre... ...tation to list your home.

Handwritten note:
Hello,
We would like
to help you with your
house.
Owl us a call.
277-Pink

Pink REALTY
Think Pink

office - (719) 277-Pink (7465)
fax - (888) 630-9087

Info @ PinkRealty.com
www.PinkRealty.com

2760 N. Academy Blvd. #
Colorado Springs, CO 809

Formal letter

Postcards

Postcards are very effective because you don't have to worry about the homeowners opening the mail. When doing postcards, your message should be very clear. You can do handwritten notes on postcards as well. Write a handwritten note, scan the note into a file, and upload to www.click2mail.com as a picture. This becomes the picture on your postcard, and it looks like you handwrote the postcard to the homeowner.

Or you can design your own postcard and order them from www.Uprinting.com. Once you get the postcards, you will need to have somebody stamp and address them. I usually use an address label for the postcards instead of hand addressing.

Addressing Your Envelope

• Use a pretty stamp like Disney, comic, animals, anything cute, but not religious.
• Place the stamp at an angle.
• Hand address the envelope in blue ink.
• Have a cute and decorative return address label that doesn't look like a formal business return address label

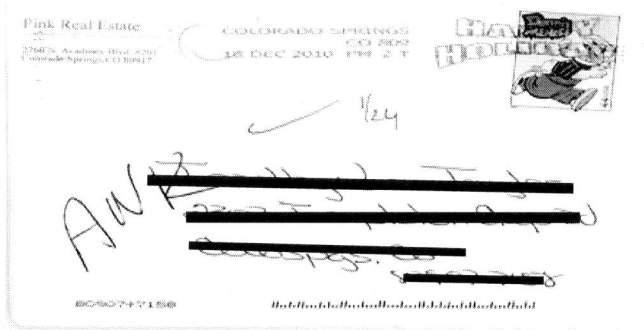

Envelopes

When you do your mailings, you can get very creative. Use a variety of different types of envelopes that are different from the standard envelopes everyone uses. And when you go door knocking, you can put your information into unique decorative or holiday bags.

- Metallic Foil Envelopes: They are very flashy and very interesting looking.

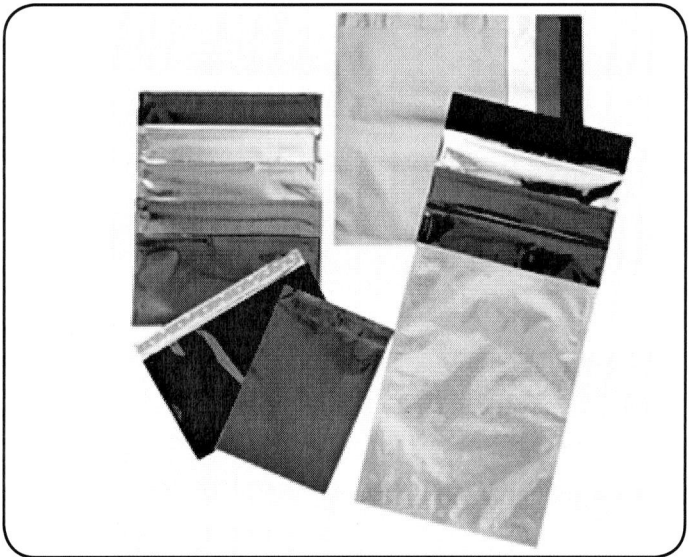

- Trick or treat bags: They are great to use during Halloween.

• Christmas Cards—During December, mail the homeowner a Christmas card with your letter inside. Handwrite a simple holiday message inside the card to personalize it. You will be surprised what an impact this makes.

• Clear zip-lock bag—This is see-through, so put a check inside that is not signed.

You can buy colored envelopes online at

• www.Envelopes.com
• www.Responsemail.com
• www.Wallet-Mailer.com
• www.envelopemail.com
• www.jampaper.com

Object Mailings (Lumpy Mail)

You can place an object inside the mail that will stick out. This makes the homeowners wonder what's inside the envelope and entices them to want to open the letter. You can place objects in the letter like a key, a compass or dice. You can put a little catch phrase associated with the objects. For example:

• This is the key to a new future.
• Do you need some direction?
• Are you struggling to find your way?
• Don't take a gamble on your foreclosure; learn your options.

You can buy small objects in bulk at:
www.orientaltrading.com.

How Often Should I Mail?

Persistence is key! Most of the time, a homeowner

wants to try to save their house from foreclosure by keeping it. They are not ready to sell. Eventually there will come a point when the homeowner wants to sell their house or realizes they don't have another option. I mail homeowners every week until their home forecloses. The homeowner is getting mail from many different companies to help them avoid foreclosure. You want to stand out from the rest of the crowd. You will stand out by mailing them weekly and by mailing them creative and unique mail. Many companies only mail the homeowner one letter. Below is how I structure my mailings:

Week 1—Introduction Letter

Week 2—Letter #1

Week 3—Postcard

Week 4—Letter #2

Week 5—Postcard

Week 6—Letter #3

Week 7—Postcard

Week 8—Letter #4

Week 9—Postcard

Week 10—Letter #5

Week 11—Postcard

Week 12—Letter #6

Week 13—Postcard

Week 14—Letter #7

Week 15—Postcard

Week 16—Letter #8

Week 17 until the date of the foreclosure—Postcard each week

Each letter is different and has a different topic of focus. For example, letter 1 may discuss the different types of short sales for each loan, letter 2 may discuss the HAFA program, letter 3 may discuss loan modifications and letter 4 may discuss bankruptcy, etc.

In my initial letter, I usually send a magnet and a business card. In each letter, I attach an article or include important information they need to know. If a homeowner calls and asks you to remove them from the mailing list, talk to them first before removing them. Find out why they want to be removed. Many times they want to be removed for a legitimate reason. Maybe the home has already been foreclosed, maybe the foreclosure was withdrawn or maybe their loan modification was approved.

If they request to be removed from your list, remove them. If you don't, they could contact the Better Business Bureau (BBB) to file a complaint. If the homeowner doesn't have a legitimate reason for wanting to be removed, try to talk to them first and tell them how you can help them before taking their name off your list.

Advertising around Town

Advertising around town is a great way to catch attention. You will notice by advertising around town, sellers will call you before they are even in foreclosure, and this will give you more time to negotiate the short sale.

Bandit Signs

Do searches online to find the sign company with the cheapest prices. Competition among these companies is high, so pricing frequently changes. Make sure you order signs that have the flutes positioned horizontally. When it is windy, the sign will bend around the stake if the flutes are vertical. You can stake the bandit signs into the ground at various intersections or you can staple them onto telephone poles. You can go to www.signstapler.com to buy a long pole with a stapler on the top. This will staple your sign high on the telephone pole so the sign police can't reach it and take it down!

We order our stakes in bulk and pre-cut from a local wood company, Home Depot or Lowes. The stakes need to be 1"x2" and 26" long, single or double bevel point on the bottom so they can be easily put into the ground. Buy some roofing nails from Home Depot or Lowes. Hire a team of laborers to put your signs together and to put them out. Make sure you give them a map showing the locations where you want your signs placed and include directions with which way you want the signs to face. I always choose major intersections with the signs facing the drivers who are stopped at a stop light or stop sign. You can place an ad on Craigslist.org for the labor help needed to get this done. I placed one ad and had 300 applicants respond to the job for $1 per sign. This price included putting the signs together and putting them out. You'll be amazed how many people will do this job for $1 per sign.

Check with local city ordinances before putting out bandit signs. Some city ordinances allow signs to be put out during certain days and/or certain times. Some city ordinances don't allow it at all and consider it illegal. In Colorado Springs, signs can go out on Fridays at noon but must be picked up by the following Monday at noon. We put our signs out every Friday, but we did not go back on Monday to take them down because so many signs got taken down or destroyed over the weekend by the people who don't like the signs being up! Many of the calls we receive are from folks who see our signs during the week and either call during a lunch hour or on their way home from work, so we're happy when there are a few signs standing after the weekend!

You may get complaint calls about your signs. It's amazing how many people actually hate signs being up around the city. If you get harassing calls about your signs in a particular area, just don't put any signs in that area. If you do have your signs out when they aren't supposed to be, you could receive a fine from the city. However, in Colorado Springs, the city doesn't have enough manpower to police the signs around town, so it rarely becomes an issue.

Put a clear message on your signs with a phone number people can remember while driving by. Make your phone number a local phone number. For example:

555-HELP	555-HOPE	555-SAVE
555-CASH	555-STOP	555-FAST

Billboards

Bus Stop Bench Signs

Bus stop bench advertising is another great way to bring in leads. This form of advertising is permanent, and you won't have to worry about anyone taking your signs down or vandalizing them. You sign a contract with a company, and they guarantee replacement of your signs if they are vandalized. However, this form of advertising is very expensive, so I recommend you be a seasoned investor before you invest in this advertising route.

Car Magnets

This is a very inexpensive way to get advertising around town. Have family members drive around with these car magnet signs.

Door Hangers

There are many websites that already have templates for "We Buy Houses" door hangers or "Avoid Foreclosure" door hangers. I prefer to create my own personal message and upload my file to www.Uprinting.com. My door hanger message is very clear: "Avoid Foreclosure 555-1000."

On the door hanger we say how we can help them, the money they can possibly get, our company name, the BBB logo, our website, testimonials and a picture. You can hire someone to put out the door hangers and pay them an amount per door hanger; however, you will need to drive the route afterwards to ensure the door hangers were placed!

Flyers

Flyers can be made very inexpensively. There are several companies online that can print your own personal custom flyers, or you can use their online templates.

Company Website and Lead Generating Websites

Create a company website and plaster it with testimonials from every client. Be sure your website includes very specific and detailed information on how you can help homeowners avoid foreclosure. Many people research companies and the various types of help they can provide when they are dealing with foreclosure.

There are many foreclosure scams out there today, so you need to make yourself and your company stand out from your competition. Get accredited with your local BBB and make sure you don't have any complaints. Also, if you affiliate yourself with a local charity, it makes your company look even better and stronger.

You can also pay lead generating websites to generate leads for you. There are many websites available that do this. For example: www.webuyhouses.com and www.cashhomebuyers.com. All you need to do is pretend you are a seller who needs to sell ASAP. Google: Avoid Foreclosure Denver, sell house fast Denver, We buy houses Denver. You will find a ton of websites. Go to each website and contact the owner to see if your area is available for an investor to purchase. Generating leads this way when you are first starting up your business is much less expensive than building a website from scratch.

Referrals

A lot of our business comes from referrals. Once you are in the business for a while and have established a good name and reputation, your referrals will grow. Past clients will refer you to their friends and family, and other professionals in the real estate industry will refer their clients to you when they know what you can do and see that you can help people save their homes from foreclosure.

Other free ways to generate leads and get deals are to network with people in related industries, such as those provided below. People in these industries have contact with distressed homeowners and people going through financial hardships. Talk with them, tell them what you do, give them flyers to pass out to their clients and tell them you will reciprocate and refer clients to them. Offer them a referral fee if a deal gets signed.

Realtors® and Real Estate Agents

Realtors® and real estate agents are a great source for short sales. You can have them look for deals for you or see if they would be a good fit for working together with you or being your buyer's agent.

Expired/Withdrawn Listings from the MLS

If you have a buyer's agent, you can have them send you a list of expired listings and withdrawals from the MLS. These homeowners may be frustrated with their realtors, so if you approach them as an instant buyer, they will probably be happy.

Mortgage Brokers

When a homeowner is in trouble with their mortgage, the first thing they do is contact a mortgage broker to see if they can refinance their house. If they are currently past due on their payments or the current value of their home is less than what they owe, they are generally turned down for the refinance. These are junk leads to mortgage brokers but great leads for you! Become friends with a lot of mortgage brokers. Tell them what you do and ask them to refer you leads. You can offer to pay them a referral fee if a deal is signed or offer to pay them a fee when the deal closes.

Real Estate Attorneys

It is good to have a couple of good real estate attorneys you can rely on who understand the foreclosure and short sale process, as well as the state laws regarding the different types of real estate closings. You want to have a good real estate attorney contact for when you have questions about changes in the laws or if you are engaging in a unique sales transaction.

Divorce Attorneys

You will find that many people going through a foreclosure may also be going through a divorce. Divorce attorneys are a great resource. Create a list of divorce attorneys in your area. Again, tell them what you do and ask them to refer their clients. Be sure to offer them a referral fee and tell them you will reciprocate and refer clients to them as well.

Probate Attorneys

Another great source for distressed property leads are probate attorneys. Generally, if the estate can't afford to maintain the house or afford the payments, it does nothing about it. If you work with the probate attorney handling the estate case and promise the estate some money for helping you buy the house, they may be willing to cooperate.

Bankruptcy Attorneys

A wonderful source for leads is bankruptcy attorneys,

if they are willing to cooperate with a short sale. You want to build a good relationship with at least one reputable bankruptcy attorney who supports short sales. If a bankruptcy attorney does not support short sales, they can make the process very difficult and can possibly stop a short sale from happening. You want a relationship with a bankruptcy attorney who is willing to provide Order of Abandonments on properties.

Accountants

Accountants are another great source for referrals, as they do have contact with people going through financial distress.

Other businesses to consider when you are looking to place flyers around town are pawn shops and second hand stores as these are businesses that homeowners frequently patronize when going through a financial hardship.

Additionally, you can contact housing centers, family and marriage counselors, homeowners' associations, business and social clubs and churches and charities that help families in distress. There are endless inexpensive ways to get your flyers placed around town and get the word out that you are here to help homeowners.

Go to the Foreclosure Court Hearings

This is the hearing where homeowners can dispute the foreclosure. In our state it's called the 120 hearing. It may be called different things in different states. You can hand out business cards at this hearing and talk with the homeowners and tell them how you can help them.

Other Marketing Ideas

- Business Cards
- Outbound calls—cold calls
- Voice broadcast
- Flyers
- Post-it notes on doors

Other means of building your business and generating leads include pursuing traditional marketing tactics. These may include the following:

TV, Radio, Newspaper

Your local newspapers, radio stations and news channels can help you market to your clients. Their creative departments can help you with company branding, creating the right message for your audience, targeting your market with the radio and television air times, etc. Oftentimes you can find someone to do the production less expensively. If you go this route, be sure to get the technical specification requirements from the station you plan to air your commercials with before starting production. While newspaper, TV and radio advertising is very effective marketing, it is very costly.

Newspaper Advertising

You can have the newspaper ads run every day or weekly. Make your ad stand out over all other ads.

- Circle your ad
- Box your ad
- Put a house design around your ad
- Make a display ad (a color ad that is typically bigger than a standard-size ad—effective, but costly)

Driving for Dollars

Drive through different neighborhoods and write down the addresses of houses that are in dire need of repair, look run-down or basically have no curb appeal. Go to the assessor's website and find out who owns these homes and start marketing to the homeowner to buy their home. Tell them you are interested in buying their home, you want to fix it up and help give the neighborhood a facelift.

Vacant Houses

Build a list of vacant homes or non-owner-occupied homes in your areas of interest that are run-down and in need of repair. The owners of these properties may soon become distressed sellers. You can build a list of vacant homes by going to the assessor's website or title companies, or you can build a list from a provider such as www.melissadata.com.

Three M's of Marketing

1. Message
2. Media
3. Market

Message

- "We'll Buy Your House Even If You Owe More than It's Worth" message
- "Save Your House from Foreclosure" message
- If you, or an investor you know, have rental properties or rent-to-own properties available, mention that you may be able to find the homeowner a new home to move into.

Media

There are so many different ways to market to homeowners, but this is how we deliver our message. With this type of marketing we do get their attention.

Market

Who is your Target Market?

•Geographic: Your target market is determined by area.

> County
> City
> Zip Code
> Neighborhood
> Area Price Point—areas where values meet your price point (e.g., $500K)

•Demographics—different types of lists

> Foreclosure list
> 60-day default list
> Probate list
> Bankruptcy list
> Divorce list

1 Step: Homeowner Calls You Directly

Long Form Approach: Tells the homeowner everything that you do and is very detailed. This way the homeowner can read the message to see if this is right for them.

2 step: 24/7 Recorded Message and You Hunt Them Down

Short Form Approach: Tells the homeowner to call a 24/7 toll-free number to receive a no-obligation recorded message for more information.

Keys to Successful Marketing

- Be different from everyone else
- Stand out like a sore thumb
- Be persistent
- Don't talk about your company; talk about how you can help the homeowner
- Mention homeowners may be able to get money
- Use testimonials with your marketing pieces—written testimonials, pictures with you and homeowners or videos with you and your satisfied homeowners
- Use keywords such as "Avoid Foreclosure" as opposed to "Stop Foreclosure." Using "Avoid Foreclosure" will get homeowners who are not yet in foreclosure to call you. Using "Stop Foreclosure" generally targets the homeowners who are already in foreclosure. Using "Avoid Foreclosure" will get you the best response.

Hire an Envelope Stuffer

Place an ad on Craigslist.org with the job description and the pay. This person will handwrite the envelope, stuff the envelope, place any objects in the envelope, put the return address label on and place the stamp on the letter. I usually pay $.27 cents per envelope for this task. For postcards, all they need to do is put a stamp on and an address label. I usually pay $.05 cents per postcard.

You will find plenty of people willing to do this job for this pay. It is ideal for stay-at-home moms and senior citizens. The work keeps them busy and earns them a little extra income. Other good candidates for this type of job are students and folks who have lost their jobs and need temporary work until they find permanent jobs.

Budget

Don't think of marketing as an expense; think of it as a return on your investment. Your marketing budget should be 10% of your expected revenue per month. Think of it as for every $2,500 you spend, you will get a $25,000 profit. If you expect to make $50,000 per month, you need to spend $5,000 per month marketing your business. You will find that the financial investment you make in marketing your business will bring you the return you are looking for. You will get so many deals you won't know what to do with them all!

Answering the Marketing Phone Calls

As the investor, you should not answer your own phone calls, but somebody needs to. You can hire an assistant to answer your phone calls, or you can outsource your calls to an answering service. Make sure you get an appointment scheduled right away. Your answering service can schedule appointments as well. If you miss one phone call, that is a potential $25K profit deal you could lose. If you don't answer on the first ring, the homeowner may move on to the next person. You have to assume the homeowner has been solicited by several competitive companies. Make sure you **ANSWER YOUR PHONE OR SOMEONE ELSE WILL!**

Your assistant should return all calls for the people who called the 24/7 phone line with your recorded message. If you don't have an assistant, you can use a voice blast system that does it for you.

Chapter 6
Screening Leads

How to Talk to Homeowners Who Need Help

When you talk with homeowners, the most important thing is to know what you're talking about! You can't sell a short sale if you don't know what a short sale is or how the process works. You need to have knowledge of the different types of loans and the different types of short sale programs so you can speak intelligently with the homeowner. You'll need to know which short sale program they would be involved in and be able to discuss all the benefits of that short sale program. You need to be able to explain why short sales are more beneficial than allowing their home to go into foreclosure. Having the knowledge you need to confidently present short sale information to a distressed homeowner is your best asset in securing a deal!

Each homeowner has their personal situation and their own story about how and why they are losing their home. Let them share their story with you. Be sensitive and understanding to their situation. People don't just choose to let their home go into foreclosure. They have a story that is heartbreaking to them, so be compassionate. People don't want to have to sell their home. They don't even want to think about having to sell their home to avoid foreclosure. Most people want to save their home by whatever means may be available. Your expertise on short sales and your keen people skills are needed. You must be a good listener. This means really listening and understanding their situation. It's providing the same compassion you would want if you were in their shoes. There may be times when you will be on the phone for more than an hour listening to their story and then another two hours when you meet them at their house for their appointment. The time you spend caring about them and their situation works in your favor.

Never pressure a homeowner into signing a deal. You want to earn their trust and have them be comfortable with you. This can take time and patience. There are so many people trying to solicit the same benefits to a homeowner, and your competition may be too eager to just get a deal signed. This can be offensive to the homeowner. Make yourself stand out from the rest of the competition by being compassionate and making the homeowners feel like you are there solely for their benefit. With all the current news and information available about foreclosure scams, you may meet homeowners who have their guard up. Use your expertise to let them know what the scams are and explain that you are not part of any of them.

Please don't charge a homeowner to work with them. They are far more willing to work with you when they know your services are free and there is no obligation. If you charge a fee for your service, it will bring you fewer future leads and may make you look like you are one of the scams! Again, be different and set yourself apart from the rest.

So You Got a Phone Call, Now What? Screening Your Leads

When you get a phone call, the most important thing to do is listen . . . and listen carefully. Let the homeowner do the talking. You shouldn't do much talking at all. The homeowner may ask you questions like, "So what services do you offer," or "What do you do?" They may ask these questions because they just saw an advertisement that said "AVOID FORECLOSURE." Personally, I don't like to jump right in and say what it is we do, because most homeowners don't want to think about selling their home. They would rather try to save their home than sell it! I usually ask them to tell me about their situation. I ask them if they are working on any solutions or ask what solutions they have already tried. This breaks the ice and opens the door to let them start talking about their specific situation. They generally start talking about their entire financial hardship and everything they have done to try to help their situation. While they tell their story, don't just sit there in silence. Engage in the conversation by giving them your listening feedback. You do this by responding with "Hmm" or "Oh" with emphasis, or say things like, "That is terrible!" or, "I can't believe that happened to you!" or "WHAT, they did THAT to you?" Show compassion and emotion! Agree with them. Be on their side. Your shared emotion comforts them and makes it easier for them to see that you really do want to help them. They need your help. They deserve your attention, listening skills, compassion and understanding. This helps earn their trust because they will see that you are truly there to help them.

Listening to the stories takes time and energy, but it is what you have to do. Once their story is told, it is time to collect information about them and their home. Once you have the information about their home, it helps you determine the deal and your exit strategy so you will know how you can best help them!

Questions to Ask to Determine the Deal and Exit Strategy

The information you need to collect from the homeowners to best assess the deals is compiled on the form shown below.

Seller Interview Questions Downloadable Form

1. Name: _____
2. Cell phone:_____
3. Home phone: _____
4. Email address:_____
5. Address of home selling:_____
6. Do you live in the home?_____
7. Is your house currently listed with a real estate agent?_____
8. Is this a single-family home, townhouse, condo or modular?_____
9. Who owns the home?_____
10. Whose name is on the loan?_____
11. Type of loan (VA, FHA, conventional):_____
12. How much do you owe on the house?_____
13. How much do you think the house is worth?_____
14. 1st mortgage info
    a. How much is owed?_____
    b. Who is the lender?_____
    c. Payment_____
    d. Current or how far behind?_____
    e. If current, what is the interest rate?_____
    f. If current, is this a fixed or variable interestrate?_
15. 2nd mortgage info

a.How much is owed?_____

b.Who is the lender? _____

c.Payment_____

d.Current or how far behind?_____

e.If current, what is the interest rate?_____

f.If current, is this a fixed or variable interest rate?____

16.Is your home in foreclosure? If so, do you know the foreclosure sale date?

17.Have you filed BK or are considering filing BK?__

18.Condition of the home—what would you do to fix it up in tip-top shape?_____

19.How many square feet? Total:___Finished:_____ Unfinished:_____

20.Year built:_____

21.How many bedrooms:___ Baths: Garages/Carport

_____

22.(If behind) Do you hold any kind of security clearance?_____

23.(If there is equity) How much are you trying to sell your house for?_____

24.What is your motivation for selling (hardship)?__

_____

_____

25.Any other notes:_____

After hearing their story and gathering the information you need on the property, you should be better able to assess their situation, the deal and how you can best help the homeowner. At this point, let the homeowner know what options they have available and how you can best help them.

Short Sale Deals Realtors Want

Any house, pretty or ugly, will be acceptable to list. However, timing is very important. You want to start the listing about one month before the foreclosure sale or earlier for VA loans and conventional loans that don't qualify for HAFA. If the homeowner qualifies for HAFA or if it's an FHA loan, then you can start the listing two weeks before the foreclosure sale date. If you end up with a deal with a foreclosure sale date right around the corner, you will need to act very quickly, and the homeowner must be willing to cooperate with you.

Short Sale Deals Investors Want

Investors, you need to decide if this is a deal you want. If it is, determine what your exit strategy will be.

• If it's an ugly house or a house that won't pass VA or FHA financing for buyers, this is ALWAYS a deal for you!

• If the house is pretty and you determine your exit strategy is to buy and hold, then this IS a deal for you.

• If it's an ugly house and you determine your exit strategy is to buy and hold, this is a deal for you.

• If you determine you can short the 2nd mortgage completely and bring the first loan current and take the loan subject to the existing financing, this IS a deal for you.

• If it's a pretty luxury house with a value of $500K or more, this IS a deal for you. The higher the value, the lower discount you will get.

What to Do When It's Not an Investor Deal

If you determine the deal isn't for you and you can't

make a profit on it, refer the deal to an agent to list the property and ask for a marketing fee. If you have a real estate license, you can list the property yourself to help the homeowner. Or, as an investor, you can work with an agent who lists short sales but hates working the short sale. In this case, you can offer to work the short sale for the agent for half the commission. Your half of the commission will be paid to you for your short sale negotiating services.

If you are not a real estate agent and chose not to be involved anymore but still refer the deal to another agent, the most that agent can do is buy you a small gift or pay you a marketing fee. They cannot legally pay you a referral fee unless you are a licensed real estate agent. They may be able to pay you a small marketing fee, but don't count on it.

You can do what I did as well. I decided I didn't like throwing away my leads, so I opened up Pink Realty to refer all our extra leads to. I trained the real estate agents how to do short sales and how to list them. Then I get half of all their commissions because I am the owner of the company. If you are interested in owning your own Pink Realty and Pink Real Estate franchise, please go to wwww. PinkShortSaleMentor.com/Licensing.

Items the Homeowner Should Have Ready for the Appointment

Below is a checklist of the items homeowners need to have ready for their appointment. They should be given this list when you are on the phone with them. It is helpful if you have your agent bring this checklist with them to the appointment to ensure they get all the documents they need at the time of the appointment or to document what is still needed and what they need to follow up with. Following this checklist is a brief description of these documents.

Checklist: Items needed from homeowners for short sales: `Downloadable Form`

☐ Last two years of tax returns—must be signed

☐ Last two years of W2s

☐ Hardship letter—must be signed and dated

☐ Bank statements—last two months

☐ All income statements (pay stubs, disability, alimony, child support, unemployment, retirement)—last two months

☐ Mortgage statement from all mortgage companies

☐ Financial worksheet completely filled out (downloadable form)

☐ If self-employed—two months of business bank statements

☐ If self-employed—two years of profit and loss statements

☐ Utility bill (HAFA only)

☐ Death certificate and estate information (if applicable)

Hardship Letter

The hardship letter is a handwritten or typed letter from the homeowners that explains in detail to the bank why they have fallen behind on their mortgage. In this letter, the homeowner also needs to specifically state that because of their financial situation, they are requesting to sell their home as a short sale.

If the homeowner has any documentation that supports their hardship, they can include these documents as part of their short sale package.

Proof of Income

The bank needs proof of the homeowner's income. They want two current months of pay stubs, social security income, unemployment income, retirement income, disability income, spousal support, child support, etc. The bank will need current proof of any type of income. If the income is received annually, the homeowner will need to provide a copy of the annual statement.

Bank Statements

The bank needs two current bank statements for each bank account. These statements must be the actual bank statements. They will not allow activity statements printed from the Internet as these do not show the homeowner's name, address or full account number. The bank must receive a copy of each statement page, front and back.

Tax Returns

The bank needs two full years of completed and signed federal tax returns with all schedules attached. Most people do not sign their own copies of their tax returns, so ensure the homeowner signs them. The bank will not accept tax returns that are not signed by the taxpayer. Many banks are requesting a completed and signed 4506T to be submitted with the short sale package. This form is a tax return request form.

Death Certificate and/or Estate Information (if applicable)

If you are dealing with a property where a homeowner has passed away or the property is in an estate, you will need to get a copy of the homeowner's death certificate and copies of the estate information. It needs to clearly state who the executor of the estate is.

Self-employed Homeowners

If a homeowner is self-employed, the lender will need two years of profit and loss statements and two current months of business bank statements.

Mortgage Statement

Have the borrowers provide you with a current copy of their mortgage statement. If there is a first and second mortgage on the property, have them give you a copy from each lender. This information is used to contact the bank at the start of the short sale process.

If the homeowners do not have mortgage statements, they will need to provide you with loan numbers and a customer service phone numbers for each lender.

HAFA Short Sales

If the homeowner is going into the HAFA program, additional documents are needed. They will need to provide a statement from their Homeowners' Association (HOA) if there is one. They need to provide a copy of a current utility bill. If the homeowners have moved out of the home, they will need to provide the last utility bill from the short sale property and a current utility bill from the property where they are now living.

Finally, if the homeowners moved for a job, they will need to obtain a letter from their employer stating when they started their position.

Missing Documentation

If the homeowner does not have certain documentation, such as bank statements or pay stubs, they must write a letter of explanation stating why they don't have the documentation. The reason can be as simple as they don't have a job or they don't have a bank account. However, each letter of explanation must be signed and dated by the homeowner and include their loan number.

The reason letters of explanation must be written for missing documentation is because the banks have an electronic checklist system to track all required documentation. If a document is missing, the file gets flagged as incomplete. Incomplete files will not move forward in the process. Letters of Explanation serve as documentation for a required item, so their checklist system can complete a file and move it forward.

Chapter 7
Preparing for the Short Sale Meeting

Investors: Why Using a Real Estate Agent Is Beneficial

When I first began investing, I did not use a real estate agent for the buying process. This meant I had to go on every appointment myself. This became very time consuming, especially when I had several appointments in one day. As an investor, if you partner with a good real estate agent for the buying process, your agent is the one who would go on these appointments for you. You still need to take time to establish a good relationship with the homeowners so they will want to keep you as the buyer for their house, but you won't need to take the time required to do the homeowner appointments.

In addition to establishing a good relationship with the homeowner, if you choose to establish a good relationship with a reputable Realtor® or real estate agent, you will need to train them to handle these appointments. This means training the agent on short sales, the short sale process and the benefits of the different types of short sales. It also means ensuring they have the necessary people skills and compassion to work with the various types of homeowners, their emotions and their financial situations. Building trust in these relationships is very important. Establish a good relationship with your buying real estate agent. Ensure both you and your buyer's real estate agents establish a good relationship with the homeowners. Stay on top of each homeowner's short sale and communicate with the homeowner regularly. Much of your success in this business will be based on the relationships you establish. It is necessary to invest the time to build and grow these relationships.

Below is a list of responsibilities your buyer's agent should handle:

- The real estate agent orders the O&E (Owner and Encumbrance Report) on the property.
- The real estate agent goes to the appointment to meet the homeowner as your buyer's agent.
- They prepare the purchase contract for you.
- They get the house under contract with your offer.
- They collect all the short sale documents from the homeowner and deliver them to you.
- They collect any required updated financial documents when they expire (every 60 days) and deliver them to you.
- They take pictures of the property and write a damage report for you. This helps when negotiating the short sale.
- They meet the BPO agent or appraiser at the property and provide them a copy of the contract. The real estate agent must point out every property defect. Additionally, your buyer's agent needs to establish a good relationship with the BPO agents and appraisers to help influence them as much as possible so the value of the property can come in close to the offer or list price. If the house does not qualify for FHA or VA financing, the buyer's agent needs to point this out so

the lender knows the house will most likely sell only to a cash buyer.

- The real estate agent will get a check at closing for their work. I give them 3% for the listing. This keeps them happy and keeps them wanting to work with you!
- And possibly negotiate the short sale for you.

As you can see, in addition to saving you a lot of valuable time, there are many other benefits to working with a buyer's agent. If you don't want to use a real estate agent, you will save the buyer's agent commission, but you will not be able to leverage your time as efficiently. I use a real estate agent because it leaves me more time to continue building my business. I don't mind paying a commission when it gives me time to grow my business and leaves me with fewer headaches and details I have to attend to.

O&E

Before each meeting, you (or your real estate agent) need to get an O&E on the property. An O&E is an Owner and Encumbrance Report on the property. It tells you what liens and judgments are attached to the property. You (or your real estate agent) need to request this from your title company. The cost for these in El Paso County, Colorado, runs about $5 per property. On the O&E you will see the deed of trust. On the deed of trust you will be able to see what type of loan the homeowner has. This is very important information to have so you know what paperwork to bring to the appointment with the homeowner.

On the next page is a snapshot of what a VA loan will look like on a Deed of Trust:

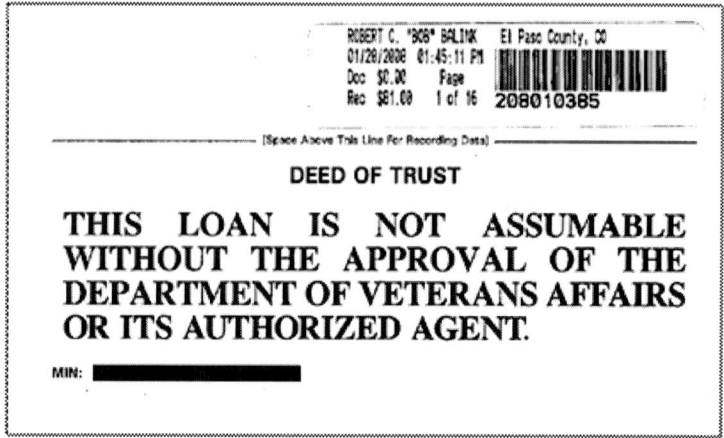

Below is a snapshot of what an FHA loan will look like on a Deed of Trust:

On a conventional loan, you won't see anything that says FHA or VA. This is how you know it's a conventional loan. On the O&E, you will also see if there are any judgments attached to the property. If the homeowner has a personal judgment against them, then it will attach to the property.

HAFA Approved Property: You Need a Listing Agent

If the property is a HAFA-approved property, you need to have a listing agent list the property, put the house in the MLS at a reduced price and flip the house to pending or under contract. This makes the property secured by you, and no other buyers can look at the house. Make sure the real estate agent puts negative comments about the condition of the property in the MLS under property remarks. Also, make sure the Agent doesn't list anything that isn't true because this could jeopardise their license.

The following is a list of property condition examples:

- House needs major TLC
- Roof must be replaced
- Plumbing is leaking
- House has structural damage
- Electrical is not working

There are several reasons for listing these types of remarks in the MLS. They make the property undesirable to other buyers, it shows the BPO agent and/or appraiser what the condition of the property is and it also lets the bank know the condition of the property when they request a copy of the MLS listing.

Real Estate Agents: Preparing for the Meeting with the Homeowner

Investors, if a real estate agent needs to list the property, make sure they do the following things:

- Prepare all standard and normal listing documents.
- In Colorado, there is a short sale addendum to the listing agreement that needs to be prepared as well.
- Get an O&E on the property from your title company. This document shows the liens and judgments on the property. This information will let you know what lien negotiations will be needed and will also let you know

what loan type you are working with.

• Collect all homeowner's financials and have the homeowners sign additional short sale documents.

• Get the house under contract with your offer.

• Price the property no higher than 25% below market, minus repairs. This will be the target BPO value and the highest the investor can pay for the house.

Real Estate Agents: Paperwork to Bring to the Appointment

• Bring a checklist for the items needed for the short sale so you can check off the documents received. It will also let you know which documents are still needed. Bring a form that will allow you to document the property condition.

• Bring a Third Party Authorization so the lender will release loan information. (Please note that some banks require that their own Third Part Authorization form be used.)

• Bring the bank's financial worksheet. (Please note that some banks require that their own Third Part Authorization form be used.)

• FHA Loans: Bring the FHA Application to Participate form (HUD Form 90036). Be sure to include the information on page 3 that includes pre-foreclosure sale program information to give to the homeowner.

• HAFA Eligible Loans: If the home is eligible for HAFA, find out if the loan is Fannie Mae, Freddie Mac or a non-Fannie Mae or non-Freddie Mac HAFA loan. You will need to bring the appropriate HAFA documents for the specific loan type you are dealing with.

- If there is a contract on the house, bring the contract with you. In Colorado, the contract must be on the standard "Contract to Buy and Sell Real Estate" contract form and must include the Short Sale Addendum.

- Bring an information packet with you. This packet should include a copy of all the documents the homeowner will be signing and will include educational resources for the homeowner. Provide as much helpful information as you can as this will make you stand out from everyone else. I provide a folder with my company logo on it and include a copy of everything they sign, information on short sales, information on the type of short sale they will be doing, foreclosure avoidance options, warnings about foreclosure scams and past client testimonials.

- Bring all the standard listing documents.

Below is a checklist that can be used by the real estate agent who is going to the listing appointment:

Checklist: Short Sale Package Items for Agents Going to Listing Appointments*:   `Downloadable Form`

☐ Last two Years of Tax Returns—must be Signed

☐ Last two Years of W2s (if you don't have, don't worry)

☐ Hardship letter—must be signed and dated

☐ Bank statements—last two months

☐ Pay stubs—last two months

☐ Mortgage statement from all mortgage companies

☐ Financial worksheet from lender—must be filled out

- ☐ Other proof of income (disability, SSI, retirement)
- ☐ If self-employed, business bank statements—last two months
- ☐ If self-employed, profit and loss statement—last two years
- ☐ Current utility bill
- ☐ Death certificate (if applicable)
- ☐ Personal representative info—estate info (if applicable)
- ☐ 4506T
- ☐ Listing agreement
- ☐ Third-party authorization
- ☐ Confidentiality authorization
- ☐ Contract
- ☐ HUD
- ☐ O&E
- ☐ HAFA agreement (conventional only)
- ☐ Application to Participate (FHA short sales)
- ☐ Proof of Funds
- ☐ Lead-based Paint Disclosure (if applicable)
- ☐ Property Disclosure
- ☐ Source of Water addendum
- ☐ Square Footage Disclosure
- ☐ Closing Instructions
- ☐ Short Sale Addendum
- ☐ FTC Disclosures
- ☐ Key

Authorization to Release Personal Identifying and Confidential Information Downloadable Form

I and_____ authorize Pink Realty, Inc. to release our personal identifying and/or confidential information to any necessary person involved with the short sale regarding our property located at_____.

I also understand that due to the nature of the transaction it is not always feasible to transmit this information in an encrypted or otherwise secured manner. As such, I further authorize Pink Realty, Inc. to fax, mail, email, verbally communicate or otherwise transmit whether verbally and/or in writing this data and provide personal identifying and/or confidential information to any person involved in the short sale transaction.

I understand that persons may include but are not limited to: mortgage companies, all lien holders including judgment holders, title companies, attorneys, your spouse or your significant other, and Pink Realty, Inc. employees.

I understand that this personal identifying and/or confidential information that may be transmitted in an unencrypted, plain text or otherwise unsecured manner may include but not be limited to my (our) name, address, social security number, bank statements, tax returns, mortgage statements, financial information and/or other similar information.

RELEASE OF LIABILITY

On this_____ day of_____, 2011_____, intending to be legally bound hereby, the undersigned agrees and does hereby release from liability and to indemnify and hold harmless Pink Realty, Inc. and any of its employees, shareholders, members, owners, managers, subcontractors and agents representing or related to Pink Realty, Inc. This release is for any and all liability for personal loss and other damages occasioned by, or in connection with, any activity associated with the aforementioned property, its liens, debt and/or short sale negotiation including but limited to damages resulting from identity theft resulting from the communication of personal identifying and/or confidential information.

_____
Borrower Signature   Date

_____
Borrower Signature   Date

147

Monica Adams

AUTHORIZATION TO RELEASE INFORMATION

Lender: _____

Lender Phone / Fax #:_____

Lender Address:_____

Account or Loan #:_____

I hereby authorize you to release any and all information regarding my loan, including interest rate, payoff amount, amount of monthly payment, late charges, penalties, to:

Please fax immediately to _____Thank you.

Borrower's Name:_____

Borrower's SSN:_____

Borrower's Signature:_____

Co-Borrower's Name:_____

Co-Borrower's SSN: _____

Co-Borrower's Signature:_____

Address of Property: _____

Date: _____

Create your own 'Done for you' Short Sale System

Financial Information Worksheet for Loan

Your name & mailing address   Co-Borrower's name & mailing address

_____   _____

_____   _____

_____   _____

How long have you owned the home? _____

Total Monthly Income (take home)_____

	Wages	Social Security	Pensions	Rent/Other Income
Mortgagor				
Co-Mortgagor				

# of Dependents_____   How long on current job? Mortgagor_____ Co-Mortgagor_____

1st Mortgage	$	Food	$
2nd Mortgage	$	Gas/Electric	$
Property taxes	$	Water/Sewer	$
Homeowner's insurance	$	Trash	$
HOA/Condo fees	$	Phones/cell phones	$
Credit card payments	$	Cable/satellite TV	$
Installment loan payments	$	Internet	$
Transportation/gas/car repairs	$	Life/health insurance	$
# of vehicles in household	$	Child support/alimony	$
Auto payments	$	Medical/dental expenses	$
Auto insurance	$	Charitable contributions	$
Day care/child care	$	Tuition	$
Other	$	Other	$

149

You must attach your two most recent pay stubs, proof of any other income and the items listed on the front of this form.

I agree that the financial information provided is an accurate statement of my/our financial status. I understand that any action taken by the Lender is in strict reliance on this information. My/our signature below grants the holder of my mortgage the authority to confirm the information that I have disclosed in this financial statement, to verify it is accurate by ordering a credit report and to contact my credit counseling representative.

_____   _____
Mortgagor's Signature   Date   Co-Mortgagor's Signature   Date

This is an attempt to collect a debt, and information obtained will be used for that purpose.

The following applies to any recipient of this notice who is entitled to the protection afforded by the 11 U.S.C. 362 of the United States Bankruptcy Code. NOTE: This is in accordance with the mortgage agreement and is not a demand for payment. It is sent only for the purpose of notifying you of the availability of assistance.

Create your own *'Done for you'* Short Sale System

Form 4506-T

(Rev. January 2011)

Department of the Treasury
Internal Revenue Service

Request for Transcript of Tax Return

► Request may be rejected if the form is incomplete or illegible.

OMB No. 1545-1872

Tip. Use Form 4506-T to order a transcript or other return information free of charge. See the product list below. You can quickly request transcripts by using our automated self-help service tools. Please visit us at IRS.gov and click on "Order a Transcript" or call 1-800-908-9946. If you need a copy of your return, use Form 4506, Request for Copy of Tax Return. There is a fee to get a copy of your return.

1a Name shown on tax return. If a joint return, enter the name shown first.

1b First social security number on tax return, individual taxpayer identification number, or employer identification number (see instructions)

2a If a joint return, enter spouse's name shown on tax return

2b Second social security number or individual taxpayer identification number if joint tax return

3 Current name, address (including apt., room, or suite no.), city, state, and ZIP code (See instructions)

4 Previous address shown on the last return filed if different from line 3 (See instructions)

5 If the transcript or tax information is to be mailed to a third party (such as a mortgage company), enter the third party's name, address, and telephone number. The IRS has no control over what the third party does with the tax information.

Caution. If the transcript is being mailed to a third party, ensure that you have filled in line 6 and line 9 before signing. Sign and date the form once you have filled in these lines. Completing these steps helps to protect your privacy.

6 Transcript requested. Enter the tax form number here (1040, 1065, 1120, etc.) and check the appropriate box below. Enter only one tax form number per request. ►

a **Return Transcript**, which includes most of the line items of a tax return as filed with the IRS. A tax return transcript does not reflect changes made to the account after the return is processed. Transcripts are only available for the following returns: Form 1040 series, Form 1065, Form 1120, Form 1120A, Form 1120H, Form 1120L, and Form 1120S. Return transcripts are available for the current year and returns processed during the prior 3 processing years. Most requests will be processed within 10 business days □

b **Account Transcript**, which contains information on the financial status of the account, such as payments made on the account, penalty assessments, and adjustments made by you or the IRS after the return was filed. Return information is limited to items such as tax liability and estimated tax payments. Account transcripts are available for most returns. Most requests will be processed within 30 calendar days □

c **Record of Account**, which is a combination of line item information and later adjustments to the account. Available for current year and 3 prior tax years. Most requests will be processed within 30 calendar days □

7 **Verification of Nonfiling**, which is proof from the IRS that you **did not** file a return for the year. Current year requests are only available after June 15th. There are no availability restrictions on prior year requests. Most requests will be processed within 10 business days □

8 Form W-2, Form 1099 series, Form 1098 series, or Form 5498 series transcript. The IRS can provide a transcript that includes data from these information returns. State or local information is not included with the Form W-2 information. The IRS may be able to provide this transcript information for up to 10 years. Information for the current year is generally not available until the year after it is filed with the IRS. For example, W-2 information for 2007, filed in 2008 will not be available from the IRS until 2009. If you need W-2 information for retirement purposes, you should contact the Social Security Administration at 1-800-772-1213. Most requests will be processed within 45 days □

Caution. If you need a copy of Form W-2 or Form 1099, you should first contact the payer. To get a copy of the Form W-2 or Form 1099 filed with your return, you must use Form 4506 and request a copy of your return, which includes all attachments.

9 Year or period requested. Enter the ending date of the year or period, using the mm/dd/yyyy format. If you are requesting more than four years or periods, you must attach another Form 4506-T. For requests relating to quarterly tax returns, such as Form 941, you must enter each quarter or tax period separately.

Signature of taxpayer(s). I declare that I am either the taxpayer whose name is shown on line 1a or 2a, or a person authorized to obtain the tax information requested. If the request applies to a joint return, **either** husband or wife must sign. If signed by a corporate officer, partner, guardian, tax matters partner, executor, receiver, administrator, trustee, or party other than the taxpayer, I certify that I have the authority to execute Form 4506-T on behalf of the taxpayer. **Note.** For transcripts being sent to a third party, this form must be received within 120 days of signature date.

Telephone number of taxpayer on line 1a or 2a

Sign Here

► **Signature** (see instructions)   Date

► **Title** (if line 1a above is a corporation, partnership, estate, or trust)

► **Spouse's signature**   Date

For Privacy Act and Paperwork Reduction Act Notice, see page 2.   Cat. No. 37667N   Form **4506-T** (Rev. 1-2011)

Preparing Your Offer to the Bank

When I write my offers to the bank, I usually create a disposable LLC. Once you have your business name, you must register your business with the state your business is located in. The cost to do this in Colorado is approximately $50. This cost may vary depending on which state you do business in. I also write up the offer using our personal name so it doesn't look like an investor is purchasing the property.

Using a Real Estate Agent to Write Up the Offer

Always use the state-approved forms when writing up a short sale offer. This is another reason I like using a real estate agent as my buyer's agent. I may not be familiar with the contracts in one particular state, but the real estate agent will know the contracts.

Earnest Money

Because you plan on writing a lot of short sale offers, you don't want to have to put down earnest money for each offer. The earnest money on my offers is in the form of a promissory note. This means that I promise to pay the earnest money right before closing.

On the next page is a sample promissory note I use for earnest money deposits:

The printed portions of this form, except differentiated additions, have been approved by the Colorado Real Estate Commission (EMP 80-5-04)

EARNEST MONEY
Promissory Note

U.S. $_____,

Date:_____

City_____ State_____

FOR VALUE RECEIVED,

_____

Name(s) of Maker(s)_____

_____, Address

Jointly and severally, promise to pay to the order of

_____

The sum of_____ Dollars,

with interest at_____per cent per annum from

_____until paid.

Both principal and interest are payable in U.S. dollars on or before_____, payable at_____ or at such other address as note holder may designate. Presentment, notice of dishonor, and protest are hereby waived. If this note is not paid when due, I/we agree to pay all reasonable costs of collection, including attorney's fees.

Maker's signature_____

Maker's signature_____

This note is given as earnest money for the contract on the following property:_____

Preparing Your Initial Offer

When making an initial offer, make sure the offer is very low. You never want to give your highest and best offer right away. The bank always counters the initial offer, whether it is a short sale offer or a retail offer. I typically calculate my initial offer as follows:

After Repair Value (ARV), minus 30%

Minus repair costs

Minus an additional security (usually $20k for my offers)

You can make your additional security amount more or less, if you'd like. It is up to you to decide this amount.

For example, if the ARV of a house is $150,000 and the repair costs are $30,000, my initial offer would be calculated as follows:

ARV	$150,000
(ARV less 30%)	$105,000
$105K less rehab costs of $30K	$75,000 = Max. Allowable Offer
Minus Extra Pad of $20,000	$55,000 = Initial Offer

How to Estimate the ARV for a Fix and Flip

When I want to estimate the ARV for my offers, I usually run comps through our local MLS service. Only real estate agents have access to the MLS. If you do not have access to the MLS, you can have your real estate agent run comps for you, or if you do a lot of business with your real estate agent, they can give you an assistant login that you will have to pay for. You can also run your own comps by using these websites:

- Local assessor's website (Google search by typing in the name of the county's assessor office, e.g., El Paso County Colorado Assessor)
- www.zillow.com (not very reliable)
- www.trullia.com
- www.Renav.com (for Colorado only)

Another option is going to the title company you use. If you do your closings with a particular title company, they will generally allow you access their database.

How to Estimate Repair Costs

When doing a short sale, I make my repair estimates for more than they should be. I do this because I don't always look at the house before writing an offer. I assume it needs everything. As a standard rule of thumb, you can use these numbers:

- Rancher 3/1/1 1000 square feet—repair estimate $25,000
- Bi-Level 4/2/1 1666 square feet—repair estimate $30,000
- Ranch with a basement—repair estimate $35,000
- Add $5,000 if the property needs a new roof
- Add $1,700 if the property needs a new furnace

These may be completely off from what the true rehabilitation costs are, but that is OK. This is only for your initial offer to the bank.

Typical repair costs for a 4/2/1 are as follows:

Type of Repair	Cost
Roof	$4,500
Furnace	$2,000
Paint Interior	$2,500
Paint Exterior	$3,500
KitchenCabinets/Countertops	$3,000
Appliances	$2,000
Skim, Texture, Prime	$2,500
Case and Base	$2,500
Windows	$175 per hole
Bathroom	$2,500 per bath
Carpet	$181 / yard
Concrete Work	$3,000
Landscaping	$1,000
Tile	$5/ft
Doors	$125/hole
Water Heater	$1,000
Garage Door w/opener	$500
Deck	$2,000
French Door	$600

Meeting the Homeowners

Investors, if you don't plan on meeting homeowners, train your real estate agents using the following information. When first meeting the homeowners as either an investor or a real estate agent, introduce yourself with confidence and a smile. Shake their hands and offer them your business card. Have the homeowners take you on a tour of their property. Be compassionate. Homeowners take pride in their homes, so even if the house is in poor condition, you want to be able to provide them with as many compliments as you can. These may include giving the homeowner compliments on the floor plan, the yard or the neighborhood. You want the homeowners to feel as good as possible regarding their home. When the house tour is done, sit down at their dining room table to begin the next step.

The homeowners may want to talk again about their hardship situation. Let them talk! You will find the first hour of the appointment may simply include going over the short sale process again, listening to their story and answering their questions. The second hour will be spent going over the short sale documents. I like to collect all the short sale paperwork from them that they were to gather, and then I like to fill out any bank documents with them. So fill out the financial worksheet with them, have them sign the Third Party Authorization and complete any FHA or HAFA specific loan paperwork. Be sure all of these documents are completely filled out, dated and signed.

Then begin going over the listing documents and contract documents. Explain each document to them. You may find that some homeowners don't care much about the listing documents or the contract to buy and sell. If you feel they don't care, you can just briefly go over these documents with them. If you are dealing with a concerned homeowner who has a lot of questions, you may need to be as detailed as you can about each document.

After all the documentation is completed and signed, prepare the homeowners for what to expect throughout the short sale process. Explain to them if a bank representative, BPO agent or appraiser calls them to get into the house, they are not to let them in. Instruct them to have these people contact the real estate agent to schedule a time to meet them at the property.

Once you are done prepping the homeowner, ask them if you can walk through the house again to take pictures. This is the time when you can take marketing pictures of the house and take pictures of everything that is wrong with the house and needs repairs. At this time, you also want to make a list of everything the house needs, including all minor repairs. Below is an example of a property checklist you can use:

Downloadable Form

Property Inspection Checklist:

Property Inspection Sheet

Street Address					Date / /
City				☐ SFR ☐ 2 Family ☐ 3 Family ☐ Other	
Rooms	Bedrooms	Baths	Sq. Ft.	☐ Vacant ☐ Occupied	

Inspection Checklist	Yes	No	Comments	Repair Cost
1. Does the house need a roof?				
2. Does the house need exterior paint?				
3. Do the windows need to be replaced?				
4. Does the foundation need repair?				
5. Does the garage need repair?				
6. Does the yard need to be cleaned up?				
7. Does the plumbing/heating need repair?				
8. Does the electric need to be updated?				
9. Does the house need to be cleaned out?				
10. Does the house need interior paint?				
11. Does the house need flooring?				
12. Does the kitchen need repairs?				
13. Does the kitchen need appliances?				
14. Do the baths need repair?				
15. Does the basement need repair?				
16. Miscellaneous repairs needed				
Additional Comments			TOTAL	

After Repaired Value	$	Asking Price	$
ARV x 70%	$	Realtor	$
(Repairs)	$	Seller	☐ Bank ☐ Estate ☐ Individual ☐ Other
MAO	$		

Offer 1	$	Date / /	Counter 1	$	Date / /
Offer 2	$	Date / /	Counter 2	$	Date / /
Offer 3	$	Date / /	Counter 3	$	Date / /

At the end of the appointment, leave them with your contact information, put the lockbox on the door and take a picture of the outside of the house. If this is a listing, you will also place your sign in the front yard.

Chapter 8
Preparing and Submitting
the Short Sale Package

A short sale package can be lengthy, so it is best to have a system that can organize your documents and fax your documents. Systems such as the one offered by Short Sale Commander (www.sscommander.infusionsoft.com/go/sschp/pink) helps streamline your short sale process so you spend less time chasing paperwork and filing notes. I use Short Sale Commander with my business, and I love it. If you want to use Short Sale Commander to organize your short sales, click on the link above, which is my "Pink Link," and Short Sale Commander will waive your set-up fee of $49! Make sure you type the code "Pink" in the discount code.

Features include
- HAFA Simplified Wizard
- 100% Web based
- Mortgage company database
- Mortgage forms library
- Auto-populated lender documents
- Document & photo storage
- Detailed task manager
- Full email & e-fax capability

- Automatic package generation
- Guest access ability
- BPO Builder to give to the BPO agents
- HUD -1 Generator
- Notify Homeowners and Agents instantly of updates

If money is tight, you can use Adobe in conjunction with an Internet fax system such as Ring Central, which can be purchased through www.RingCentral.com. We scan each individual document and save them into separate files for each property. We create folders for each property and create five sub-folders for each property folder. Then all scanned documents are organized and saved under the proper sub-folder for easy viewing and retrieval. The sub-folders we use are listed below:

- Buyer Documents
- Short Sale Documents
- Title Company Documents
- Listing Documents
- Property Photos

Check your documents after you have scanned them into a PDF file to make sure they are readable. If you can't read the documents, the bank won't be able to read them either. If they can't read them, they will require you to resend readable documents. To save yourself the time and redundancy, make sure your documents are readable before sending them to the bank.

Using Adobe Acrobat software is very convenient for preparing your short sale package for the bank. For example, you can combine all short sale documents together, create a header and footer that includes the loan number and a page number, extract pages the bank does not need or pages you don't want to send, circle items you want to make sure the negotiator sees and use the white-out function and the typewriter function to add or erase notes.

Your short sale package can be in any order; however, we organize our packages in the following document order:

   •Cover Page containing the following information:
> To Information: Who the package is being sent to
> Regarding: (e.g., short sale package)
> From Information: Your name and contact information
> Borrower's name
> Borrower's loan number
> Borrower's Social Security number(s)
> Property address
> A short and simple message to the bank
  •Third Party Authorization
  •Contract to buy and sell
  •HUD-1
  •Proof of funds
  •Listing Agreement (fax if HAFA property—must be listed with a real estate agent)
  •FSBO request (if transaction is a For Sale By Owner, have homeowner write a statement saying they wish to sell the house FSBO)
  •Hardship Letter
  •Financial Worksheet (use lender specific form if required)
  •FHA or HAFA documents (if applicable)

•Proof of income for the last two months (this includes all pay stubs, unemployment statement, Social Security income, disability income, retirement income, spousal support, child support, etc.—any and all types of income must be sent in)

•Bank statements from the last two months (must be copies of their actual bank statements and not activity statements downloaded from the Internet; statements must include homeowner's name and account number)

•Last two years of federal tax returns (must be signed and dated and include all schedules)

•4506T

•Current utility bill (HAFA only)

•HOA statement (HAFA only)

•RMA (HAFA only)

•Any additional documentation such as a death certificate, estate information, power of attorney and/or any items related to their hardship.

NOTE: Make sure all documents that require signatures and dates are signed and dated by the homeowners. Make sure you have a header and footer that contain the loan number on each page.

The banks only want to see documentation that is pertinent to the short sale. They don't want to see every outstanding bill, medical bill or utility bill. If you send in a package that includes the documents listed above, your package will most likely be about 100 pages long! Don't overwhelm the banks with any more documentation than they need. The negotiator will pull a credit report that will show all outstanding debts and verify the homeowner isn't trying to mislead the bank. The cleaner and leaner your short sale package is, the better.

Step 1: Gather Lender Information

•Get lender information. You will need to contact each lien holder on the property to get the following:

•Short sale department phone number

•Short sale department fax number

•Third Party Authorization fax number

•Find out if the lender uses the Equator System (Bank of America and GMAC are two banks that do)

Step 2: Gather Lien/Judgment Information

If there are any judgments or other liens on the property, such as HOA liens, you will need to contact the attorney's, lenders and/or associations to request their fax number so you can submit a Third Party Authorization to them as well.

Step 3: Fax the Third Party Authorizations

Fax in a Third Party Authorization to release loan/lien information to each lien holder. The Third Party Authorization fax number is generally different than the lender's short sale department fax number.

Step 4: Fax the Short Sale Package

Fax the short sale package to each mortgage holder (1st and 2nd, if applicable). If there are multiple mortgages on the property, you will need to fax the short sale package to each lien holder. Create two separate short sale packages— one for each lender—and make sure the header and footer have the correct loan number at the top and bottom of each page that corresponds to the bank you are faxing the short sale package to.

Step 5: Follow Up

Be sure to follow up on both your Third Party Authorizations and your short sale packages. Two days after you fax everything in, call the bank to make sure all documents were received. Some banks take longer than two days to image and upload the documents into their system, so if the documents have not yet been uploaded, you will need to continue following up until you know the bank has received the entire package.

Short Sale Package Tips

1. Make sure your short sale package is complete! When talking with the homeowner on the phone prior to the initial appointment, give them a complete list of all required documents needed so they can gather the information and have it ready for their appointment. While you are at this appointment, ensure you have all the required documentation. This will save you a lot of time. If the homeowner is missing specific documentation, have them write a statement explaining why the documentation is missing. The only items on the above list that can be replaced with a letter of explanation are proof of income, bank statements and tax returns. (Sample letters are included at the end of this chapter.) Make sure you handwrite or type in large letters what the item is supposed to be (e.g., Reason for No Paystubs, Reason for No Tax Returns, Reason for No Bank Statements).

Everything must be provided by the homeowner and should be collected at the time of the initial appointment. The financial worksheet and the hardship letter should be filled out and completed at the time of the appointment. Most homeowners want the process to be as simple as possible, so they prefer that you fill out the paperwork for them so all they have to do is sign the documents.

If the homeowners are missing a tax return, but they did file their taxes, ask them to get a copy from their local IRS office. The cost for this is around $10 per tax year. If they can't afford the fee, have the homeowners write a letter of explanation for the reason their taxes are missing and have them complete a 4506T form.

A 4506T is a tax transcript request form. It authorizes the bank to pull the taxes themselves from the IRS. You will find that some banks want both the taxes and a 4506T form filled out, because they want to verify the borrower didn't try to change their tax return for their own benefit.

2. Fax the entire short sale package all at once! Once your short sale package is complete with all required documentation, you are ready to submit the short sale package to the lender. It is much more beneficial to fax the entire short sale package at one time. When the bank receives all the required documents at once, it speeds up the short sale process. If you send several faxes with a few items here and there, you risk documents being lost, misfiled, etc. Banks prefer receiving the entire package all at once.

The only time it makes sense to fax in an incomplete package is when the house is about to be foreclosed upon and you are trying to get the foreclosure sale date postponed.

3. Use an online fax program—this is faster and much more convenient that using a standard fax machine. With the system we use, Ring Central, I open the selected PDF short sale file, click on "Print," and select "Ring Central Fax" as the printer choice. This brings up a dialogue box that allows me to enter the fax number, contact person's name, company name and a cover letter memo. A very simple process! No more faxing one page at a time with pages getting stuck in a fax machine.

Once the fax has been sent, you get an email that confirms whether the fax was submitted successfully or if it failed.

4. Save all your email confirmations. Be sure to keep all your fax confirmations in an email folder. I organize my email inbox with a folder for each property. This way all emails pertaining to a specific property are filed in the appropriate email folder. Save all fax confirmations, because banks often ask for the date when you faxed documents.

Example Letter for No Pay Stubs
Reason for NO PAY STUBS

1/1/11

Dear Wells Fargo,

The reason I have no pay stubs to provide is because I was laid off of work 2 months ago and I have not been able to find a job. I am currently not getting unemployment pay.

Thanks,

Sally Seller

Example Letter for No Bank Statement
Reason for NO BANK STATEMENTS

1/1/11

Dear Wells Fargo,

I currently do not have any bank statements because I don't have a bank account. My bank closed out my account due to insufficient funds. I also don't have a job to deposit any money into a bank account. Please attach this letter under your bank statement file to serve as my explanation for no bank statements.

Thanks so much for your understanding in this matter.

John Doe

Example Letter for Explanation for No Tax Returns
Explanation for NO TAX RETURNS

1/1/11

Dear Wells Fargo,

I cannot provide any tax returns because I have not been able to file my taxes for the last 2 years. I owe the IRS money and I have no money to give them, therefore I have been putting off filing my taxes. I will provide you a 4506T so you can confirm I have not filed my taxes.

Thanks for your understanding,

Patty Smith

Example Letter for FSBO transaction
Explanation for NO LISTING AGREEMENT

1/1/11

Dear Wells Fargo,

I currently do not have my property listed with a real estate agent. I do have my property listed For Sale by Owner and that is how I was able to find a buyer for my property. I would like to entertain this offer first before I consider listing my property with a real estate agent. By doing a For Sale by Owner transaction you will save money on the commission.

Thank you for your consideration.

Sally Seller

Hardship Letters

Please take a few minutes to talk to the homeowners about the hardship letter they will need to write. Explain to them that they must briefly state in the letter what hardship or difficulty occurred that caused them to default on their mortgage payments. If it was a series of events that brought about their financial crisis, then they should begin chronologically with the first event, second event, etc., and explain how the combination of the series of events created the default. Let them know if the bank can't understand their hardship, they won't be able to help them. Wherever possible, provide supporting evidence for the hardship (e.g., copy of their pink slip for unemployment, separation agreement for marital problems, death certificate of wage-earning spouse, etc.).

It is important that the hardship letter conveys exactly

what caused the homeowner to fall behind on their mortgage payments. If you find that you and a homeowner are stuck on how to explain a hardship, please contact me, and I will offer suggestions on how to best present the hardship.

Other Samples of Hardship Letters*:

Hardship Sample Letter #1

1/1/11

To Whom It May Concern:

I am writing this letter to share some of the hardships I have endured over the past year. As you know, my property is located at _____ . I have tried to sell the property and have received no offers. The market is flooded with homes for sale in this area. I urge you to please accept the offer being submitted by Pink Real Estate, they are my only hope.

I have been diagnosed with cancer and have been on chemotherapy since February, this has caused stress to my family and me. I have not been able to keep up with all of the repairs on my house or any of my bills. My medical bills are outrageous and it's making me go under.

I am in the clothing industry and things have basically stopped since September 2009. I am currently looking for another field in which to work. So far, I haven't had much success. I am 2 months behind on my car, electric, and phone, etc. Attached are copies of my late notices.

I need to sell quickly and need your help.

Sincerely,

Sally Seller

Hardship Sample Letter #2

June 5, 2011

Bank Name & Address

Re: Short Sale – Property Address

Dear Lender:

I am writing this letter asking for your assistance in the sale of my home. I am starting to have trouble trying to make ends meet. In November 2010, my daughter and grandson moved back in with me and my son, as her husband deployed to Iraq. But, prior to deploying he filed for divorce, this was an unknown situation by my daughter. My son-in-law has yet to pay any support to my daughter and grandson. I have been trying through various agencies to get this corrected. This is becoming a financial burden on me. My ex-wife refuses to assist me in any way with our kids and our grandchild. Also having my daughter and grandson living with me has severely limited my ability to make needed upgrades/repairs to the house.

In February 2010 I had to file a Chapter 7 Bankruptcy, because my ex-wife was not making house payments or refinancing our family home, the divorce court awarded my ex-wife the house. At that time the mortgage for that home was under my VA benefits and in my name. Since it was in my name the mortgage company was coming to me for payment and not her. That was the only recourse I had to stop them from coming to me for payment. This is also why I cannot afford to allow the house to go into foreclosure. My current position as a contractor at Ft. Carson is threatening lay-offs. The job currently does not pay well. I recently accepted a new job. This new job will require that I move to Phoenix, AZ. This move will cost me over $2,000 and I can't even afford this now. With my son, daughter and grandson it will be impossible for me to have the house in Colorado and also pay to move, rent an apartment, pay for gas, rent storage space (if needed) and try to find a new house to purchase.

I will be out of a job for two weeks while I move. I can't make another payment on my mortgage because I will need to pay for moving expenses. I also need to sell my house NOW and can't afford to have the house sit on the market for 6 months like the other houses that have been sitting and not selling in my neighborhood. I cannot make two house payments; I am already living paycheck to paycheck. My house is currently listed and I have not received any offers. Pink Real Estate has offered to buy my house subject to approval of Option One accepting a short pay on my loan. If this short pay does not go through, I would end up still owing around $20,000 to the bank to pay off the house, closing costs, real estate agent fees, etc. I have no other funds to make up the difference between the balance owed and the purchase offer price. I will receive no cash or other consideration from this sale.

Thanks so much for your help.
John Doe

Hardship Sample Letter #3

Date
Lender
Attn: Bank Rep, Loss Mitigation
Re: 1234 Main Street – Short Sale
I am writing to ask for your assistance in trying to

sell my home. On September 10th of last year, I was in a car accident and was severely injured. The person who hit my car was uninsured. I have been out of work due to my medical problems. It is for this reason that I have not made my November, December and January payments. I have enclosed a copy of the accident report verifying the date of my injury. I've also attached a letter from my doctor indicating that I will be unable to return to work for several months.

I need your help in order to keep my home from foreclosure. I have tried listing the property with a real estate agent, but have had little success because the house is in need of repairs and I am unable to fix up the property. It does not show well and I have not had any suitable offers, except from Ira Investor.

Ira Investor has offered me $150,000, subject to approval of Wells Fargo accepting a short pay on my loan. I have no other funds to make up the difference between the balance owed and the purchase offer price. I will receive no cash or other consideration from this sale.

My telephone number is (555) 333-4444 and the best time of the day to reach me is between 12 p.m. and 5 p.m., as I am in physical therapy in the mornings.

Thank you very much for your consideration and assistance in helping me save my home from foreclosure.

Respectfully,
Sally Seller

Hardship Sample Letter #4

Date:

Lender Name and Loan #:

Dear Wells Fargo:

I am writing to ask for assistance in trying to sell my home. My property at 123 Any St. in Colorado Springs, CO 80906 was occupied with renters until they moved out because they couldn't afford the rent. We listed the home in the newspaper for several weeks and found no one who can afford the rent. Unfortunately this was a big expense for us and we also cannot afford the rent! The house is now listed on the MLS for sale. I am writing this letter to share some of the hardships we have endured over the past several months as we are having trouble trying to make ends meet.

In September 2010 I found out I was pregnant with our second child, which was great except we had no health insurance since it was a preexisting condition. The job's health insurance plan covered our family, but we had to pay for all of its cost plus a percentage of the bills. Shortly after all of this I lost my job and my pregnancy already showing made it difficult for me to find another job. This left my husband to take care of all the bills, and we have a large house payment as well as a truck payment. Unfortunately we also have credit card debt and were recently audited by the IRS for the past two years, in which we owe almost five thousand dollars with interest. I had our baby April 27th 2011, the insurance company covered a percentage of my bills after the deductible but they will not cover our baby's bills. Also the health insurance company will not allow our baby to be on the plan for six months, so we had to discontinue our coverage.

I need your help in order to keep our home from foreclosure. We cannot afford the repairs to fix up the home or pay for the utilities. Pink Real Estate has offered to purchase our house subject to approval of you, the Wells Fargo, accepting a short pay on my loan. I will receive no cash or other consideration from this sale.

Thank you very much for your consideration and assistance in helping us save our home from foreclosure.

Sincerely,

Homeowner's Name

Using a Software Program to Track Short Sales

Using a good industry software program is the best and most convenient way to track your leads and short sales. So, if you have the money to invest in a good tracking system, this is what we recommend. We use Short Sale Commander to track all our leads. You can track non-short sale leads in this database as well.

You can sign up to try a free trial at www.sscommander. infusionsoft.com/go/sschp/pink.

Systems such as this one allow you to do everything electronically so you don't need paper copies of documents. You can track loan numbers, borrower's names, Social Security numbers, addresses, bank phone numbers and all conversation notes saved with date and time stamps next to them. You can also assign yourself tasks to help keep yourself organized.

Every day when you log in, you will have the list of phone calls you need to make that day and appointments you need to go on, and it can also track all upcoming foreclosure dates. Our cost is $100 per month for five users. Your cost will vary depending on how many users you have.

If You Have No Money for a System

If you are just starting out and you don't have the money to invest in a system, you can start the same way I did. I used a manila file folder for each property and kept hard copies of every document for that property in the appropriate property file. On the top of the file I included all the homeowner's important contact information and all the lender's information, including loan number and phone numbers. I documented every phone call and every fax with date and time on a piece of paper that I kept in the file. I put important reminders for phone calls and appointments in my Outlook calendar to remind me to call banks and ask them to let me know which properties had a foreclosure sale date coming up.

If you are doing a lot of volume, this manual system will become cumbersome very quickly. Therefore, I don't recommend using this type of system unless you are just starting out and working only a few properties.

Once you've had a few closings and made some money, I recommend investing in a software program designed to handle short sales. It will make your life a lot easier.

Chapter 9
Different Types of Short Sales

Overview of Conventional Loans

Many of the conventional loans that homeowners have today are 80/20 loans. This means when the homeowner got their mortgage, 80% of the mortgage went to the first mortgage and 20% went toward the second mortgage. Some 80/20 conventional loans have both mortgages with the same company, and some have a different lenders for the first and second mortgages. In most cases, the second is completely over-encumbered because the homeowner is upside down on their house (they owe more on the mortgages than the home is worth). The second mortgage usually gets wiped off at foreclosure. It is easier to negotiate a short sale when both the first and second mortgages are with the same mortgage company. In cases where the homeowner has a second mortgage lender that is the same as the first mortgage lender and they pursue a short sale, the second mortgage lender already knows they will get $3,000 or 10% of the sales price. When you have a second mortgage lender that is different than the first mortgage lender, there can sometimes be a fight between the two mortgage companies.

Questions to Ask the Homeowner

When starting a conventional short sale, you need to find out if the home is in foreclosure and if so, what the foreclosure sale date is. This lets you determine how much time you have. You also want to find out if the homeowner is eligible to apply for the HAFA program. To do this, you need to ask the homeowner the following questions:

- Is this your primary residence?
- Do you currently live in the property?
- If you don't live in the property, when did you move out?

If the property is not their primary residence, they will not be eligible for the HAFA program. If they moved out within the last year and have not purchased another property, they are still eligible to apply for the HAFA program.

What Is a Traditional Conventional Short Sale?

If the homeowner is not eligible for the HAFA program, you will be doing a traditional short sale. The homeowner will not get any financial incentive for doing the short sale, and they will not be guaranteed a deficiency waiver. When you are doing a traditional short sale, the lender will need a complete short sale package with an offer before they will start the short sale or consider a postponement of the foreclosure sale date.

Investors, we don't recommend starting a short sale on a conventional loan if the foreclosure date is less than two weeks away, as you will need a completed short sale package, including an offer and the HUD-1 in the lender's hands before they will postpone the foreclosure sale date. Sometimes, depending on the bank, the imaging system they use and how organized they are, it can take up to two weeks for the lender to receive your short sale package.

It also depends on whether the bank uses a new system called "Equator." The Equator system organizes the short sale into stages, and you upload certain documents in a particular order. The first information the system asks for is the purchase price. If the purchase price does not meet or exceed the market value they have in their system, the offer is immediately rejected. If the purchase price is accepted, the system requests the HUD-1, purchase contract and listing agreement. With each stage of document uploads, they are reviewed and approved. Once approved, you are required to upload the next batch of documents.

While this system organizes the short sale for the lender, it oftentimes eliminates your chance to get an offer approved before the foreclosure sale date. Lenders currently using the Equator system are Wells Fargo, GMAC and Bank of America.

Below are several screen shots from the Equator system.

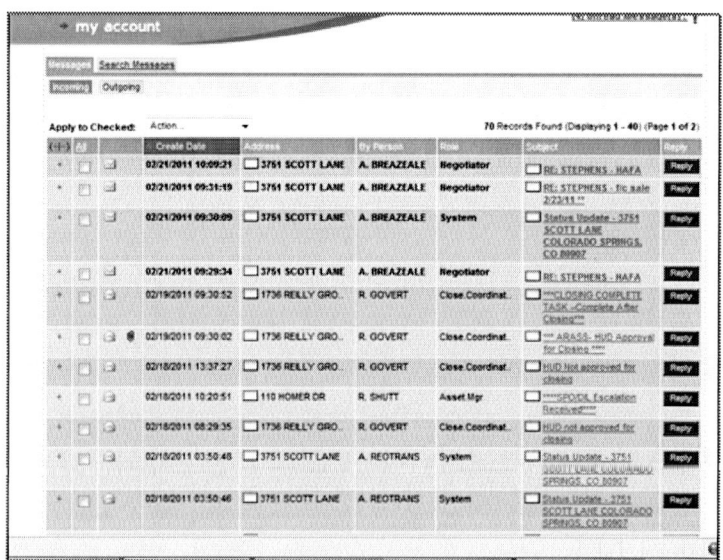

Figure 1: Equator Message Screen

Figure 2: Equator Properties Screen

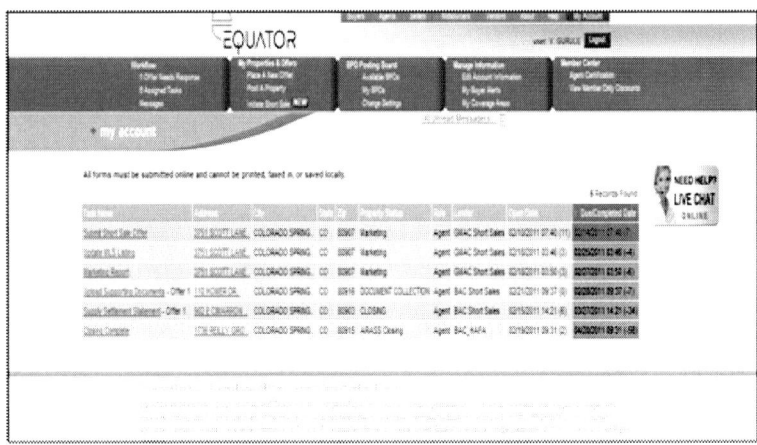

Figure 3: Equator Task Screen

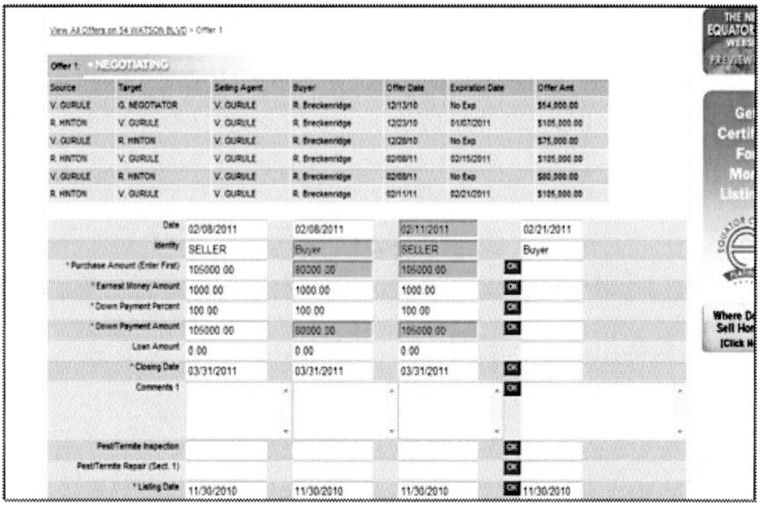

Figure 4: Equator Screen to Counter Offer

Each bank follows its own short sale process and, while some banks move through their process quickly and efficiently, other lenders are slow and inefficient. Therefore, it is important to learn which bank you are dealing with and which short sale system they use or what short sale process they follow. If a homeowner has a foreclosure date that is two weeks away and they have a conventional loan, we don't recommend signing the deal as you won't have enough time to get everything submitted to the bank. So, with traditional loans we recommend sticking to our "two-week rule."

I have started short sales just days before a foreclosure sale date and have been able to postpone the date, but that is only because I was either dealing with a bank that was organized and had an efficient short sale system in place, or because I had an inside contact (a good negotiator I had previously worked with) who could help me push the file through to get the foreclosure date postponed.

Know the Investor

When you are doing a traditional short sale with a conventional loan, the bank will have an investor behind the loan. The investor may be Fannie Mae, Freddie Mac or a private investor. The mortgage may also have Private Mortgage Insurance (PMI) on the loan. The bank could also just be the servicer for the loan and therefore, they are simply the go-between for you and the investor. The servicer or mortgage company is required to follow the investor's guidelines. Investor guidelines continuously change. For example, if there is no approved offer, Fannie Mae is not allowed to postpone a foreclosure sale. This guideline is constantly changing.

If your offer meets a certain net, you may be able to get an in-house approval from the servicer. If the offer is below the investor's net requirement, the offer will need to be submitted to the investor for their approval, and this takes more time. In order for the servicer to know what the minimum net requirement is, they need to get a value on the property. To do this, they either hire a third-party agent to do a Broker Price Opinion (BPO) on the property or they order an appraisal. A BPO agent is typically a real estate agent who runs comparables on the property and then looks at the property to determine what the value is for the bank. Most lenders doing a traditional conventional short sale will order a BPO instead of an appraisal to save money.

FHA Short Sales

Whenever someone has an FHA loan and they want

to do a short sale, they must be approved to participate in the FHA short sale program, which is called the Pre-Foreclosure Sale Program (PFSP). This is the only short sale they can do. The homeowner cannot do a regular short sale. This is a HUD loan and therefore the servicers must follow HUD guidelines. FHA short sales are personally one of my favorite short sales to do because the banks tell you how much they need to net, and the net proceeds go from 88% of appraised value down to 84%. The requirements to be eligible for the PFSP program are listed below.

Requirements

- The property must be the homeowner's primary residence.
- The homeowners must be occupying the home.
- If the homeowners have moved out, their reason for moving must be a valid reason approved by FHA.
- The homeowner must be 31 days or more behind on their mortgage payments.
- Their income must have gone down or their expenses must have gone up.

Details of the PFSP

- The program lasts four months.
- If the mortgage company is registered with HUD as a Tier 1 servicer, the program will automatically renew two additional months if necessary.
- The foreclosure sale date will be postponed during the time a homeowner is in the program.
- The homeowner is given a $1,000 seller incentive if they sell their house in 90 days or less. The incentive

goes down to $750 if the house gets sold after 90 days.

• Tier 1—The net to HUD is 88% of appraisal value between days 0 and 30 from the Approval to Participate date.

• Tier 2—The net to HUD is 86% of appraisal value between days 31 and 60 from the Approval to Participate date.

• Tier 3—The net to HUD is 84% of appraisal value between days 61 and 90 from the Approval to Participate date.

• You do not need an offer on the house to be eligible for the program.

• The home must be in habitable condition.

• The homeowner must maintain the property and keep it in marketable condition.

FHA Short Sale Process

Once the bank gets a completed short sale package, they assign a negotiator to the file regardless of whether or not there is an offer on the property. Oftentimes, when you call the loss mitigation department, you will realize many of the lender's representatives know little or nothing about the PFSP. They fight and argue with you, claiming there needs to be an offer on the property before they will consider the file for a short sale. This is not true! They also fight and argue with you claiming they cannot postpone the foreclosure sale date without an offer. Again, this is not true! If the homeowner has submitted their Application to Participate in the Pre-Foreclosure Sale Program, the bank must postpone the foreclosure sale date to allow them time to get him into the program.

If you find lenders are giving you trouble, tell them you will report them to HUD for violating HUD guidelines. This gets the lenders in trouble. So threatening to report them generally pushes the representative to get you in touch with a representative or supervisor that handles and understands FHA loans.

If you still can't get anywhere with the lender, report them to HUD! HUD will open up a case ticket and assign a HUD negotiator to the case to intervene. A HUD negotiator will call the bank and intervene until the issue is resolved. In order to speak to HUD regarding the issue, you will need to submit a Third Party Authorization to them so you are authorized on the account. This authorization will require the homeowner's name and FHA case number (not the lender's loan number). This can be found on the O&E on the top right-hand corner of the Deed of Trust. It will say "FHA Case #_____."

HUD Contact Information
- HUD Loss Mitigation Phone: 866-449-1661
- Authorization Fax: 918-935-2994
- FHA National Servicing Center: 800-Call-FHA

Get Your File Assigned an FHA Negotiator

If everything goes well and the HUD negotiator resolves your issue, the next step is to have the mortgage company assign your file to an FHA negotiator. Depending on the bank, this process can take up to 30 days. Once the file is assigned to a negotiator, they order an FHA appraisal on the property. A BPO is not accepted for FHA loans. In order to do an FHA short sale, the bank must use the value of the property that was determined by the certified FHA appraiser.

Approval to Participate (ATP) Is Issued

The value of the appraisal will determine the list price for the property. Once the appraisal is done and back to the FHA negotiator (generally one week or less), the negotiator determines whether or not the homeowner is eligible for the FHA Pre-Foreclosure Sale Program. When it is determined the homeowner is eligible, the negotiator issues the Approval to Participate in the Pre-Foreclosure Sale Program. This is referred to as the ATP. The ATP outlines the program details; it states what the appraised value is, what the net proceeds requirement is and how long the homeowner has to find a buyer for the property.

The net to the bank within the first 30 days must be at least 88% of the appraised value. This means if the appraisal came back at $150,000, the net to the bank needs to be $132,000. This net gets reduced to 86% of the appraised value between days 31 and 60 and to 84% between days 61 and 90. This is the lowest the net proceeds requirement will go.

If you can't pay the minimum net proceeds for the property, you can keep the property listed with a real estate agent and drop the price. This will show the bank that the listing agent tried to get a buyer, but there were still no offers. You can reduce the price of the house even if the net will be lower than the required net. I have had offers get accepted that were lower than the net requirements.

If an offer comes in close to the net, say at 82%, you can

try to get a variance with HUD to accept the offer. If you think the appraised value came back too high and there is no way you will be able to get a buyer at that price, you can dispute the appraised value. The mortgage company can ask the appraiser to re-appraise the property, or they can order a new appraisal. You will probably have to provide them with sold comps within the last six months to justify your reasons for wanting a new appraisal.

Buyer's Closing Costs

HUD will pay 1% in closing costs only if the buyer is getting an FHA loan. If the buyer is not getting an FHA loan, they will not pay any closing costs! Knowing this will save you a lot of time. You can, however, request a variance with HUD to pay 1% in closing costs for a VA or conventional buyer. I recommend putting the following in the MLS real estate agent remarks: "Approved FHA short sale."

This way the buyer's agents will show the property, and if they are familiar with short sales, they will understand how closing costs are paid.

If you get an offer in, counter the offer right away if they are asking for the full closing costs, as it will never get accepted with HUD. These are their guidelines, and a variance will not be accepted. This is the only down side to an FHA short sale. Most buyers expect all closing costs to be paid. The only way a buyer can get more closing costs paid is if the seller gifts their seller incentive to the buyer to be used toward their closing costs. This means that the seller will not get their seller incentive.

In almost all instances, when a buyer is not a cash buyer, the seller gives up their incentive to save the deal.

Secondary Liens

If there are secondary liens on the property, HUD will pay up to $2,500 for the secondary liens to be released. If there are judgments on the property but no second mortgage, $2,500 can be applied toward the judgments. To give you an example, if there is a second mortgage and a judgment, and the second mortgage lender accepts $2,000 to release the lien and the judgment wants $1,000 to satisfy their lien, you will be short $500. Therefore, the additional money needed will have to come from the seller incentive. This reduces their incentive but pays off their debt.

FHA Loan Modification Agreement or Partial Claims

Always make sure to order an O&E before doing any short sale. If you see anything on an FHA loan that looks like a loan modification agreement or a partial claim of any sort, these will need to be paid in full with the sales proceeds. If the homeowner did a loan modification agreement and HUD did a claim for $7,000, the full $7,000 will need to be paid in full in addition to giving the first mortgage their required net. Having to pay these can make it very difficult to sell the house.

Judgments

If there is a judgment on an FHA loan, the bank will need to immediately see a lien release of the judgment or intent to release the judgment against the property. If you don't have this, it could make the house unmarketable, and the bank won't allow the homeowner to be in the Pre-Foreclosure Sale Program.

Required Listing Agreement Disclosure

The Listing Agreement must include the cancellation clause, which reads as follows:

"Seller may cancel this Agreement prior to the ending date of the listing period without advance notice to the Broker, and without payment of a commission or any other consideration if the property is conveyed to the mortgage insurer or the mortgage holder. The sale completion is subject to approval by the mortgagee."

FHA Application to Participate

FHA Approval to Participate:

Downloadable Form

Approval to Participate	U. S. Department of Housing	OMB Approval No 2502-0464
Pre-foreclosure Sale Procedure	and Urban Development	(exp. 10/31/2012)
Property Sales Information	Office of Housing	
Property Occupancy & Maintenance	Federal Housing Commissioner	

Public reporting burden for this collection of information is estimated to average 9 minutes per response, including the time for reviewing instructions, searching existing data sources, gathering and maintaining the data needed, and completing and reviewing the collection of information. This information is required to obtain benefits. HUD may not collect this information, and you are not required to complete this form, unless it displays a currently valid OMB control number

Section 204 of the National Housing Act authorizes the Secretary to pay an insurance claim that bridges the gap between the fair market value proceeds from the HUD-approved third party sale of a property. The respondent's may be lenders (mortgagee's), counselors and homeowners who are attempting to sell their properties prior to foreclosure. The Privacy Act of 1974 pledges assurances of confidentiality to respondents. HUD generally discloses this data only in response to a Freedom of Information request

Mortgagee Contact Person and Phone Number	Control Number	FHA Case Number	Date
Homeowner Name(s)		Property Address	
Homeowner Signature(s)			

Homeowner(s): Please Read This Information Carefully.

Approval to Participate

Your interest to participate in the HUD Pre-foreclosure Sale procedure has been approved. By signing this form and returning to the above referenced mortgagee within 7 days, you are agreeing to abide by the following conditions of the program

Property Sales Information

The property must be listed for sale with a licensed Realtor unrelated to you within 7 days of your receipt of this letter for a list price at or near $_____ which is the "AS IS" value indicated on the appraisal of your property. The listing agreement must include the following specific cancellation clause in the event the terms of a sale are not acceptable to HUD. "Seller may cancel this agreement prior to the ending date of the listing period without advance notice to the broker, and without payment of a commission or any other consideration if the property is conveyed to the insurer or the mortgage holder." The sale completion is subject to approval (under HUD guidelines) by the mortgagee

Your deadline to obtain a signed Contract of Sale from a qualified buyer is _____ If you have not been able to obtain an acceptable contract by that date, your mortgagee must recommence foreclosure or accept a deed-in-lieu of foreclosure

Acceptable Terms of Sale

Program criteria require that "net" amount payable to HUD as a result of this sale, after allowable expenses will be at least $_____ You must submit your proposed Contract of Sale for approval to the Mortgagee Contact named above. The sale must be an "arm's length" transaction, the buyer cannot be a member of your family, business associate, or other favored party. No hidden terms or special understandings can exist between you, the buyer, appraiser, sales agent or mortgagee. If you negotiate with a buyer to pay for discount points, a home warranty, repairs not required for a new mortgage, transfer taxes or

other costs normally paid by the buyer, you must pay for these expenses. You must also pay prorated real estate taxes and assessments at closing. Your mortgagee can explain which sales costs may be deducted from HUD's sale proceeds

Relocation Services

A relocation service affiliated with your employer may contribute a fixed sum towards the proceeds of the PFS, without altering the arm's length nature of the sale. This contribution simply reduces the shortfall between the proceeds and the amount owed on the mortgage note. As with any other PFS, such a transaction must result in the outright sale of the property and cancellation of the FHA mortgage insurance.

Occupancy and Property Maintenance

You are responsible for property maintenance and repair until closing. This includes but is not limited to cutting the grass, snow removal, regular interior and exterior cleaning, immediate repair of broken doors and windows, and paying utility bills as they become due. If the property is vacant or becomes vacant during marketing, you must inform your mortgagee immediately and ensure that the property is protected from freeze damage by "winterizing" plumbing pipes. You may arrange with your sales agent to provide property maintenance but you will continue to be responsible for the condition of the home until it is sold. Damage and repair expenses resulting from fire, flood or other natural causes must be reported immediately to the insurance company and to your mortgagee

Borrower's Incentive Compensation

If you successfully close a sale of your home under this procedure, you will be paid compensation of $750 at closing. Your compensation will increase to $1,000 if the sale of your property closes on or before _____ You may elect to receive cash or apply some or all of the compensation to sales costs not paid by HUD, for example, discount points, or home warranty plans. You may also use it to pay off junior liens

Questions concerning any of this information, or your responsibilities in the Pre-foreclosure Sale procedure, must be directed to the contact person at your mortgagee's office at the above telephone number.

form HUD 90045 (6/2005)
ref. Handbook 4330.1

FHA Request for Variance

| Request for Variance
Pre-foreclosure Sale Program | U. S. Department of Housing
and Urban Development
Office of Housing
Federal Housing Commissioner | OMB Approval No.2502-0464
(exp. 10/31/2012) |

Public reporting burden for this collection of information is estimated to average 15 minutes per response, including the time for reviewing instructions, searching existing data sources, gathering and maintaining the data needed, and completing and reviewing the collection of information. This information is required to obtain benefits. HUD may not collect this information, and you are not required to complete this form, unless it displays a currently valid OMB control number.

Section 204 of the National Housing Act authorizes the Secretary to pay an insurance claim that bridges the gap between the fair market value proceeds from the HUD-approved third party sale of a property. The respondent's maybe lenders (mortgagee's), counselors and homeowners who are attempting to sell their properties prior to foreclosure. The Privacy Act of 1974 pledges assurances of confidentiality to respondents. HUD generally discloses this data only in response to a Freedom of Information request.

Mortgagee Name and ID No:	Date of Request:	Name & Telephone No. of Contact Person:	FHA Case Number:
Homeowner Name(s):		Property Address:	
Homeowner Name(s):			

Mark one, as appropriate: The following variance is requested, for reason indicated below:

☐ Approval of the subject homeowner's participation in the Pre-foreclosure Sale procedure has been withheld due to surchargable damage.

☐ Approval of a proposed contract of sale has been withheld because the estimated net sale proceeds are less than the required 84 percent of "FMV" appraised value of the subject property. A copy of the HUD-1 is attached.

"FMV" Appraised Value	Gross Sales Price	Estimated Net Sales Proceeds	Ratio of estimated Net Sale Proceeds to "FMV" appraised value (as percent)
$	$	$	%

☐ Request variance from other criterion (identify the criterion)

Justification for requesting HUD approval of this variance from customary Pre-foreclosure Sale procedure.

Local HUD Office Response: Comments (if any)

☐ Granted ☐ Denied	
Signature & Title of HUD Official:	Date:

FHA 90051 – Sales Contract Review

Sales Contract Review
Pre-foreclosure Sale Program

U. S. Department of Housing and Urban Development
Office of Housing
Federal Housing Commissioner

OMB Approval No. 2502-0164
(exp. 10/31/2012)

Public reporting burden for this collection of information is estimated to average 9 minutes per response, including the time for reviewing instructions, searching existing data sources, gathering and maintaining the data needed, and completing and reviewing the collection of information. This information is required to obtain benefits. HUD may not collect this information, and you are not required to complete this form, unless it displays a currently valid OMB control number.

Section 204 of the National Housing Act authorizes the Secretary to pay an insurance claim that bridges the gap between the fair market value proceeds from the HUD-approved third party sale of a property. The respondent's maybe lenders (mortgagee's), counselors and homeowners who are attempting to sell their properties prior to foreclosure. The Privacy Act of 1974 pledges assurances of confidentiality to respondents. HUD generally discloses this data only in response to a Freedom of Information request.

Mortgagee Contact Person		Phone Number	Account Control Number	FHA Case Number
Homeowner Name(s)		Property Address		
Homeowner Name(s)				

Date of Sales Contract	Date contract Received by Mortgagee	Sales Agent and Firm	Phone Number	Sales Commission & Rate
Offered By		Address		

Listing Price	Price Offered	Appraised Value	90% of Appraised Value	Estimated Net Sales Proceeds
$	$	$	$	$

Mortgagee (or HUD) Review of the Sales Contract

The Sales Contract offered by the individuals listed above is:

☐   Accepted

☐   Rejected (List reasons below)

This Sales Contract is rejected for the following reasons(s).

_____

Mortgagee Signature and Date

form HUD 90051 (06/2005)
ref. Handbook 4330.1

FHA 90052 – Closing Worksheet

Closing Worksheet
Pre-foreclosure Sale Program

U. S. Department of Housing and Urban Development
Office of Housing
Federal Housing Commissioner

OMB Approval No.2502-0464
(exp. 10/31/2012)

Public reporting burden for this collection of information is estimated to average 58 minutes per response, including the time for reviewing instructions, searching existing data sources, gathering and maintaining the data needed, and completing and reviewing the collection of information. This information is required to obtain benefits. HUD may not collect this information, and you are not required to complete this form, unless it displays a currently valid OMB control number.

Section 204 of the National Housing Act authorizes the Secretary to pay an insurance claim that bridges the gap between the fair market value proceeds from the HUD-approved third party sale of a property. The respondent's maybe lenders (mortgagee's), counselors and homeowners who are attempting to sell their properties prior to foreclosure. The Privacy Act of 1974 pledges assurances of confidentiality to respondents. HUD generally discloses this data only in response to a Freedom of Information request.

Mortgagee Contact Person	Phone Number	Account/Control Number	FHA Case Number

Homeowner Name(s):	Property Address:
Homeowner Name(s):	

Mortgagee (or HUD) Approval of the Sales Contract is a Pre-Condition of the Sale

Name of Purchaser	Address	Phone Number
Name of Purchaser	Address	Phone Number

Type of Financing (mark one) ☐ FHA ☐ VA ☐ Conventional ☐ Other	Date Contract Approved	Selling Price $	Sales Commission %

Payable from Sale Proceeds

Sales Commission	$	
(Local & State transfer taxes/stamps, etc.)	$	
(Lien discharge (must not exceed $1,000) (insert item)	$	
(insert item)	$	
Consideration to seller (basic amount=$750. Addition amount (normally $250) is paid if closing occurs within 90 days of start of participation in Pre-foreclosure sale Procedure)	$	
Total Amount Payable from Sales Proceeds (Add column of items)	$	Deduct all payments form Proceeds from selling price **New proceeds to Mortgagee:** $
Total amount paid to seller	Seller's Initials & Date	*(By initialing, seller acknowledges receipt of amount specified)
Sale's Agent/Broker's Signature & Date**		**By signing, the Agent/Broker certifies that there are no hidden terms or special understanding with the buyer, seller, appraiser, closing agent or mortgagee
Mortgagee's Authorizing Official's Signature & Date X		Closing Agent's Signature & Date X

(Attach copy of Settlement Statement)

form HUD-90052 (06/2003)
ref Handbook 4330.1

FHA Preforeclosure Fact Sheet

PREFORECLOSURE SALES PROGRAM

The Preforeclosure Sale Program allows a Mortgagor in default to sell his or her home and use the sales proceeds to satisfy the mortgage debt, even if the proceeds are less than the amount owed. Ref: Mortgagee Letters 2003-19 and 2008-43.

FACTS

- Outright sale of mortgaged property to a third party and must be an "arms length" transaction.
- Outstanding indebtedness includes: unpaid principal balance + delinquent interest + Partial Claim (if applicable).
- HUD will pay up to $1,000 incentive to the Mortgagor if closed within 3 months from the date of application, thereafter, the incentive is reduced to $750.
- HUD will pay an additional amount up to $1,500 for the discharge of junior liens after the Mortgagor's incentive has been applied.
- HUD allows all reasonable cost of the sale including up to 6% sales commission, local/state transfer tax stamp and other customary closing cost.
- HUD allows up to 1% of the buyer's mortgage amount for closing costs to be included in the "Seller's Costs" on the HUD-1 for all transactions that involve a new FHA-insured mortgage.
- Tiered Net Sales Proceeds requirement is applicable as follows:
  - For the first 30 days of marketing, Mortgagees may only approve offers that will result in minimum net sale proceeds of 88% of the "As-Is" appraised Fair Market Value.
  - During the next 30 days of marketing, Mortgagees may only approve offers that will result in minimum net sale proceeds of 86% of the "As-Is" appraised Fair Market Value.
  - For the duration of the Preforeclosure Sale marketing period, Mortgagees may only approve offers that will result in minimum net sale proceeds of 84% of the "As-Is" appraised Fair Market Value.
- Unacceptable Settlement Costs:
  - Repair reimbursements or allowances;
  - Home Warranty Fees;
  - Discount points or loan fees for non FHA-financing; and
  - Lender's title Insurance fee
- Property Condition:
  - Properties that have sustained damage may be eligible for the PFS option.
  - If the cause of the damage is fire, flood, earthquake, tornado, boiler explosion (for condominium's only) or mortgagee neglect (i.e., surchargeable damages as defined in 24 CFR Part § 203.378) mortgagees must obtain prior approval from the NSC at the address above.
  - Prior to seeking this approval, the mortgagee must obtain the government's estimate

Revised – February 4, 2009

of the cost to repair the surchargeable damage by contacting the HUD Management and Marketing (M&M) Contractor with jurisdiction for the geographic area where the property is located.

- A list of M&M Contractors can be found on the Internet at:
  http://www.hud.gov/offices/hsg/sfh/reo/mm/mminfo.cfm.
- **Under no circumstance** should the Mortgagor be encouraged to default on their mortgage for the purpose of participating in the Preforeclosure Sale Program.

ELIGIBILITY

- The property must be owner-occupied, no "walk-a ways" or investment properties. Exceptions: when it is verifiable that the need to vacate was related to the cause of default (job loss, transfer, divorce, death), and the subject property was not purchased as rental investment, or used as a rental for more than 18months.
- The Mortgagor must be 31 days or more delinquent at the time of the Preforeclosure Sale closing.
- The Mortgagor must provide documentation substantiating a reduction in income or an increase in living expense, and documentation that verifies the Mortgagors need to vacate the property (if applicable).

PROCEDURES

(1) Mortgagors who express an interest in the Preforeclosure Sale Option or who have been identified by the Mortgagee as a qualified candidate for the Preforeclosure Sale Program must be mailed a copy of the revised *Information Disclosure* Form HUD-90035.

(2) The Mortgagee must obtain a standard "As Is" FHA appraisal which has been completed in accordance with the requirements of HUD Handbook 4150.2 (Valuation Analysis for Single Family One-to Four-Unit Dwellings). To this end, Mortgagees must:

- Obtain a standard electronically-formatted appraisal from an appraiser on FHA's Appraiser Roster. The selected appraiser must not share any business interest with the Mortgagor or the Mortgagor's agent. Appraisals obtained by the buyer, seller, real estate agent, or other interested parties may not be used to establish the Fair Market Value of the property for the Preforeclosure Sale Program. It is also important to note that:
  - The appraisal must contain an "As-Is" Fair Market Value for the subject property;
  - The appraisal will be valid for six (6) months; and
  - Distress sales may not be used by the appraiser to establish comparable values unless they represent the only comparables within reasonable proximity of the subject property.
- Provide a copy of the appraisal to the homeowner, sales agent, or HUD, upon request.
- Mortgagees are reminded that in accordance with HUD regulations at 24 CFR Part § 203.365 (c) they are responsible for the accuracy of all documentation used in the PFS decision, including accurate and complete appraisal information.

In an effort to ensure that the most current Fair Market Value is used for the Preforeclosure Sale, a Mortgagee may obtain a new FHA appraisal, even if the property was appraised by an FHA Roster Appraiser within the preceding six (6) months.

Revised – February 4, 2009

To be reimbursed through HUD's claim filing process, the cost of the appraisal must be reasonable and customary for the market area where the appraisal is performed. The appraisal must be retained in the claim servicing file, even if the Preforeclosure Sale is not approved or completed.

(3) The Mortgagee must obtain a title search or preliminary report verifying that the title is not impaired with un-resolvable title problems or with junior liens that cannot be discharged as permitted by HUD.

(4) When an application is accepted an *Approval to Participate* form is used. The date of this form becomes the starting date of the PFS participation. The *Approval to Participate* form must include the date by which a signed contract for sale must be obtained and minimum acceptable net sales price.

- The Mortgagor agrees to show good faith in attempting to market and sell the property.
- The Mortgagor must perform all normal property maintenance and repairs until closing of the Preforeclosure Sale.
- The Mortgagor must list the property with a licensed real estate broker, unrelated to the Mortgagor. The listing agreement must include a specific cancellation clause in the event the terms of the sale are not acceptable to HUD.

(5) The Mortgagee delays foreclosure to allow pursuit of the Preforeclosure Sale.

(6) The Preforeclosure Sale period shall be four (4) months beginning upon Mortgagee approval (automatically extended two months for Mortgagees in Tier 1, or there is a signed Contract of Sale, but settlement can not occurred by the end of the fourth month).

(7) The Mortgagee should review marketing efforts with the Mortgagor and or the Real Estate Broker/Agent on a monthly basis.

(8) The sale closing must occur within six months (6), eight (8) months if Mortgagee is in Tier 1, from the date the Mortgagee notified the Mortgagor in writing of approval to participate in the Preforeclosure Sale Program.

If you have any question you may contact NSC at:

National Servicing Center
www.hud.gov/offices/hsg/sfh/nsc/nschome.cfm
E-mail: hsg-lossmit @ hud.gov
1-888-297-8685

Frequently Asked Questions:
http://www.hud.gov/offices/hsg/sfh/nsc/faqnsctc.cfm
PFS Forms: http://www.hud.gov/offices/hsg/sfh/nsc/lmmltrs.cfm

Revised: February 4, 2009

VA Short Sales

A VA short sale follows a similar process to conventional short sales where the homeowner is not going into the HAFA program. There is no incentive for the homeowner, and there must be an offer on the property to pursue the short sale. A primary difference between a VA short sale and a traditional conventional short sale is that the bank orders a VA appraisal. A BPO is not accepted on VA loans. The net proceeds on a VA short sale must be 88.13% of the VA appraisal. Additionally, the lender will pay 6% commissions and all buyers' and sellers' customary closing costs.

A VA appraisal is good for six months. The lender will not order a new appraisal until the current appraisal on file is six months old. VA appraisals are done using non-distressed sales comparables, so values oftentimes come in at a higher value that what would typically be seen on a BPO. VA appraisals are also very difficult to dispute. If you do need to dispute a VA appraisal, the process needs to be handled with the VA regional office that did the appraisal. This process is called a "reconsideration of value." Unless there are current sales comparables available to justify lowering the value, I do not recommend trying to dispute the appraised value. You will be wasting your time.

Program Requirements

- VA appraisal must be obtained.
- The property must be sold for fair market value.
- The homeowner must have a financial hardship.
- If the loan was originated on or before 12/31/89, the seller must be willing to sign a promissory note for the

deficiency.
- Closing costs must be reasonable and customary.
- There must be a sales contract on the property before the homeowner can be considered for the program.

Benefits

There are benefits for veterans who do a VA short sale.
- The lender does not pursue the homeowner for the deficiency. The VA guarantees the loan. They pay the lender and take the loss.
- Homeowner gets $1500 at closing for moving expenses.
- The borrower is eligible for another VA loan; however, there are contingencies. The VA will require that the borrower repay the deficiency amount due on the prior loan to restore their full eligibility, or the VA may reduce the veteran's eligibility amount by the deficiency amount. For example, if the homeowner qualifies for a VA loan in the amount of $200K but the deficiency of the short sale was $50K, the VA may ask the borrower to pay back the $50K deficiency before giving them the loan, or they may reduce their qualifying amount of the new loan to $150K. The same is true if the veteran loses a home to foreclosure. The veteran will need to pay back the amount the VA lost in the foreclosure to restore their full eligibility, or their eligibility will be reduced by the amount of the loss. [25]

HAFA Short Sales

There are three different types of HAFA short sale programs:

25 www.benefits.va.gov/homeloans/faqelig.asp

1. HAFA for Freddie Mac loans

2. HAFA for Fannie Mae loans

3. HAFA for non-Freddie Mac and non-Fannie Mae loans

To find additional information on the HAFA programs and to find out which program you want to qualify a homeowner for, visit www.makinghomeaffordable.gov and, under the Get Assistance tab, select "Loan Look Up." Once you know which program you will be working with, you will need to review the guidelines for that program, because each different HAFA program has different guidelines and requirements. Much of the information on the different HAFA programs was taken from the HAFA guidelines. You can find a complete set of the HAFA guidelines at the following websites:

- www.efanniemae.com/sf/servicing/hafa/ (Fannie Mae HAFA)
- www.freddiemac.com/singlefamily/service/hafa. html (Freddie Mac HAFA)
- www.hmpadmin.com/portal/programs/ foreclosure_alternatives.jsp (non-Fannie and non-Freddie)

While the programs are complicated, if you spend time learning all the HAFA guidelines and stay on top of the continual changes, you will stay ahead of the banks. This will give you the upper hand and will help you be successful with these cases.

The HAFA program was created under "Making Home Affordable" to help homeowners who didn't qualify for HAMP (Home Affordable Modification Program). HAMP is the loan modification program. Because many homeowners were not qualifying for a loan modification, President Obama created the HAFA (Home Affordable Foreclosure Alternatives) program under HAMP so homeowners had alternative options to help them avoid foreclosure.

By providing alternative options to foreclosure, this program helps homeowners, servicers, investors and the community. The program offers financial incentives to both servicers and homeowners who participate in HAFA. The program is intended to reduce the lengthy foreclosure proceeding process. It helps keep the value of the properties higher because it allows for faster short sale approval and property maintenance to keep down vandalism and property deterioration.

Unlike the process for many short sales and deeds-in-lieu of foreclosure, HAFA sets clear timelines to keep the process efficient. Mortgage servicers must evaluate homeowners for HAFA within 30 days after one of the eligibility criteria is met. If the homeowner is eligible, the servicer will send a Short Sale Agreement (SSA)—a contract between the homeowner and the servicer—that will include:

- A list price approved by the servicer.
- The length of time the property will be marketed for sale.
- An agreement releasing the homeowner from all future liability after the property is sold.
- The amount of the monthly mortgage payment, if any, that the borrower will be required to pay during the term of the SSA.
- Information about $3,000 in relocation assistance after closing.

- An agreement that so long as the borrower performs in accordance with the terms of the SSA, the servicer will not complete a foreclosure sale.

HAFA: Non-Fannie Mae and Non-Freddie Mac Eligibility

- The property is the borrower's principal residence.
- The mortgage loan is a first lien mortgage originated on or before January 1, 2009.
- The mortgage is delinquent or default is reasonably foreseeable.
- The current unpaid principal balance is equal to or less than $729,750.
- The house can be vacant and rented to a non-borrower within 12 months. It must have been considered your primary residence. The borrower cannot have purchased another 1- to 4-unit property during that 12-month period.

Every potentially eligible borrower must be considered for HAFA before the borrower's loan is referred to foreclosure or the servicer allows a pending foreclosure sale to be conducted. Servicers must consider possible HAMP-eligible borrowers for HAFA within 30 calendar days of the date the borrower

- Does not qualify for a Trial Period Plan.
- Does not successfully complete a Trial Period Plan.
- Is delinquent on a HAMP modification by missing at least two consecutive payments.
- Requests a short sale or DIL.

Borrower Obligations

The borrower must sign and return the SSA within 14 calendar days from its Effective Date, along with a copy of the real estate broker listing agreement and information regarding any subordinate liens. In returning and signing the SSA, the borrower agrees to

- Provide all information and sign documents required to verify program eligibility.
- Cooperate with the listing broker to actively market the property and respond to servicer inquiries.
- Maintain the interior and exterior of the property in a manner that facilitates marketability.
- Work to clear any liens or other impediments to title that would prevent conveyance.
- Make the monthly payment stipulated in the SSA, if applicable.

Cause for Termination

- The borrower's financial situation improves significantly, the borrower qualifies for a modification or the borrower brings the account current or pays the mortgage in full.
- The borrower or the listing broker fails to act in good faith in listing, marketing and/or closing the sale, or otherwise fails to abide by the terms of the SSA.
- A significant change occurs to the property condition and/or value.
- There is evidence of fraud or misrepresentation.
- The borrower files for bankruptcy and the Bankruptcy Court declines to approve the SSA.
- Litigation is initiated or threatened that could affect title to the property or interfere with a valid

conveyance.

- The borrower fails to make the monthly payment stipulated in the SSA, if applicable.

Request for Approval of Short Sale

Within three business days following receipt of an executed purchase offer, the borrower or the listing broker should deliver to the servicer a completed RASS describing the terms of the sale transaction. With the RASS, the borrower must submit to the servicer:

- A copy of the executed sales contract and all addenda.* **(See Note Below)**
- Buyer's documentation of funds or buyer's pre-approval or commitment letter on letterhead from a lender.
- All information regarding the status of subordinate liens and/or negotiations with subordinate lien holders.

*NOTE: There are required HAFA clauses that need to be included in the Listing Agreement and Contract to Buy and Sell. These are listed below:

Exclusion Clause—Listing Agreement

"Seller may cancel this Agreement prior to the ending date of the listing period without advance notice to the broker, and without payment of a commission or any other consideration, if the property is conveyed to the mortgage insurer or the mortgage holder."

Contingency Clause—Listing Agreement and Sales Contract

"Sale of the property is contingent on written agreement

to all sale terms by the mortgage holder and the mortgage insurer (if applicable)."

Sales Contract Language—Sales Contract

"Seller and Buyer each represent that the sale is an 'arm's length' transaction and the Seller and Buyer are unrelated to each other by family, marriage or commercial enterprise." "The Buyer agrees not to sell the property within 90 days of closing this sale."

Approval or Disapproval of Sale

Within ten business days of receipt of the RASS and all required attachments, the servicer must indicate its approval or disapproval of the proposed sale by signing the appropriate section of the RASS and mailing it to the borrower.

The servicer must approve a RASS if the net sale proceeds available for payment to the servicer are equal to or exceed the minimum net determined by the servicer prior to the execution or extension of the SSA and all other sales terms and conditions in the SSA have been met. Additionally, the servicer may not require, as a condition of approving a short sale, a reduction in the real estate commission below the commission stated in the SSA.

The servicer may require that the sale closing take place within a reasonable period following acceptance of the RASS, but in no event may the servicer require that a transaction close in less than 45 calendar days from the date of the sales contract without the consent of the borrower.

Monica Adams

General Terms and Conditions

Suspension of Foreclosure Sales

At the servicer's discretion, the servicer may initiate foreclosure or continue with an existing foreclosure proceeding during the HAFA process, but may not complete a foreclosure sale

- While determining the borrower's eligibility and qualification for HAFA.
- While awaiting the timely return of a fully executed SSA.
- During the term of a fully executed SSA.
- Pending transfer of property ownership based on an approved sales contract per the RASS or Alternative RASS.
- Pending transfer of property ownership via a DIL by the date specified in the SSA or DIL Agreement.

Payment Forbearance

The servicer will identify in the SSA, Alternative RASS or DIL Agreement the amount of the monthly mortgage payment, if any, that the borrower is required to make during the term of the applicable agreement and pending transfer of property ownership, as applicable. In no event may the amount of the borrower's monthly payment exceed the equivalent of 31 percent of the borrower's gross monthly income. Servicers must develop a written policy in accordance with investor requirements that identifies the circumstances under which they will require monthly payments and how that payment will be determined. Any requirement for the borrower to make monthly payments must be in accordance with applicable laws, rules and regulations.

Release of Subordinate Liens

It is the responsibility of the borrower to deliver clear marketable title to the purchaser or investor and to work with the listing broker, settlement agent and/or lien holders to clear title impediments. The servicer may, but is not required to, negotiate with subordinate lien holders on behalf of the borrower. The servicer, on behalf of the investor, will authorize the settlement agent to allow a portion of the gross sale proceeds as payment(s) to subordinate mortgage/lien holder(s) in exchange for a lien release and full release of borrower liability.

Each lien holder, in order of priority, may be paid no more than six percent (6%) of the unpaid principle balance of their loan, until the $6,000 aggregate cap is reached. Payments will be made at closing from the gross sale proceeds and must be reflected on the HUD-1 Settlement Statement. Investors are eligible for incentive reimbursement for up to one-third of the cost to extinguish subordinate liens as described in the Incentive Compensation section of the HAFA Supplemental Directive .[26]

Prior to releasing any funds to subordinate mortgage/lien holder(s), the servicer through its agent must obtain written commitment from the subordinate lien holder that it will release the borrower from all claims and liability relating to the subordinate lien in exchange for receiving the agreed-upon payoff amount. Although servicers have discretion to draft policies and procedures for ensuring that

26 https://www.hmpadmin.com/portal/programs/docs/hafa/sd0909r.pdf

the commitment of subordinate lien holders is documented prior to closing and such documentation is retained in the servicing file, they would be in compliance with HAFA guidelines if they further required the closing attorney or agent to either confirm that they are in receipt of this commitment from subordinate lien holders on the HUD-1 Settlement Statement, or request that a copy of the written commitment provided by the subordinate lien holder be sent to the servicer with the HUD-1 Settlement Statement that is provided in advance of the closing.

Subordinate mortgage/lien holder(s) may not require contributions from either the real estate agent or borrower as a condition for releasing its lien and releasing the borrower from personal liability. In addition, any payments to subordinate mortgage/lien holder(s) related to the short sale or DIL must be reflected on the HUD-1 Settlement Statement, as applicable.

Release of First Mortgage Lien

The servicer should follow local or state laws or regulations to time the release of its first mortgage lien after receipt of sale proceeds from a short sale or delivery of the deed and property in a DIL transaction. If local or state law does not require release within a specified time from the date the servicer receives payment and satisfies the mortgage, the servicer must release its first mortgage lien within 30 business days. Additionally, the investor must waive all rights to seek a deficiency judgment and may not require the borrower to sign a promissory note for the deficiency.

Mortgage Insurer Approval

For loans that have mortgage insurance coverage, the servicer/investor must obtain mortgage insurer approval for HAFA foreclosure alternatives. A mortgage loan does not qualify for HAFA unless the mortgage insurer waives any right to collect additional sums (cash contribution or a promissory note) from the borrower.

Borrower Relocation Assistance

Following the successful closing of a short sale or DIL, the borrower shall be entitled to an incentive payment of $3,000 to assist with relocation expenses. In a short sale transaction, the servicer must instruct the settlement agent to pay the borrower from sale proceeds at the same time that all other payments, including the payoff to the servicer, are disbursed by the settlement agent. The amount paid to the borrower must appear on the HUD-1 Settlement Statement.

Servicer Incentive

The servicer will be paid $1,500 to cover administrative and processing costs for a short sale or DIL completed in accordance with the requirements of HAFA and the applicable documents. Investors may elect to pay additional incentive compensation to servicers which will not affect the HAFA servicer incentive.

Freddie Mac HAFA

Mortgage and Borrower Eligibility

The following mortgages are eligible for HAFA:

- First-lien mortgages, owned, guaranteed, or

securitized by Freddie Mac that were originated on or before January 1, 2009

- Eligible properties are single family, 1–4 units, and primary residences, including condos, guide-eligible manufactured homes and negotiated conforming jumbos
- Mortgaged property that is not abandoned, condemned, or vacant without an applicable exception

Borrowers may be eligible for the following initiative if they meet the following requirements:

- Borrowers must be more than 60 days delinquent and have cash reserves less than the greater of $5,000 or three times their current monthly mortgage payment.
- Borrowers must have first been considered for a HAMP modification and then for other Freddie Mac home retention options under Guide Chapter B65, but were either ineligible, did not complete or declined the modification.
- Borrowers may be in foreclosure, in pending litigation involving the mortgage or in active bankruptcy.
- Borrowers must be able to convey a clear, marketable title to the mortgaged property.

Fannie Mae HAFA

HAFA Eligibility Considerations

Servicers may not consider a borrower for HAFA until the borrower has been evaluated for a HAMP modification (including, but not limited to, providing all required income documentation) in accordance with the eligibility criteria for HAMP as outlined in the Servicing Guide, Part VII, Section 610.01: HAMP Eligibility, and any supplemental HAMP policy guidance. Once a borrower has met all of the eligibility criteria for HAMP, the borrower must be considered for a HAFA short sale or DIL (after all home retention options have been considered) if the borrower

- Was not offered a trial modification due to inability to meet the HAMP qualifications (for example, did not pass the net present value (NPV) evaluation or meet the target monthly mortgage payment ratio based on verified income).
- Failed to complete the trial period successfully.
- Became two consecutive payments (31 or more days) delinquent on the modified mortgage loan.
- Requests a short sale or DIL.

Without Fannie Mae's prior written consent, a servicer must not consider or solicit a borrower for a Fannie Mae HAFA short sale or DIL with respect to a mortgage loan if

- A foreclosure sale is scheduled to be held within 60 days of the borrower's request for a Fannie Mae HAFA short sale or DIL, or a determination that a borrower is ineligible for HAMP.
- A foreclosure proceeding could be initiated and reasonably be expected to result in a foreclosure sale being held within 60 days of the borrower's request for a Fannie Mae HAFA short sale or DIL, or a determination that a borrower is ineligible for HAMP.
- The mortgage loan is secured by a property in Florida on which foreclosure proceedings are pending, judgment has been obtained or a hearing on summary

judgment or trial is scheduled within 60 days.

Evaluation of the Borrower's Financial Condition

The servicer must evaluate the borrower's financial condition for the Fannie Mae HAFA program using the guidelines noted below, to determine whether the borrower has an ability to contribute meaningfully to reducing the potential loss on the mortgage loan. The servicer must determine if the borrower has

- The ability to continue making the mortgage payments but chooses not to do so.
- Substantial unencumbered assets or significant cash reserves equal to or exceeding three times the borrower's total monthly mortgage payment (including tax and insurance payments) or $5,000, whichever is greater.
- High surplus income.

Downloadable Form

Request for Modification and Affidavit (RMA)

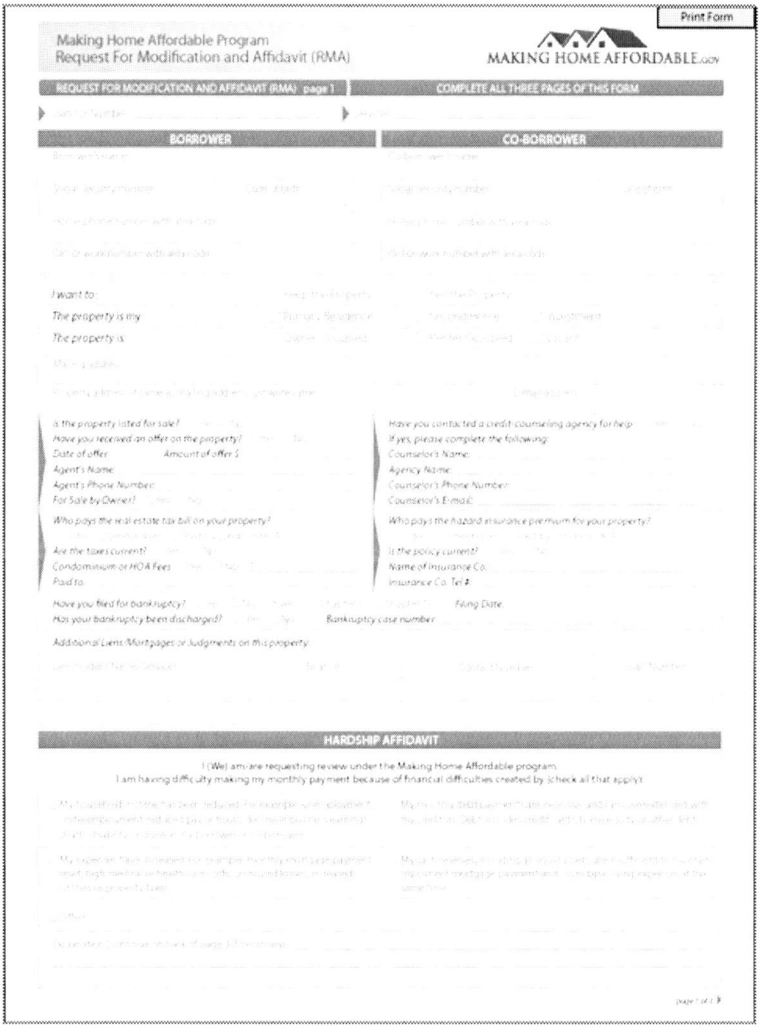

Print Form

Making Home Affordable Program
Request For Modification and Affidavit (RMA)

MAKING HOME AFFORDABLE.GOV

REQUEST FOR MODIFICATION AND AFFIDAVIT (RMA) page 1 | COMPLETE ALL THREE PAGES OF THIS FORM

BORROWER | CO-BORROWER

I want to:
The property is my
The property is:

Is the property listed for sale?
Have you received an offer on the property?
Date of offer Amount of offer $
Agent's Name:
Agent's Phone Number:
For Sale by Owner?
Who pays the real estate tax bill on your property?
Are the taxes current?
Condominium or HOA Fees
Paid to:

Have you contacted a credit-counseling agency for help
If yes, please complete the following:
Counselor's Name:
Agency Name:
Counselor's Phone Number:
Counselor's E-mail:
Who pays the hazard insurance premium for your property?
Is the policy current?
Name of Insurance Co.:
Insurance Co. Tel #:

Have you filed for bankruptcy? Filing Date:
Has your bankruptcy been discharged? Bankruptcy case number

Additional Liens/Mortgages or Judgments on this property:

HARDSHIP AFFIDAVIT

I (We) am/are requesting review under the Making Home Affordable program.
I am having difficulty making my monthly payment because of financial difficulties created by (check all that apply):

Monica Adams

REQUEST FOR MODIFICATION AND AFFIDAVIT (RMA) page 2	**COMPLETE ALL THREE PAGES OF THIS FORM**

INCOME/EXPENSES FOR HOUSEHOLD[1]   *Number of People in Household:*

Monthly Household Income		Monthly Household Expenses/Debt		Household Assets	
Monthly Gross Wages	$	First Mortgage Payment	$	Checking Account(s)	$
Overtime	$	Second Mortgage Payment	$	Checking Account(s)	$
Child Support / Alimony / Separation[2]	$	Insurance	$	Savings/ Money Market	$
Social Security/SSDI	$	Property Taxes	$	CDs	$
Other monthly income from pensions, annuities or retirement plans	$	Credit Cards / Installment Loan(s) (total minimum payment per month)	$	Stocks / Bonds	$
Tips, commissions, bonus and self-employed income	$	Alimony, child support payments	$	Other Cash on Hand	$
Rents Received	$	Net Rental Expenses	$	Other Real Estate (estimated value)	$
Unemployment Income	$	HOA/Condo Fees/Property Maintenance	$	Other _____	$
Food Stamps/Welfare	$	Car Payments	$	Other _____	$
Other (investment income, royalties, interest, dividends, etc.)	$	Other _____	$	Do not include the value of life insurance or retirement plans when calculating assets (401k, pension funds, annuities, IRAs, Keogh plans, etc.)	
Total (Gross Income)	**$**	**Total Debt/Expenses**	**$**	**Total Assets**	**$**

INCOME MUST BE DOCUMENTED

[1] *Include combined income and expenses from the borrower and co-borrower (if any). If you include income and expenses from a household member who is not a borrower, please specify using the back of this form if necessary.*
[2] *You are not required to disclose Child Support, Alimony or Separation Maintenance income, unless you choose to have it considered by your servicer.*

INFORMATION FOR GOVERNMENT MONITORING PURPOSES

The following information is requested by the federal government in order to monitor compliance with federal statutes that prohibit discrimination in housing. **You are not required to furnish this information, but are encouraged to do so. The law provides that a lender or servicer may not discriminate either on the basis of this information, or on whether you choose to furnish it.** If you furnish the information, please provide both ethnicity and race. For race, you may check more than one designation. If you do not furnish ethnicity, race, or sex, the lender or servicer is required to note the information on the basis of visual observation or surname if you have made this request for a loan modification in person. **If you do not wish to furnish the information, please check the box below.**

BORROWER	☐ I do not wish to furnish this information	CO-BORROWER	☐ I do not wish to furnish this information
Ethnicity:	☐ Hispanic or Latino ☐ Not Hispanic or Latino	Ethnicity:	☐ Hispanic or Latino ☐ Not Hispanic or Latino
Race:	☐ American Indian or Alaska Native ☐ Asian ☐ Black or African American ☐ Native Hawaiian or Other Pacific Islander ☐ White	Race:	☐ American Indian or Alaska Native ☐ Asian ☐ Black or African American ☐ Native Hawaiian or Other Pacific Islander ☐ White
Sex:	☐ Female ☐ Male	Sex:	☐ Female ☐ Male

To be completed by interviewer		Name/Address of Interviewer's Employer
This request was taken by: ☐ Face-to-face interview ☐ Mail ☐ Telephone ☐ Internet	Interviewer's Name (print or type) & ID Number Interviewer's Signature Date Interviewer's Phone Number (include area code)	

Overview of All Three HAFA

HAFA OVERVIEW	HAFA	Fannie Mae	Freddie Mac
Program Dates	April 5, 2010–Dec. 31, 2012	August 1, 2010–Dec. 31, 2012	August 1, 2010–Dec. 31, 2012
Borrower Forms Short Sale Approval	SSA	Form 184	Form 1135
Borrower Forms Request for Approval of Short Sale	RASS	Form 184a	Form 1136
Borrower Forms Alternate Request for Approval of Short Sale	Alternate RASS	Form 185	*NOTE: Borrowers must have first been considered for a
Borrower Relocation Assistance	$3,000	$3,000	$3,000
Servicer Incentive Due after reporting period	$1,500	SS: $2,000 DIL: $1,500	SS: $2,000 DIL: $1,500
Investor Incentive Aggregate	$6,000 cap	$6,000 cap	$6,000 cap
Eligibility Requirements 1	Principal residence (1 year rule to be vacant and can't buy another house in that year)	Relocated or transferred more than 100 miles and has not purchased another unit within 90 days	Principal residence (90 day rule—justifiable employer relocation)
Eligibility Requirements 2	First lien non-GSE mortgage	First lien mortgage owned by Fannie Mae	First lien mortgage owned by Freddie Mac
Eligibility Requirements 3	Originated prior to January 1, 2009	Originated prior to January 1, 2009	Originated prior to January 1, 2009
Eligibility Requirements 4	Is delinquent or default is foreseeable	Is delinquent or default is foreseeable	Borrower must be 60 days delinquent
Eligibility Requirements 5	Current unpaid principal balance is equal or less than $729,750	Current unpaid principal balance is equal or less than $729,750	Current unpaid principal balance is equal or less than $729,750
Eligibility Requirements 6	No requirement—just got rid beginning Feb 1st	Total monthly mortgage payment exceeds 31% of gross income	Cash reserves must be less than the greater of either $5,000 or 3 times their current monthly mortgage payment

Chapter 10
Calling Banks and Negotiating Tactics

Finding a Short Sale Company Name

Investors, you should never let the banks know you are the buyer when you negotiate your short sales! If you intend to negotiate your own short sales, you need to create a company exclusively for this purpose. My short sale company name is Pink Short Sale Team. When we call the banks, we refer ourselves as the Pink Short Sale Team and we work on behalf of the agents. The agents hired the Pink Short Sale Team to negotiate the short sale. All of the Pink Realty agents use the Pink Short Sale Team for their negotiations as well. This is very common, as most agents do not negotiate their own short sales. A lot of big players either hire an assistant to do the work or hire a short sale negotiating company like a title company or a national company to do their short sales. You can also create your own short sale company. Some company name examples might be Short Sale Solutions, Short Sale Alliance, Colorado Springs Short Sale Team and Short Sale Mitigation.

Calling the Banks and Starting the Short Sale

Regardless of what all the other short sale programs teach you, I always submit my short sale package immediately, especially if it's FHA or HAFA. It's always best to get as much done as possible before there is a buyer for the property. This way all the leg work is done, and once you have a buyer, you should be able to get an approval letter quickly. With FHA and HAFA, the banks order an appraisal or BPO right away. For these loan types, this is good. Just make sure the house is priced at the value at which you need the BPO value to come in. The BPO agents and appraisers look at the current list price and usually come in near that price. If the loan is conventional (non-HAFA approved) or VA, however, you don't want the banks to order the BPO or appraisal until you have an offer.

Agent Gets an Offer – Preparing the Buyer (Agents Only)

Real estate agents, when you get an offer on the property, it is very important to talk to the buyer's agent when they submit the offer. Make sure they know where you are in the short sale process and find out if the buyer is patient and willing to wait until the short sale is finished. You also want to make sure the buyer understands the home is being sold "as-is" and the homeowner is not in a financial position to make any repairs to the property.

Finally, make sure there are no dates on the offer and make sure they put SSA+ the number of days (Short Sale Approval plus) for the dates. This way while you are working on the contract, you don't get out of contract and give the buyer a bigger excuse to want to walk away from the deal.

Once you are under contract, make sure you update the buyer's agent once a week on the progress of the short sale. This way they know you haven't forgotten them. You need to cater to both the buyer's agent and the buyer, as you don't want the buyer to walk.

Negotiating Tactics – Tricks for Getting What You Want

Tactic #1: Be Nice Until Nice Doesn't Work

Kill them with kindness is the way to start out with the banks. This tactic is a good way to start. Unfortunately, there are banks that will give you a hard time. When this happens, move to the next level and get firm. If this still doesn't work, you might have to impress them with progress and take it, once again, to the next level.

While it is good to remain professional, there are times when being rude might get you further along the process, but not always. You need to do whatever is needed to get your job done! I have personally reached the point of yelling and have forgotten all "ladylike" behavior. You are not friends with the bank representatives. This is business, and you need to do what needs to be done to be successful at your business.

If all you have to do is be nice, the ball is in your court. Compliments have moved mountains, and telling negotiators they are awesome, helpful and wonderful can do wonders. When I have a good experience with a negotiator, I take that to the next level as well. I tell them they deserve a raise and ask for their manager's contact information so I can write a letter or send an email to compliment their employee. This flatters them and provides me with an additional supervisor contact that I just might need in the future.

So, go ahead and butter them up . . . Call them "Sweetie," heighten their egos, kiss their butts! Flattery can oftentimes get you exactly what you need.

Tactic #2: Be Aggressive and Tell Them How You Feel

I have been known to get into it with negotiators. I have been known to be aggressive and let my frustrations out. I will create drama and explain how a file has been so frustrating I have lost sleep over it and now I'm having nightmares about it.

I tell them, "I don't know how you put up with the investor. I feel really sorry for you because after you have to deal with them, you have to deal with people like me."

With my anger, I add humor that generally results in both of us laughing, and the negotiator ends up on my side. This, however, isn't always the case. After you let the negotiator have it, you have to hope they don't hang up on you!

Negotiating short sales requires some good people and character skills. You never know what kind of bank representative you will get on the other end of the phone. You may get a representative who is fully knowledgeable and has their act together, or you may get a newly hired trainee who is still struggling to read the script in front of them. Sometimes you get someone who cares and sometimes you don't.

The representative might be in a good mood or a bad mood. The more you negotiate, the more you'll learn which tactics will work best for the personality on the other end of the phone.

Tactic #3: Threaten to Turn the Bank in to the Officials

Threatening the lenders is another negotiation

technique. When you know a particular lender is not following the correct guidelines, you can threaten to turn that lender in to the authorities. The more familiar and knowledgeable you are with the different guidelines, the easier it will be to know when the lenders are following them and when they are not. Depending on the type of loan you are working with, you can file complaints with the appropriate agencies (the Treasury Office, FTC, HUD, VA, etc.)

During a short sale negotiation involving a conventional, non-Fannie and non-Freddie Mac loan with GMAC, I was dealing with a situation where the bank forced the house into foreclosure without giving the homeowner an opportunity to do a short sale. The house foreclosed at $455K, and we had a cash offer of $450K. No one bought the house at the auction, so it gave us the opportunity to try and rescind the sale. In Colorado, you have eight business days to rescind a sale. We went to rescind the sale and report the bank for foreclosing on the house without allowing the homeowner to try for a successful short sale.

The investor on this loan wanted a $50K cash contribution from the seller. This was ridiculous because the amount to bring the loan current was $25K! Regardless, the investor insisted on receiving a $50K cash contribution. In my discussions with the negotiator, I said the investor was setting the homeowner up for failure with the short sale and explained that GMAC was not following the guidelines issued by the U.S. Treasury Office, which clearly states foreclosure sales must be postponed when there is a short sale in review. Despite this, the foreclosure date was not postponed and the house went to foreclosure. I continued to explain to her that the government is now prosecuting those who don't follow proper guidelines. I told her I filed a complaint and received a case number with the FTC and they are actively investigating this case. Despite all of our efforts, the lender closed the short sale file because the homeowner was not willing to pay a $50K cash contribution at closing.

I sent an email to the negotiator and copied the complaint department of the U.S. Treasury Office and copied a press release from the FTC in the email. As a result of this email, the negotiator's supervisor contacted my short sale facilitator. She explained to the supervisor what the negotiator had done, and the supervisor said she would call the investor to see what she could do.

The next day was Friday, and we only had two business days left to rescind the sale. I emailed the supervisor to find out if she had heard anything back from the investor and was told the investor still wanted the $50K cash contribution from the seller. I completely lost my temper and said, "This investor allowed this house to be foreclosed on without even reviewing the offer. GMAC is supposed to follow guidelines issued by the Treasury Office and postpone all foreclosure sales when there is a short sale in review. Your negotiator did not do this!"

I then told the supervisor that the government is now prosecuting those who don't follow these guidelines and I have filed the complaint with the FTC and they are actively investigating this case. Going through the case again, I explained this investor is setting the homeowner up for failure with the short sale. The amount to bring the loan current is $25K and he is asking for a $50K cash contribution. This is crazy; if he had that kind of money he wouldn't be losing his house and two other properties to foreclosure.

I said, "You know this is crazy. You can't tell me you don't think this is a crazy request." I also told her I felt sorry for her. I couldn't believe she had to deal with this mentality day after day. Again, I said, "This is crazy, how do you put up with this?"

At this point, things began to shift. The supervisor said she would approach the investor with the option of having the homeowner sign a promissory note for the $50K. I said that was OK, as it was a better option than having the owner pay $50K up front. I also knew the homeowner was planning on filing bankruptcy when this transaction was over, so I knew the homeowner would agree to the promissory note.

I received a phone call from the supervisor a few hours later. She said the investor refused the promissory note but said if the borrower was willing to sign an approval letter that gives the investor the right to come after the homeowner for the deficiency, then he said he would go ahead and rescind the sale. I let her know that was agreeable and I thought the homeowner would agree as well. Then I was told we had to close on that next Monday and get the investor the sales proceeds the same day. Fortunately, this was a cash deal and that was not a problem.

This was the most difficult negotiation we ever had to work through, but we managed to get it done! Most short sales are not this difficult, but you will come across a few that are very hard and frustrating. As long as you fight back using guidelines to prove that the lenders and investors are not following them, you have the recourse of filing a complaint with the appropriate agencies. With the state of the housing market, you will get assistance and support. Most importantly, **DON'T GIVE UP! FIGHT UNTIL YOU CAN'T FIGHT ANYMORE!** This is how we win more short sales than anybody else. **NEVER GIVE UP!**

Tactic #4: Persistence

Being consistent and persistent is a critical component of short sale negotiation success. You need to always be proactive with your short sale files and stay on top of the banks. Be persistent calling the banks. If you are constantly in contact with the bank representatives and negotiators, they get to know you and learn you will not go away. Your persistence will teach them that you are the "thorn in their side" or the "gnat in their face" that doesn't go away. This reputation generally works in your favor because they learn to get you what you want because they know you won't go away. So, set your daily tasks every day and make those calls to the bank. Stay on top of your files and ahead of the banks. Your success depends on it!

Ensuring the Foreclosure Sale Date Gets Postponed

It is also very important to remain organized so you can stay on top of all your foreclosure sale dates. In El Paso County, foreclosure sales are held on Wednesdays at 10 a.m.

The process of how a bank postpones their foreclosure dates involves several steps. The negotiator needs to send a postponement request to the foreclosure department to initiate the postponement. In some instances, the negotiator needs to get permission from the investor on the loan to postpone the foreclosure sale. Once the request gets to the foreclosure department and the file is reviewed for postponement, they notify the attorney handling the foreclosure. The attorney then notifies the Public Trustee to postpone the sale.

In other states, the attorney notifies the sheriff or the court. It depends on who handles the foreclosure action in that state. In Colorado, how quickly the Public Trustee is notified will depend on who the attorney is. In Colorado Springs, if the attorney is Castle Meinhold, they may have the postponement request already, but have not yet notified the Public Trustee. They generally send bulk notifications for all their postponements electronically to the Public Trustee the Monday before the foreclosure sale date.

In El Paso County, you need to continuously check the Public Trustee's website at www.elpasopublictrustee. com to confirm the postponement. If you don't see a postponement posted on the website, contact the lender's attorney handling the foreclosure to find out the current status of the foreclosure sale. If the attorney still sees no postponement request, you need to call the bank back to ensure they have initiated the postponement request. You want to start working with the bank to postpone the foreclosure sale at least two weeks prior to the sale date. The more you work with the lenders and their various negotiators, the more you may see that many don't start the postponement request until two to three days before the sale. If you do not yet have a negotiator assigned, they generally start the request a week before the sale.

When you call the bank, ask them what foreclosure

date they have in their system. They generally have a system in place that can tell you what the sale date is. If they say they don't have a current sale date, this usually means they don't have one currently scheduled, but they can get one assigned at any time. Be sure to tell the bank that according to the foreclosure attorney and the Public Trustee, the sale date is scheduled for next week, and ask them to submit a request to postpone the foreclosure sale date. They will typically make the request for you or they may ask you to request this from your negotiator.

We have approximately 100 active short sale files and have at least ten files scheduled to go to foreclosure each week. Depending on the status of the short sale, eight to nine of these are automatically postponed, but we usually have to struggle with one or two to get them postponed. We generally see a struggle when we start the short sale too close to the foreclosure date, when the investor won't postpone the foreclosure date because the offer wasn't received in time or the offer made doesn't meet their net requirement.

If you have a difficult file, you may find you are on the phone for hours trying every avenue possible to get the sale postponed. You will be sending email and faxes and leaving voice messages for every contact you have with the lender. You may find yourself calling and talking to people in all departments from customer service all the way up to the Office of the President. Request to speak with a supervisor or a manager in the foreclosure department. Don't hang up until you can speak to a real live person who can help with your situation. This may involve using serious negotiation techniques because sometimes the banks just won't to postpone the sale. If you need to, find out who the investor is and call them for help in postponing the foreclosure sale.

Don't give up! Do what you have to do. It might mean getting aggressive on the phone, it might mean begging and groveling, but don't take no for an answer. Keep calling and don't give up until you know the sale has started. Even if the house forecloses, you still don't have to give up. In Colorado, you have eight business days to get the lender or investor to rescind the sale. In El Paso County, that is the second Monday following the foreclosure sale. Rescinding a sale is very difficult to do and most banks won't do it, so be on top of your game and start addressing the foreclosure sale dates early. You do not want to have to try and rescind a sale unless it is a last resort.

The BPO/Appraisal

A BPO stands for Brokers Price Opinion. This is a third party real estate agent's opinion of the value of the property. A BPO or an appraisal can either be your worst nightmare or your biggest asset. A BPO can ruin a short sale if the value comes in too high. Your goal is to get the BPO to come in as low as possible, even if the value is a lot lower than the offer. You always want to meet the BPO agent or appraiser at the property. You do not want the BPO agent to go to the property by themselves. Provide them with the lowest comps you can find, show them the offer and the negative feedback from the showing, show them all the property damage and tell them everything about the house that makes the property unmarketable.

If you do not currently have an offer on the property,

you can say, "I can't get a buyer for this house. I keep lowering the price, but I just can't sell it. What price do you think I should list it at?" You want to be the BPO agent's best friend because if they are a good BPO agent, they will come back and do other houses for you. Once you really get to know them, you will no longer have to meet them at each house. You will be able to simply talk to them over the phone about a property if you feel they will do a good job for you.

Preparing for the BPO

The BPO is the most critical part of the short sale. If the BPO comes in too high, you will have a fight on your hands. Again, always meet the BPO agent or appraiser at the property. This is very important. You don't want to set your deal up for failure.

Before meeting the BPO agent at the property, you should prepare a BPO package.

- Take pictures of all the property damage.
- Write down everything that needs to be fixed in the house.
- Run low comps on the property. They can be active, sold, under contract, pending or short sale under contract. Make sure they are low, low, low!
- Notate anything that could affect the resale of the house (e.g., property is next to train tracks, house sits on a T, house is on a busy street, house is in the middle of nowhere, it backs up to businesses, there are sexual predators living next door, house is in a high crime area).
- Get a high contractor estimate for any repairs that need to be done to the house.

- Print out the showing history and feedback on the property, if applicable.
- Print out any inspection reports, if applicable.
- Print out the buyer's copy of an appraisal, if applicable.
- Print news articles on market conditions, days on the market, sexual predators in the area, crime, etc.—anything that may help.

BPO Package

Summary Page

The BPO package that you present to the BPO agent should have a summary page that explains the deal in detail to the BPO agent. This summary page should include the following:

- Property address
- Reason for default (hardship)
- Anything that will affect resale of the house
- Contract price and type of buyer (VA, FHA, Conventional, CASH)

Additional Property Information

- Contractor estimate
- Comparables
- Showing feedback and history
- Inspection report
- Appraisal
- Any articles that may help

At the BPO

- Don't dress in a business suit or drive the most

expensive car you own. You don't want to look like you are there to take advantage of the homeowner and capitalize on the deal. You want them to think you are a normal person and you just want to make a living.

- Arrive 15 minutes early or more.
- Take off all expensive jewelry.
- Prepare your BPO package prior to the appointment.
- Never miss an appointment.
- Make sure the homeowner is not there for the BPO and they remove any expensive vehicles or conceal them with a cover.
- Look up active foreclosures, short sales in the neighborhood and competition.

Things to Say to the BPO/Appraiser

- Days on market for that area
- Days on market for subject house
- Showing remarks
- Repairs needed and costs
- Functional obsolescence
- Marketing issues

Become friends with the BPO agent and build a rapport with them. Walk through the house with them and show them all the damage. Make sure the BPO agents take pictures of everything that needs to be repaired. You will notice that some BPO agents are easier to work with than others. Some agents are happy to take your package and value the property where you need it to be to get the deal done. Other BPO agents may refuse to accept any documents from you.

If the BPO agent asks how much is owed on the property, tell them you have no clue, but tell them what the offer on the property is and tell them this is the best offer you have received. Tell the BPO agent you need their help and tell them you need the BPO to come in as close as possible to your offer amount or the house will go to foreclosure. Say something like, "I know the offer may be low, but that's OK. Anything you can do to help will definitely help us. We can try working with the buyer later, but we really do need the value to come in as low as humanly possible to save the deal."

Talk about the homeowner and their hardship and everything they have tried to do to save their house from foreclosure. Tell the BPO agent if the bank takes this house back they are going to have to compete with these listings and possibly more by that time. When the BPO is over, ask them what they thought of the house and where they think the property value will come in.

Outsourcing the BPO

You can have a separate agent do your BPOs. You can have your buyer's agent meet the BPO agent, or you can hire a BPO agent to be your own BPO agent, but you want a friendly BPO agent. You can outsource the BPO to the home inspector, contractor, appraiser, etc. Pay them 10–15% of the commission. They will get more money doing this than working for the bank.

I have a friend who is an investor, as well as a BPO agent. He meets the bank's BPO agent at the property for me. Before he goes to the house, he takes his pictures and gets the contractor estimate prepared for me. He then emails me the contractor's estimate for repairs and I put that on my contractor's estimate sheet.

My BPO agent prepares all the documents and has everything ready for when he meets the BPO agent. When he meets the bank's BPO agent at the property, he influences the agent to come in as low as possible. I pay my BPO agent 10% of the listing agent's commission.

Chapter 11
Negotiating Junior Liens, IRS Liens, Judgments and Bankruptcy

Judgments

As you begin to negotiate short sales, you will quickly realize that about four out of five homeowners will have outstanding judgments or liens against their property. This is common because homeowners who are behind on their mortgage are generally behind on other bills as well. Creditors will file a judgment against the person, and when this happens, the judgment attaches to the property. Creditors work every angle to get their money, and they understand that short sales are big right now and most of the time they will get some money if the homeowner sells their home on a short sale.

Before you can actually negotiate the lien, you need to contact the creditor, get their fax number and send in a Third Party Authorization. Be sure to include the case number of the judgment and the name of the company. Once you are authorized, the first thing you need to verify is whether the person listed in the judgment is actually the same person as the homeowner doing the short sale. The best way to verify this is by their Social Security numbers. If the Social Security numbers do not match, you need to contact the title company and let them know the judgment is not against the person in title. The title company may call to verify this, or they will ask to have a personal information sheet completed and signed by the homeowner. Then they will research to verify the information. Once the title company confirms that it isn't the same person, they will remove the judgment from the title commitment.

I usually ask for a lien release because creditors generally won't issue a full satisfaction. Occasionally you will get them to do this, but not usually. You will also see that these creditors like to play hardball. They usually won't settle for 6%, but that is generally where I start with my offer. Anything higher than that is usually out of pocket for the agents, buyer or seller. If you are an investor who is buying the property, you should be the one to pay the judgment. Your goal in negotiating these liens is to get the amount as low as possible so it's less out of pocket for you. The creditor will call back with an amount, and it is usually 50% of the total debt. This is pretty fair for them. Tell the creditor, "OK, I will need to present this to the bank and the buyers to see what they can do, but it's not looking promising." Oftentimes, you will have to go back to the creditor three or more times before you can settle on a final amount. Each time you are coming up on the offer and they are coming down. Eventually you settle with a happy medium.

When you are negotiating, try to come up with a creative story for why the lien can't be paid. For example, tell the creditor the real estate agents can't pay the extra money because they are already paying the outstanding water bill and the HOA lien from their commissions. Tell them there are multiple judgments against the property and the real estate agents are already contributing money toward all of them. Be sure to let them know the buyers don't have the money to pay them. Generally they can't because they struggle to come up with the earnest money needed. The homeowners obviously don't have the money or they would have paid the liens and their mortgage!

You can also explain the homeowner's hardship. We had one homeowner who suffered a severe hardship. He was put in the hospital for two months because of diabetes and while he was in the hospital, he got laid off from his job because he wasn't able to work. When he got out of the hospital, he had continuing medical expenses and no income. It was a very sad situation, and we explained it to the creditors.

Tell them what the hardship is and use tones of voice that make it sound very bad. It is easy to bring in your emotions because generally the homeowner's situation is so bad that you do really feel sorry for them.

Be persistent. Go back several times, letting them know no more money is available for the liens. The closer you get to a foreclosure date, the more flexible they tend to become. Once an amount is agreed upon, ask them to fax over a payoff good for 30 days or more and the lien release. I try to get lien releases immediately. This way I have the amounts needed for the HUD-1 and for the real estate agents so they know potentially what will be coming out of their commissions if the buyers, sellers or the lender can't pay the lien. If the lien release expires, that's OK; you can generally get an extension without a problem. Most of the time if you tell the lien holder why you haven't closed yet, they will grant extensions. When negotiating IRS liens, you will follow the same process as negotiating any other lien. In many cases, you will find that negotiating IRS liens can be easier than negotiating a lien for something else, such as a judgment filed for a past due credit card balance or a Homeowner's Association lien. In my experience, I have never had a case where the IRS did not release a lien. They understand that their lien is over-encumbered and they have no choice but to release the lien. They have other ways to collect their money. I have also seen the IRS release a $100,000 lien for $0.

Negotiating Second and Third Mortgages

Having to negotiate both second and third mortgages can be difficult at times when the loans are not with the same lender. Second mortgage lenders can get greedy and insist on more than 10%. It is common for the first mortgage lender to give the second mortgage 10%; however, there are times when you will see a second mortgage lender want a much higher amount. They can play hardball and when they do this, you have to play hardball back. As you near the end of the negotiations with the first mortgage lender, the second mortgage lender usually accepts the final offer.

When you are negotiating with the second mortgage lender, you can say, "Would you rather get some money now or let the house foreclose and get nothing? The house will foreclose in two weeks and when it does, you won't get anything. The first mortgage is offering to pay you $3,000 to release the lien so we can close and avoid foreclosure. Will you accept this?" If they say "No, we want $6,000 and we would rather let it foreclose than take less," then just say, "OK, I guess that is what will happen because the buyers have no money to pay the difference, the real estate agents will not give up their commissions for this and the seller has no money to contribute. If the seller had the money, he would have paid this. He is losing his house because he lost his job and hasn't been able to find another job. His wife got angry and divorced him, leaving him to try to cover all expenses without a job. The poor guy was left with nothing. Can you imagine if that happened to you?" The reason for saying things like this is to try to gain compassion from the negotiator so they feel something or can relate to something. If they get attached to the case, they tend to do a better job of negotiating the deal for the investor they are working for.

If the negotiator remains difficult or stubborn, you are most likely dealing with an experienced negotiator who is good at finagling money out of people. Stand your ground and don't give up. Walk away from the conversation. Say, "OK, let me see what I can do for you." Go back to the first mortgage lender and explain the situation you are having with the second lender. Ask if they are willing to negotiate with the second lender or if they will give them more money. Sometimes the first lender may offer more if the second lender is being difficult. If the first will offer more, call the second and let them know you got a deal for them from the first.

When the first is willing to offer more, the second usually takes it. If the first won't offer more and won't speak to the second lender, call again in a week and offer the same amount again. Explain to them you spoke with the first lender and they are not willing to increase their offer amount because they have to follow their investor guidelines and per their investor, this is the maximum amount they will allow. After explaining this, you can say, "The buyers want to close in 30 days. Can we please make this happen so we can help the homeowner avoid foreclosure?"

Timing can be important when dealing with second mortgages. There will come a time with the second when they will be willing to negotiate, so continue to follow up and call them. They may have a minimum quota to meet by the end of the month, and if they don't meet that quota, they lose their bonus. I've actually had banks call me five days before the end of the month, asking, "If we approved this offer, can you close by the end of the month?" I would tell them yes, since I was a cash buyer. If you don't have a cash buyer for the property, you would not be able to close that quickly, as the buyer is getting a loan and the lender needs to do an appraisal and an inspection. You can tell them you can close next month so it reflects on your next month's closing books. The lender will usually say OK.

PMI and Promissory Notes

Private Mortgage Insurance is referred to as PMI. You won't come across this very often, but when you do have a loan with PMI, it means you have to get the short sale approved by both the lender you are working with and the PMI Company. PMI companies typically ask for a promissory note to cover a deficiency.

A promissory note is when the bank asks the borrower to sign a promise to pay back the difference of what is owed or an amount less than what is owed. These notes are generally interest free—principal payments only—and they are typically very low and are not secured against any property. What I usually tell homeowners is if they can't pay the promissory note, they are in no worse shape than they are now in foreclosure. I have them sign it and if they can't pay it, again, they are really not in any worse shape. If the homeowner were to file bankruptcy, it would wipe the promissory note out and they wouldn't have to pay it. I haven't seen a request for a promissory note on a loan with PMI since 2009. They used to be asked for frequently, but they are no longer common. This is most likely because no one has the money to pay them.

Bankruptcy and Short Sales

If your homeowner is currently in bankruptcy, the bank cannot foreclose on their property unless a Relief of Stay has been filed. A property can be in active bankruptcy status for a year or longer. This halts all foreclosure proceedings. The banks cannot speak to the borrower during this time, and they won't speak to you either. You will need to contact the lender to find out what documentation they require in order to speak to them on the homeowner's behalf. They generally want an authorization from the bankruptcy attorney that authorizes you to speak to them regarding a short sale. Once the bank receives this documentation, they will speak with you.

Continually follow up to check the status of the bankruptcy. If a Relief of Stay has been filed, the bank can foreclose on the property. If you see a Relief of Stay has been filed, please stay in constant communication with the bank to make sure they do not foreclose.

Before you get an approval letter, you will need to contact the title company to find out if you can actually close or if you will need an Order of Abandonment from the court. The title company can check for you, and in most cases, you will need to get an Order of Abandonment. This usually costs an additional $500–$700 on top of what the homeowner has already paid for bankruptcy fees. Therefore, I usually tell the homeowners up front to make sure they save their money for this, as they may need it at the time of closing. In many cases, I pay for this to get the deal closed.

You will need to call the bankruptcy attorney to let him know you have a short sale approval and need an Order of Abandonment. Some bankruptcy attorneys do not want to do this. You will see that some attorneys are very uncooperative and don't want to do it. If you have a good relationship with a bankruptcy attorney who you know will do this, you can refer the homeowner to this attorney.

The process for an Order of Abandonment can take two to four weeks. I would not initiate this process until you have an approval letter from the lender, because there is a good chance you will be paying for it. If you initiate it before closing, it could initiate a Relief of Stay which means the bank can foreclose.

Overview of Chapter 13 Bankruptcy [27]

In Chapter 13 bankruptcy, you keep your property but pay back all or a portion of your debts over a three- to five-year period. This is unlike Chapter 7 bankruptcy, where most of your debts are cancelled but you may have to surrender some property to the bankruptcy trustee to pay your creditors. Because you end up paying most of your debts over time in Chapter 13 bankruptcy, it is also called reorganization bankruptcy.

27   www.nolo.com/legal-encyclopedia/chapter-13-bankruptcy-overview-30099.html

Overview of Chapter 7 Bankruptcy [28]

In Chapter 7 bankruptcy, the bankruptcy trustee cancels many (or all) of your debts. At the same time it might also sell (liquidate) some of your property to pay your creditors. Chapter 7 bankruptcy is also called a "straight" or "liquidation" bankruptcy and is so named because the law is contained in Chapter 7 of the Federal Bankruptcy Code.

Bankruptcy—Side-by-side Comparison [29]

	Chapter 7	Chapter 13
Who Qualifies	Any debtor who earns less than the state median income and who, it is determined, can't pay more than 25% of their non-priority unsecured debt.	Any debtor who earns in excess of the state median income and is able to repay 25% of his or her "non-priority unsecured debt."
Effect on foreclosure	Typically delayed three to four months.	Delayed three to four months; possibly avoided
What happens to your property	You can keep all property that is legally exempt; non-exempt property must be sold to repay your creditors; property secured by liens (e.g., house, cars) must be reaffirmed if you want to keep the property. If not reaffirmed, must be surrendered to the lender.	You keep your property; however, then you must repay your unsecured creditor an amount equal to the value of your nonexempt property.
What happens to your mortgage	Bankruptcy will discharge the liability you owe on your mortgage; however, it does not release the lien. If you stop making your payments, the lender will foreclose on the property to get the security interest back. You must continue making payments on the loan to avoid foreclosure.	Your 1st mortgage will probably remain intact. A 2nd or 3rd mortgage may be eliminated depending on your home's value. Back payments can be made over time. If your lender has not filed for foreclosure at the time you file, your home can't be taken from you while under bankruptcy protection. If they filed prior to your filing bankruptcy, the lender can foreclose on your home while you are going through bankruptcy.
What happens to your debt	Most debts are wiped out (discharged); some (such as child support and back taxes) survive.	Based on your income and total debt, you propose a repayment plan to the court to repay a percentage of your total debt over a 3- to 5-year period. If you finish the plan, the balance of your debt is wiped out
How long it takes	Three to four months	Three to five years
Will you need a lawyer	No, but it is recommended	No, but recommended; will probably get better results.

28   www.nolo.com/legal-encyclopedia/chapter-7-bankruptcy-overview-29571.html
29   Chart sourced from The Foreclosure Survival Guide, by Attorney Stephen Elias, 2nd Edition, Berkley:Nolo, p. 14.

The Automatic Stay

Filing for Chapter 7 bankruptcy puts into effect an "Order for Relief," formally known as the "automatic stay." The automatic stay immediately stops most creditors from trying to collect what you owe them. This means that temporarily your creditors cannot legally garnish your wages, empty your bank account, go after your car, house or other property or cut off your utility service or welfare benefits.

Chapter 12
Bank Counter Offers

The Bank Just Countered Your Offer! Now What?

A counter offer from the lender is expected with nearly every short sale. Even if you have a rock solid offer at full price, the lender will still counter the offer. Always go back to the buyer and let them know what the bank countered the offer to. If you have a retail buyer, you will be surprised how many will come up on their offer.

First offers are generally low, leaving the buyers with room to go higher, and when you are dealing with a short sale that takes several months, the buyers generally do not want to risk starting over with another property. To avoid losing the deal, the buyers generally come up on their offer.

More Negotiating Tactics

It's time to start negotiating with the lender. Ask them to provide you a net. Tell them you may be able to work around fees and commissions to make the current offer work for them. Sometimes they will give you a net and sometimes they won't. You may have to call them several times until you get that one person who will tell you what they are looking for.

If the offer is still not in the ballpark, you can ask the bank to do a value dispute. You can provide three sold comparables and three active comparables and provide contractor estimates that are higher than what the bank actually needs to justify your position. I usually write these contractor estimates up because I don't want to waste their time. You can buy a "Contract Estimate for Repairs" at Home Depot or Office Depot. I tell my contractor what I am doing and which property the estimate is for. I then tell him, "This property may be your next project if the bank accepts the offer."

You can also get together with a licensed contractor and use their form to fill out the estimate. They generally let you do this if you give them a lot of business and they are your contractor for fix and flip properties.

On the next page is a copy of a commercial Property Inspection Sheet:

Stephens & Associates, Inc.
General Contractor, El Paso County License No. ▮▮▮

▮▮▮▮▮▮▮▮▮ Colorado Springs, CO 80918

Page 1 of 2

CONTRACT
Proposal & Acceptance

SUBMITTED TO	DATE	CLIENT PHONE NUMBER	ALTERNATE PHONE NUMBER
COS Homes X	12/21/10		

JOB STREET ADDRESS	CLIENT STREET ADDRESS
54 Watson Blvd	

JOB CITY	STATE	ZIP	CLIENT CITY	STATE	ZIP
Colorado Springs, CO 80911					

WE WILL PERFORM AS **GENERAL CONTRACTORS** ☒ YES ☐ NO **IF NO, WE WILL** PROVIDE THE FOLLOWING WORK

☐ SITE PREP ☐ ELECTRICAL ☐ LANDSCAPING
☐ FOUNDATION ☐ PLUMBING ☐ PAINTING
☐ STRUCTURAL ☐ HVAC ☐ IMPROVMENTS
☐ ROOFING ☐ CONC/PAVING ☐ _____

We respectfully submit the following Specifications and Estimate for:

#		
1.	Drywall Repair: replace, texture, prime as required	$1500
2.	Replace all casing and baseboards	$1500
3.	Replace damaged floor in kitchen and bath	$1500
4.	Replace damaged doors with white 6 pannel hollow core doors	$1500
5.	Paint Interior	$2000
6.	Carpet and Pad - 1800sf/6&1/2"/37oz	$3000
7.	Replace Roof	$4000
8.	Replace non standard plumbing in d/s bathroom as needed	$1000
9.	Replace dated kitchen cabinets	$2000
10.	Replace old non functional kitchen appliances	$2000
11.	Replace bathtub, surround, toilet, and vanity with mirror u/s and d/s	$3000
12.	Repaint exterior of the house	$2500
13.	Basic Landscape	$1000
14.	Replace out of code Electrical Box. Current is recalled federal pacific stablok	$1000
15.	Re-Pour Damaged Driveway	$2000

WE OFFER TO FURNISH ☐ MATERIALS, ☐ LABOR, OR ☐ MATERIALS AND LABOR AND COMPLETE THE WORK SPECIFIED ABOVE

FOR THE SUM OF _____ See Page 2 _____ ($_____) WITH

PAYMENTS TO BE MADE AS FOLLOWS: _____

All material is guaranteed to be as specified. All work to be completed in a workmanlike manner according to standard practices. Any alteration or deviation from the above specifications involving extra cost will be executed only upon written orders and will be and extra charge over and above the estimate. All agreements are contingent upon strikes, accidents, or delays beyond our control. Owner shall carry fire, tornado, and other necessary insurance. Our workers are fully covered by workers compensation insurance.

Contractor Signature _____

Date __12/21/2010__

OFFER SHALL BE VOID IF NOT ACCEPTED IN __30__ DAYS.

ACCEPTANCE:
THE ABOVE PRICES, SPECIFICATIONS, AND CONDITIONS ARE SATISFACTORY AND ARE HEREBY ACCEPTED. YOU ARE AUTHORIZED TO DO THE WORK AS SPECIFIED. PAYMENT WILL BE MADE AS OUTLINED ABOVE.

Authorized Signature _____ Date _____

Stephens & Associates, Inc.
General Contractor, El Paso County License No. ████

████████, Colorado Springs, CO 80918

Page 2 of 2

CONTRACT
Proposal & Acceptance

SUBMITTED TO	DATE	CLIENT PHONE NUMBER	ALTERNATE PHONE NUMBER
COS Homes II	12/21/2010	████	

JOB STREET ADDRESS		CLIENT STREET ADDRESS	
4060 Colony Hills Circle			

JOB CITY	STATE	ZIP	CLIENT CITY	STATE	ZIP
Colorado Springs, CO 80916					

WE WILL PERFORM AS **GENERAL CONTRACTORS** [X] YES [ ] NO **IF NO, WE WILL** PROVIDE THE FOLLOWING WORK

[ ] SITE PREP [ ] ELECTRICAL [ ] LANDSCAPING
[ ] FOUNDATION [ ] PLUMBING [ ] PAINTING
[ ] STRUCTURAL [ ] HVAC [ ] IMPROVMENTS
[ ] ROOFING [ ] CONC/PAVING [ ]

We respectfully submit the following Specifications and Estimate for:

1	new flooring in kitchen-existing is generally shot	$1000
2	new bathrooms (both bathrooms)-existing just old/nasty, unmarketable	$5000
3	new exterior doors	$1000
4	new interior doors	$2000
5	new trim/case/base	$2000
6	new electrical outlets/switches	$500
7	New electrical box-federal pacific	$1200
8	texture/prime/paint throughout	$2500
9	about half of basement needs to be re-drywalled	$2000
10	furnace needs to be replaced	$2000
11	extensive drywall repair due to homeowner patched	$1000
12		
13		
14		
15		

WE OFFER TO FURNISH [ ] MATERIALS, [X] LABOR, OR [X] MATERIALS AND LABOR AND COMPLETE THE WORK SPECIFIED ABOVE

FOR THE SUM OF Forty-Nine Thousand Dollars and Two hundred ($ 49,200) WITH

PAYMENTS TO BE MADE AS FOLLOWS: 5 payments of $9840

All material is guaranteed to be as specified. All work to be completed in a workmanlike manner according to standard practices. Any alteration or deviation from the above specifications involving extra cost will be executed only upon written orders and will be and extra charge over and above the estimate. All agreements are contingent upon strikes, accidents, or delays beyond our control. Owner shall carry fire, tornado, and other necessary insurance. Our workers are fully covered by workers compensation insurance.

Contractor Signature ████

Date 12/21/10

OFFER SHALL BE VOID IF NOT ACCEPTED IN 30 DAYS.

ACCEPTANCE:
THE ABOVE PRICES, SPECIFICATIONS, AND CONDITIONS ARE SATISFACTORY AND ARE HEREBY ACCEPTED. YOU ARE AUTHORIZED TO DO THE WORK AS SPECIFIED. PAYMENT WILL BE MADE AS OUTLINED ABOVE.

Authorized Signature _____ Date _____

If these tactics still don't work, ask the negotiator if you can send pictures of the house by email. Send pictures you think the BPO agent might have missed. You can explain things to the negotiator like, "The BPO agent wouldn't have known the furnace was broken, or the roof needed replacing or the boiler system wasn't functional. These types of things require an inspection or property disclosure, and I don't think the BPO agent could have even considered these items."

If you still get nowhere, I would ask if they will accept an appraisal. If they will accept an appraisal, it will be at your expense. I have never had a bank refuse an appraisal. I always use the same appraiser—one I have a good, solid relationship with. Before I pay for the appraisal, I contact him and explain the situation, tell him the condition of the house and let him know what my current offer is and the maximum amount I can pay for the house. I give him the details about the damage to the property and provide him with any evidence I have (e.g., contractor estimates, inspection reports). Then I ask him to run preliminary comparables to see if he can come up with a value that is close to my offer. If he says yes, I send him out to do the appraisal. To order an appraisal, I usually pay $350–$400 depending on how difficult the appraisal will be.

You are taking a risk ordering an appraisal because it is money out of your pocket and you have no approval letter from the lender, but doing this generally works in your favor. Before you pay for the appraisal, make sure you do these two things:

- Get a written approval from the lender that states they will use the buyer's appraisal as the current market value.

• Have the appraiser run preliminary comparables to see if the numbers can come in where you need them to be.

HUD-1 Overview

I have my title company prepare my HUD-1s for me. This way they can pull any outstanding HOA bills, liens and outstanding water bills that need to be paid at closing. I review the HUDs before sending them to the lender's negotiator. Make sure the title company puts the settlement date about three months out in case the short sale takes that long. If there are second mortgages, I generally give them 10% on the HUD. If there are judgments or liens, you can put the full amount on the HUD for now until you get a negotiated pay-off with them.

On the right side of the HUD is the seller's closing costs and on the left side of the HUD is the buyer's closing costs. In a short sale, the right side is also the bank's side listing the costs the lender will pay out of the proceeds of the sale. Make sure all applicable fees are on the HUD you submit to the lender, as you will most likely not be able to add additional expenses later. So be sure all liens and judgments are on the HUD. Make sure all past due water bills are included, as well as past HOA dues or liens. It is good to pad these costs a little in case the fees have increased by the time you get to closing.

Additionally, if you want to charge the short sale lender a short sale negotiation fee, you can. My title company, Unified Title Company, has the short sale fee recorded as their closing fee and title insurance fee. So it looks like the closing fee and title insurance are just a little high. The title company collects this fee and then reimburses the money to your short sale company or the short sale company you hired.

Below is an example of a HUD-1 Settlement Statement.

HUD-1 Settlement Statements*: **Downloadable Form**

A. Settlement Statement — U.S. Department of Housing and Urban Development — OMB No. 2502-0265

B. Type of Loan

1. ☐ FHA 2. ☐ FmHA 3. ☐ Conv. Unins.	6. File Number	7. Loan Number	8. Mortgage Ins Case Number
4. ☐ VA 5. ☐ Conv. Ins. 6. ☐ Seller Finance 8433 UTC			
7. ☒ Cash Sale			

C. Note: This form is furnished to give you a statement of actual settlement costs. Amounts paid to and by the settlement agent are shown. Items marked "(p.o.c.)" were paid outside the closing; they are shown here for informational purposes and are not included in the totals.

D. Name & Address of Borrower	E. Name & Address of Seller	F. Name & Address of Lender
Glenn Madore	John Robert Macfarlane, IV	
	3414A Daly Street	
	Twentynine Palms, CA 92277	

G. Property Location	H. Settlement Agent Name
Lot 16, Bridle Pass Sub No 2, County of El Paso, State of Colorado.	Unified Title Company, LLC
5563 Mountain Garland Drive	1720 Jet Stream Drive, Ste 105
Colorado Springs, CO 80918	Colorado Springs, CO 80921

Place of Settlement	I. Settlement Date
Unified Title Company, LLC (JS)	4/24/2010
1720 Jet Stream Drive, Ste 105	Fund
Colorado Springs, CO 80921	

J. Summary of Borrower's Transaction		K. Summary of Seller's Transaction	
100. Gross Amount Due from Borrower		**400. Gross Amount Due to Seller**	
101. Contract Sales Price	$212,000.00	401. Contract Sales Price	$212,000.00
102. Personal Property		402. Personal Property	
103. Settlement Charges to borrower	$15,610.20	403.	
104.		404.	
105.		405.	
Adjustments for items paid by seller in advance		**Adjustments for items paid by seller in advance**	
106. City property taxes		406. City property taxes	
107. County Property Taxes		407. County Property Taxes	
108. Assessment Taxes		408. Assessment Taxes	
109. School property taxes		409. School property taxes	
110. HOA Dues		410. HOA Dues	
111. Other Taxes		411. Other Taxes	
112.		412.	
113.		413.	
114.		414.	
115.		415.	
116.		416.	
120. Gross Amount Due From Borrower	$227,610.20	**420. Gross Amount Due to Seller**	$212,000.00
200. Amounts Paid By Or In Behalf Of Borrower		**500. Reductions In Amount Due to Seller**	
201. Deposit or earnest money	$1,000.00	501. Excess Deposit	
202. Principal amount of new loan(s)		502. Settlement Charges to Seller (line 1400)	
203. Existing loan(s) taken subject to		503. Existing Loan(s) Taken Subject to	
204. Loan Amount 2nd Lien		504. 1st Payoff	$210,000.00
205.		505. 1st Payoff	$2,000.00
206.		506.	
207.		507.	
208.		508.	
209.		509.	
Adjustments for items unpaid by seller		**Adjustments for items unpaid by seller**	
210. City property taxes		510. City property taxes	
211. County Property Taxes		511. County Property Taxes	
212. Assessment Taxes		512. Assessment Taxes	
213. School property taxes		513. School property taxes	
214. HOA Dues		514. HOA Dues	
215. Other Taxes		515. Other Taxes	
216.		516.	
217.		517.	
218.		518.	
219.		519.	
220. Total Paid By/For Borrower	$1,000.00	**520. Total Reduction Amount Due Seller**	$212,000.00
300. Cash At Settlement From/To Borrower		**600. Cash At Settlement To/From Seller**	
301. Gross Amount due from Borrower (line 120)	$227,610.20	601. Gross Amount due to seller (line 420)	$212,000.00
302. Less amounts paid by/for borrower (line 220)	$1,000.00	602. Less reductions in amt. due seller (line 520)	$212,000.00
303. Cash From Borrower	$226,610.20	**603. Cash From Seller**	$0.00

Section 5 of the Real Estate Settlement Procedures Act (RESPA) requires the following: • HUD must develop a Special Information Booklet to help persons borrowing money to finance the purchase of residential real estate to better understand the nature and costs of real estate settlement services. • Each lender must provide the booklet to all applicants from whom it receives or for whom it prepares a written application to borrow money to finance the purchase of residential real estate. • Lenders must prepare and distribute with the booklet a Good Faith Estimate of the settlement costs that the borrower is likely to incur in connection with the settlement. These disclosures are mandatory.

Section 4(a) of RESPA mandates that HUD develop and prescribe this standard form to be used at the time of loan settlement to provide full disclosure of all charges imposed upon the borrower and seller. These are third party disclosures that are designed to provide the borrower with pertinent information during the settlement process in order to be a better shopper. The Public Reporting Burden for this collection of information is estimated to average one hour per response, including the time for reviewing instructions, searching existing data sources, gathering and maintaining the data needed, and completing and reviewing the collection of information. This agency may not collect this information, and you are not required to complete this form, unless it displays a currently valid OMB control number. The information requested does not lend itself to confidentiality.

Previous Editions are Obsolete — Page 1 — Form HUD-1 (3/86) Handbook 4305.2

File No. 84316 TC

L. Settlement Charges

			Paid From Borrower's Funds at Settlement	Paid From Seller's Funds at Settlement
700. Total Sales/Broker's Commission based on price $212,000.00 @ 6 % = $12,720.00				
Division of Commission (line 700) as follows:				
701. $6,360.00	to	Pink Realty		
702. $6,360.00	to			
703. Commission Paid at Settlement			$12,720.00	$0.00
800. Items Payable in Connection with Loan				
801. Loan Origination Fee %	to			
802. Loan Discount %	to			
803. Appraisal Fee	to			
804. Credit Report	to			
805. Lender's Inspection Fee	to			
806. Mortgage Insurance Application	to			
807. Assumption Fee				
900. Items Required by Lender To Be Paid in Advance				
901. Interest from 4/25/2010 to 5/1/2010 @ $6/day				
902. Mortgage Insurance Premium for months	to			
903. Hazard Insurance Premium for years	to			
1000. Reserves Deposited With Lender				
1001. Hazard insurance	months @	per month		
1002. Mortgage insurance	months @	per month		
1003. City property taxes	months @	per month		
1004. County Property Taxes	months @	per month		
1005. Assessment Taxes	months @	per month		
1006. School property taxes	months @	per month		
1007. HOA Dues	months @	per month		
1008. Other Taxes	months @	per month		
1011. Aggregate Adjustment				
1100. Title Charges				
1101. Settlement or closing fee	to	Unified Title Company, LLC (JS)	$200.00	
1102. Abstract or title search	to			
1103. Title examination	to			
1104. Title insurance binder	to			
1105. Document preparation	to			
1106. Notary fees	to			
1107. Attorney's fees	to			
(includes above items numbers:)				
1108. Title insurance	to	Unified Title Company, LLC (JS)	$985.00	
(includes above items numbers:)				
1109. Lender's coverage	$0.00 $25.00			
1110. Owner's coverage	$212,000.00 $1,084.00			
1111. Courier/Messenger Fee	to	Unified Title Company, LLC (JS)	$50.00	
1112. Release Processing Fee	to	Unified Title Company, LLC (JS)	$60.00	
1113. Wire/Check Fee	to			
1114. Loan Closing Fee	to			
1115. E-mail loan doc fee	to			
1116. E-Recording/Mailing and Processing Fee	to			
1117. Tax Certificate	to	Unified Title Company, LLC (JS)	$25.00	
1118. 110% Hold Open End	to	Unified Title Company, LLC (JS)	$99.00	
1200. Government Recording and Transfer Charges				
1201. Recording Fees Deed Mortgage Rel.	to			
1202. City/county tax/stamps Deed Mortgage	to			
1203. State tax stamps Deed $23.20 Mortgage	to		$23.20	
1204. Certified Copies	to			
1205. E-Recording Fee	to			
1300. Additional Settlement Charges				
1301. Survey	to			
1302. Pest Inspection	to			
1303. Stormwater	to	City of Colorado Springs Stormwater Enterprises	$100.00	
1304. Payoff	to	Greentree	POC (B) $8,600.00	
1305. 2009 Est. Taxes	to	El Paso County Treasurer	$1,350.00	
1400. Total Settlement Charges (enter on lines 103, Section J and 502, Section K)			$15,630.20	

Previous Editions are Obsolete   Page 2   form HUD-1 (3/86) Handbook 4305.2

Approval Letter Received—Staying on Track!

Once you get your approval letter, it is very important to read through it entirely. See if the bank forgot to approve any charges. You will find that banks will want to cut commissions or reduce or omit other fees. Look over everything carefully to make sure it is accurate and there are no discrepancies.

Once it is reviewed, forward the approval letter to the title company agent so they can work up the HUD-1 statement for a closing in 30 days or less to see if you will be short any money. If you are short, you need to contact the negotiator immediately and request a revised approval letter. They may deny your request and refuse to pay certain charges. This happens frequently. There are some fees lenders won't pay for, such as release fees and the endorsement for OEC plain language. Sometimes you can ask the seller if they can pay these minimal fees. If not, maybe the buyer can pay the fees. If no one is willing to pay the fees, you may have to pay them yourself to get the deal closed. Make sure you close by the deadline on the approval letter. If at any point you feel you can't meet the deadline, contact the negotiator as soon as possible and let her know why the deadline can't be met.

Additionally, you will want to read through the approval letter to see if they just did a lien release or a full satisfaction. If they did a full satisfaction, they won't pursue the deficiency after the sale. If they did a lien release only, this means the lender reserves the right to pursue the homeowner for the deficiency balance. If this is the case, ask the homeowner to write a request to the lender waiving the deficiency and explain the reason why. Send this to the negotiator to see if they are willing to do this. In some instances they are willing to waive the deficiency, so it is worth the effort to try.

You will also want to make sure the bank didn't sneak in a promissory note or a cash contribution at closing. Bank of America once tried to sneak in a $3K cash contribution, and we didn't see it until closing. As a result, we ended up having to pay that amount at closing.

Approval Letter Examples

Chase

J.P.Morgan

To: jennifer zemler
From: kevin siefert
Date: September 21, 02:03:42 PM GMT
Subj: ████████████████
Pages: 3

EXTREMELY IMPORTANT
PLEASE READ CAREFULLY

This is not the final approval for the referenced sale. The final proposed HUD-1 settlement statement MUST be faxed to Chase no later than 72 hours before the closing date for review and approval and so that we may issue closing instructions. Arm's Length Affidavit and/or any other closing documents that may be required. Please refer to the Conditional Approval Letter for complete instructions and requirements.

Regards,
Kevin Siefert
614-422-7464
614-961-3757 fax

This transmission may contain information that is privileged, confidential, legally privileged, and or exempt from disclosure under applicable law. If you are not the intended recipient, you are hereby notified that any disclosure, copying, distribution, or use of the information contained herein (including any reliance thereon) is STRICTLY PROHIBITED. Although this transmission and any attachments are believed to be free of any virus or other defect that might affect any computer system into which it is received and opened, it is the responsibility of the recipient to ensure that it is virus free and no responsibility is accepted by JPMorgan Chase & Co., its subsidiaries and affiliates, as applicable, for any loss or damage arising in any way from its use. If you received this transmission in error, please immediately contact the sender and destroy the material in its entirety, whether in electronic or hard copy format. Thank you.

CHASE ○

Chase Home Finance LLC (OH4-7129)
3415 Vision Drive
Columbus, OH 43219-6009

September 21, 2010

Unified Title
Attn: Jennifer Zemler
1720 Jet Stream Dr. Ste 105
Colorado Springs, CO 80921
Phone Number: 719-488-9777
Fax Number: 866-534-6667

Conditional Approval of Sales Contract

Chase Home Finance LLC Account: 1793582313

Borrower(s)/Seller(s):

Property address:

Buyer(s):

Dear Closing Agent:

Chase Home Finance LLC (the "Lender") has preliminarily approved of the sales contract pertaining to the above-referenced Property for $63,500.00 between the Seller and the Buyer. Please be advised this is not the final approval for the referenced sale. Once the HUD-1 is approved, closing instructions will be issued and the closing may occur. The Property must be free of liens at the time of closing. Please be aware that should the sale on the Property proceed as outlined, our acceptance of this Short Sale will be reported to the various credit reporting agencies and may have an adverse effect on the Seller's credit. Proceeding with this transaction may have implications on the Seller's state or federal tax liability; the Seller may consult a tax advisor for additional information.

Below we have detailed both the expected seller closing costs and the minimum amount of proceeds to be received by Chase Home Finance LLC.

Expected Seller Closing Costs	
Realtor Commission	$3,600.00
Closing Fee	$265.00
Title Insurance	$680.00
Junior Lien Payoff	$2,000.00
Tax Proration	$748.39
Total Seller Closing Costs	**$7,293.39**

Expected Credits	
Total Credits	**$0.00**

Minimum Net Proceeds to Lender	
Sales Price	$63,500.00
- Total Closing Costs	$7,293.39
+ Total Credits	$0.00
Total Minimum Net Proceeds to Be Received by the Lender	**$56,206.61**

AFFIDAVIT OF "ARM'S LENGTH TRANSACTION"

Pursuant to a residential purchase agreement ("Agreement"), the parties identified below as "Seller(s)" and "Buyer(s)," respectively, are involved in a real estate transaction whereby the real property ("Property") referenced below will be sold by Seller(s) to Buyer(s). Property address: _____

("Lender") holds a deed of trust or mortgage against the Property. In order to complete the sale of the Property, Seller(s) and Buyer(s) have jointly asked Lender to discount the total amount owed on the loan which is secured by the deed of trust or mortgage. Lender, in consideration for the representations made below by Seller(s), Buyer(s), and their respective agents, agrees to a short sale on tile express condition that Seller(s), Buyers, and their respective agents (including, without limitation, real estate agents, escrow agents, brokerages and title agents) each truthfully represents, affirms, and states as follows:

1. The purchase and sale transaction reflected in the Agreement is an "Arm's Length Transaction," meaning that the transaction has been negotiated by unrelated parties, each of whom is acting in his or her own self-interest, and that the sale price is based on fair market value of the Property. With respect to those persons signing this affidavit as an agent for either Seller(s), Buyer(s), or both, those agents are acting in the best interests of their respective principal(s).
2. No Buyer or agent of Buyer(s) agents is a family member or business associate of the Seller(s) or the borrower(s) or the mortgagee(s).
3. No Buyer or agent of Buyer(s) shares a business interest with the Seller(s) or the borrower(s) or the mortgagee(s).
4. There are no hidden terms or hidden agreements or special understandings between the Seller(s) and the Buyer(s) or among their respective agents which are not reflected in the Agreement or the escrow instructions associated with this transaction.
5. There is no agreement, whether oral, written, or implied, between the Seller(s) and the Buyers and/or their respective agents which allows the Seller(s) to remain in the property as tenants or to regain ownership of the Property at any time after the consummation of this sale transaction.
6. The Seller(s) shall not receive any proceeds from the sale of the Property reflected in the Agreement, except as is reflected in the final estimated closing statement which shall be provided to Lender for approval prior to the close of escrow.
7. No agent of either the Seller(s) or the Buyer(s) shall receive any proceeds from this transaction except as is reflected in the final estimated closing statement which shall be provided to Lender for approval prior to the close of escrow.
8. Each signatory to this Affidavit expressly acknowledges that Lender is relying upon the representations made herein as consideration for discounting the payoff on the loan(s) which is/are secured by a deed of trust or mortgage encumbering the Property.
9. Each signatory to this Affidavit expressly acknowledges that any misrepresentation made by him or her may subject him or her to civil liability.

I declare under penalty of perjury that all statements made in this Affidavit are true and correct.

Additionally, I/We fully understand that it is a Federal crime punishable by fine or imprisonment, or both, to knowingly and willfully make any false statements concerning any of the above facts as applicable under the provisions of Title 18, United States Code, Section 1001, et seq.

_____	_____	_____	_____
Seller	Date	Seller	Date
_____		_____	
Print Name		Print Name	

_____	_____	_____	_____
Buyer	Date	Buyer	Date
_____		_____	
Print Name		Print Name	

_____	_____	_____	_____
Seller's Broker	Date	Buyer's Broker	Date
_____		_____	
Print Name and Brokerage		Print Name and Brokerage	

Final HUD Approval

Make sure you thoroughly read through all your approval letters. The negotiator will typically require a final HUD approval 72 hours prior to closing. They want to check all the final numbers and approve or disapprove any fees. The lender wants to make sure you didn't sneak in extra fees that were never approved.

Do a Final Walkthrough

On the day of closing, make sure you do a walkthrough of the house to make sure pipes didn't freeze, the house didn't burn down, the house didn't get vandalized, etc.

Chapter 13
Working with Real Estate Agents

Finding Deals – Using Real Estate Agents

Real estate agents are a great resource for finding short sale deals. Real estate agents absolutely hate doing short sales because it's a lot of work for them to call the banks day after day and risk not getting a commission or having their commissions cut. So many real estate agents are discouraged from doing short sales, and they usually refer them to another real estate agent and get a small percentage for the referral. Here are some reasons why real estate agents hate short sales:

- They have to wait for a buyer.
- Once they have the buyer, the short sale process takes three months or longer.
- Buyers get discouraged and walk.
- Buyers walk because of inspection issues.
- Real estate agents can't negotiate a successful short sale because the second wants more than the first will allow.
- Real estate agents don't understand how to negotiate the short sale.
- Their listing has judgments and no one to pay them.
- Real estate agents end up paying any shortage, getting their commissions slashed by banks and working for

$1 an hour by the time the deal is complete.

- Short sales take forever to close.
- Real estate agents get frustrated calling the banks every day and getting nowhere.
- Sellers get frustrated and withdraw their listings.

While these are the many reasons real estate agents don't like short sales, these are also the reasons you can use to find a real estate agent who will bring their short sale deals to you. You need to explain to the real estate agent the benefits of using you and how they will actually get paid more money.

Below are the many benefits real estate agents gain by using you:

- You can guarantee their full commission.
- You don't walk because it takes too long.
- You don't walk because of inspection issues.
- You do the short sale negotiations for free.
- You have an instant buyer.
- You can pay the difference between what the second wants and what the first will give the second.
- You can pay for the judgments.
- The short sales close faster because you know how to successfully get them done.

Contacting Real Estate Agents

Call agents in your area! Tell them what you do and how you can benefit them. Tell them you specialize in short sale transactions; that you buy short sales and negotiate them for real estate agents for free. Explain the benefits to them when they do a short sale with you. Let them know that if they have listings on properties that need work, you are interested in buying those properties. Or if they have or know of a property that is not listed, ask them not to list the property and they can be your buyer's agent.

When it's possible, only have the real estate agent list the property if the homeowners qualify for HAFA. You can also let them know you buy higher end luxury homes where the amounts owed on the mortgage are $500K and higher. You can call real estate agents who currently have short sales listed, and you can call managing brokers of real estate companies and ask if you can give a presentation to the real estate agents at their next office meeting. This will get your message across to all the real estate agents in the office at once.

Scenarios – Working with Real Estate Agents

Fix and Flip Referral – Property Already Listed

If the real estate agent has a deal that is a fix and flip and it is already listed with them, ask the real estate agent to prepare a buyer's agent contract for you so they can possibly get more than a 3% commission. Make sure the real estate agent changes the list price in the MLS to be close to what the contract price is and mark the property under contract. This will prevent other buyers from making offers on the property.

In Colorado, we have a short sale addendum. In the short sale addendum you can mark that this shall be the only offer considered, and it locks your contract in so the seller cannot accept higher offers.

Fix and Flip Referral – Property Not Listed

Find out of this is an eligible HAFA deal. If it is, then

the referring real estate agent should list the property. Have the real estate agent prepare a contract for you to buy the property. Make sure the list price is close to your offer price. Have the real estate agent put the house under contract immediately.

If this is a non-HAFA deal, ask the real estate agent to be your buyer's agent, and the transaction will be a FSBO for the homeowner. The real estate agent will present your offer and get all the short sale documents to you.

Luxury Home – Property Listed

This is a special transaction because with this type of deal you are going to resell the property immediately. If the real estate agent has the property listed, you will ask them to remove the listing from the MLS. They will still represent their seller, but it is very detrimental to have the property listed in the MLS because of the BPO. You need the BPO to come back as low as possible.

Tell the real estate agent that you intend to resell the property to a retail buyer so you will need to get the property listed with another real estate agent after the BPO is done. That real estate agent will represent you to find you a buyer. Ask the initial listing agent to prepare the contract for you to buy the house to get the property under contract. Make sure your double closing provisions are in the contract. Find another real estate agent to list the property for you once the BPO is complete. The list price should be a quick sell price and one of the lowest in the neighborhood. Ask your real estate agent what they can sell the house at in 30 days and list it at that price. You want to get a buyer as soon as possible.

Luxury Home – Property Not Listed

Instead of listing the property, ask the real estate agent to have this transaction be a FSBO transaction, and the real estate agent can be your buyer's agent. Once the BPO gets done, you will have the same real estate agent list the property for you as the seller to find an end buyer. You can use this same real estate agent for both the buy and sell transaction because the same real estate agent is representing the same party. You, the investor, are the buyer and the seller. A real estate agent cannot represent two different parties as represented in the previous example, where you had to use a different real estate agent to relist the property for you. You want to build a good relationship with the real estate agent, so you do not want them to risk losing their real estate license.

Scenarios – Buyer's Agent Finds Short Sale Agent to Work with You

Fix and Flip – Property Already Listed

Have your buyer's agent prepare the contract to buy the house and present it to the listing real estate agent. Make sure the price in the MLS is close to what the contract price is. Have your buyer's agent make sure the listing agent changes the property in the MLS to "under contract."

Fix and Flip – Property Not Listed

Ask your buyer's agent if they can pay the referring real estate agent a referral fee from their commission at closing and have you and your buyer's agent take care of everything from this point forward. If they don't want to do this, they can list the property and your buyer's agent prepares the contract. Again, make sure the price in the MLS is close to contract price and is changed to "under contract."

Luxury Home – Property Listed

Have your buyer's agent contact the listing agent to have the property removed from the MLS. Once the BPO is done, your buyer's agent will list the property for you as the seller. They will work on finding you an end buyer.

Luxury Home – Property Not Listed

Have your buyer's agent ask the referring real estate agent if you can pay them a referral fee at the time of closing. If not, have them get a listing agreement prepared with the seller that includes directions to not put the property in the MLS. Once the BPO is complete, have your buyer's agent list the property for you as the seller.

Chapter 14
Exit Strategies

Exit Strategies for Investors

I strongly recommend getting legal advice before starting a short sale. I am very familiar with Colorado laws; however, I am not as familiar with the laws of other states. Some state laws may allow you to sell a property immediately and possibly do a double closing. Other states, like Colorado, now prohibit reselling the property immediately if the Foreclosure Protection Act (FPA) applies. In Colorado, you must wait fifteen days before you can resell the property. So please, before reselling the property, contact a real estate attorney in the state you are working in to see if there are any resell laws that pertain to that state.

You should always know what your exit strategy will be before signing up any deal. In most cases, your exit strategy will be to wholesale the property or to do a fix and flip. With my business model, I generally use a short sale with the following exit strategies:

1. Fix and flip
2. Buy as a keeper
3. Buy and hold 90 days and then sell

I don't participate in double closings or buy and resell transactions. With the changing laws, it has become more and more difficult to do this. Short sale banks are demanding contract addendums to be signed that state "No flipping is allowed" and the property can't be resold for thirty to ninety days. Even if you do full disclosure, the short sale banks are still considering this fraud. I don't want to be investigated for fraud, so I always hold on to the property for 90 days before selling the property again.

Wholesaling the Deal – Varies State by State

The best way to do this is by writing up the contract in an LLC name that you want to sell to your end buyer. So make sure that you only write up one offer under that LLC name. You are going to get an approval letter with that LLC name. Next make sure you have a cash buyer lined up at a certain price. Basically you are going to sign all the buying docs. If you wholesale your deal, you won't have to use any of your own money. Your wholesale buyer uses their money to fund the transaction, and you keep the spread. Once the closing is done, you generate a document that says you are now selling your ownership interest in the LLC to your wholesale buyer. The wholesale buyer cuts you a check for the difference between what you bought the property for and the amount you agreed to sell it to him for.

*Note: In Colorado you could be in violation of the 14 rule. So you may want to do one of the following things:

1. Add your end wholesale buyer as a member of the LLC before purchasing the property. You can do this for a fee of around $1,000. This fee needs to be a non refundable fee. This buys their interest into the LLC. After day fifteen you can remove your membership interest in the LLC giving the full control of the LLC to

your wholesale buyer. Make sure that whatever spread was yours is given to you at this time. The spread is the amount you had under contract with the bank and the price your wholesale buyer agreed to purchase the property for.

2. You can have your end wholesale buyer become a lender on the property. They will lend you the money for fifteen days to purchase the property and then after day fifteen you transfer the title to your end buyer who loaned you the money.

3. Before you receive the approval, do an amendment to the contract to change the name to your wholesale buyer's name or LLC name. Your end wholesale buyer will close at your purchase price with the bank. Have an agreement in writing from your wholesale buyer that he will pay you $X,XXX for the wholesale fee or short sale negotiation fee. The $X,XXX amount is the amount you would have collected on your wholesale. Have your buyer write you a check for this amount at closing, before closing, or after closing.

Fix and Flip

This is a great way for flippers to get cheap properties and not have to have a bidding war with other investors on the MLS. Your deal may be on the MLS, but you are under contract or pending in the MLS, so all potential buyers go away. You buy the house the same way you would normally buy any fix and flip. Either you will buy it with your own cash, or you will get a hard money lender or private money lender, and they secure their note and deed of trust against the property.

Double Closings and Simultaneous Closings

Let's define the difference between the two so there isn't any confusion:

- **Simultaneous Closing:** This is where you have a closing back to back within the same day and you don't use any of your funds to close on the transaction. Your funds come from your end buyer; these funds get channeled to the mortgages to pay off their lien, and you keep the spread between what their payoff is and what you sold the house for.

- **Double Closing:** You can close in the same day, but you use your own funds and buy the house and then instantly sell the property.

Simultaneous closings used to be the popular way to go for investors. They could be in and out of a deal with no money and make a quick spread; however, the short sale banks have caught on and now require buyers to sign anti-flip agreements, or they include language in their approval letters that requires you to agree not to sell the house within "x" days. Some banks haven't started doing this yet, but in Colorado, effective January 1, 2011, double closings are illegal if the Colorado Foreclosure Protection Act applies. You must first purchase the property with cash and hold the property in your name or an LLC name for fourteen days before you can resell the property. The only other way to get around this is if you assign your contract to another person for a fee or you sell the other end person the LLC interest. It's going to be more difficult to assign your contract because you will need to get a new approval letter in the name that you assigned the contract to. This means you're going to have to give an excuse to the bank why the buyer suddenly changed. Hopefully the lender will agree to give you a new approval letter instead of closing the file. Selling the LLC interest is the best way to do this.

If you are doing a simultaneous closing using your buyer's funds to channel through to your closing, then this isn't an issue. You won't even have to come to closing with any money at all. (Only some states allow this. Please check with your state regulations or consult an attorney.)

Buy and Resell

You can buy and resell quickly and still make a decent spread. Just be careful not to break any laws. Once you buy the property, immediately get it listed for sale again at a much higher price. Or you can get the property listed immediately after the BPO has been done. Make sure your list price is lower than any other price in the neighborhood so you can sell the house quickly.

You will have a hard money lender or a private money lender funding your deal until you get the house sold. You will need to hold on to the house for two weeks to three months, depending on how you bought the property. If you bought the house and the homeowners were in the HAFA program, you can't sell the house for 90 days. If the bank had a clause that says you can't resell for 30 days, then you need to hold the property an additional 30 days. If you violate the bank's minimum hold time, you could risk having the money being wired back.

Don't break any laws! You don't want to be investigated for fraud and end up in jail. Violating these rules could mean jail time.

Short the 2nd, Bring the 1st Current and Take Subject to the 1st

Let's say the first mortgage has some equity, but the second mortgage is high. You can short the second mortgage to a few thousand dollars and then bring the first mortgage current and buy the property subject to the first mortgage. This means the first mortgage will still be in place on the property, but you own the house and you make the payments on the mortgage.

Some exit strategies with this route could be to do a fix and flip and not have to get a hard money loan. You would just need to keep making the payments on the first mortgage. Or, if you wanted a nice, long-term "keeper" property, you could rent the property for enough to make the mortgage payment and maybe a little more. This deal does require cash down to bring the loan current, but if you have the money and like keepers, this is a good option and a great way to long-term wealth.

Buy and Hold

Here are some possibilities if you just shorted a very nice house that doesn't need much work. If you have the cash yourself, you can buy it and keep it as a rental and have long-term passive income. If you are qualified for a loan, you can get a loan and cash flow the property. If you don't qualify for a loan, you can find another credit partner, and he or she can get the loan on the property and you both split the profits.

A common strategy we use is buying the property with a hard money lender and then refinancing the property with a portfolio lender. The hard money loan will need to include the purchase and rehab. This way when you do the refinance, you are out of pocket no money at all. But in order to do the refinance, you must qualify for a loan and have six months' reserves in your bank account for the property you are buying.

Lenders in Colorado who are doing these transactions for us are Pine Financial for hard money and Denver Mortgage Company for the refinance. Here is their information:

> Pine Financial Group
> Kevin Amolsch
> www.pinefinancialgroup.com
> (303) 835-4445

> Denver Mortgage Company
> www.DenverMortgageCompany.com
> (303) 763-7676

Successful Double Closings or Buy and Resell

It is very important to use proper disclosure when doing a double closing. The last thing you want to do is get into trouble and end up in prison for fraud. This is a very serious issue, and you want to make sure you do everything right.

Before doing a double closing, you need to do research on the foreclosure laws in your state. Colorado has a 14-day rule now regarding short sales. If you sell in 14 days or less on a short sale where the Colorado Foreclosure Protection Act is applicable, you must give full disclosure before you can resell a short sale property. Full disclosure must be given to the homeowner, buyer, buyer's lender, and short sale bank.

I highly recommend you contact an attorney for legal advice in each state in which you wish to do a double closing. In Colorado, I use Bill Goldberg. He can be contacted at (303) 320-3636, or email him at billgoldberglaw@yahoo.com. **If you are my mentor student or order my home study course, I do provide the disclosures. However, I do not participate in double closings or simultaneous closings.**

The best properties to buy and sell again are the higher-end properties. You can get a substantial discount on houses with a loan amount of $500K or more. The discounts are more substantial if the property has a large second mortgage. After the short sale lender approves a few thousand dollars to the second mortgage and the first mortgage is shorted a little, you end up with a house that has a lot of equity.

But you can also do this method with houses that need a lot of work. You can get a good discount on those because they need work, and if you happen to find a buyer who wants to buy a rehab or you sell to another investor, you should be good. Always use the state-approved forms on the A-B and B-C transactions.

You will need transactional funding in the middle to do this. This will cost money for holding costs. There are many transactional funding lenders out there. See if you can find one that will cover the costs up front and just take the profit on the B-C closing. Another thing you can do is see if they will partner with you on the transaction and split the profit.

Anti Flip Waivers from the Lender

GMAC has an anti-flip waiver. It says no flipping schemes are allowed and the property cannot be resold within 90 days. Below is a copy of GMAC's Anti-Flip Affidavit:

GMAC's Anti-Flip Waiver: Affidavit

State of _____

County of _____

Property Address:_____

Property flips occur when ownership of one property changes several times in a brief period of time. Property flipping becomes illegal and a fraud for profit scheme when a home is purchased and resold within a short time frame at an artificially inflated value. For the purposes of this statement, a short time frame is defined as a period extending ninety (90) days from the date of the short sale transaction.

BUYER represents, along with BUYER real estate agent, that I/ WE are not involved in a for profit scheme to flip the property and that there are no current agreements, written or otherwise, to immediately re-sell the Property at a higher price, and that no transactions of this nature will take place within ninety (90) days of the date of closing on the short sale transaction.

I/WE represent that there are no relationships between any parties involved in the transaction, including BUYER, SELLER, FINANCING COMPANY OR INSTITUTION, NEGOTIATOR, or REAL ESTATE AGENT.

I/WE understand that any information associated with the short sale may be made available to federal, state, and/or local law enforcement agencies for such action within their jurisdiction as they deem appropriate if illegality related to this short sale is discovered.

_____ _____
BUYER   Date

_____ _____
BUYER'S Agent   Date

_____ _____
FINANCING PARTY'S   Date
Agent
Subscribed and sworn to before me this _____day of _____
_____, 20____.
Notary Public
My commission expires: _____

Bank of America's Short Sale Purchase Contract Addendum

Bank of America also has a Short Sale Purchase Contract Addendum that needs to be signed by all applicable parties as well. A copy of this document is shown below.

Realtor / Broker Listing Agent Certification

Subject to and including the terms and condition contained in the attached Short Sale Purchase Contract Addendum Seller(s') Broker/Real Estate Agent_____ and Buyer ('s') Broker/Real Estate Agent _____ (hereinafter referred to as "Brokers") further acknowledge and agree as follows:

1. Brokers' hereby acknowledged and agree that Bank of America is not the property seller, but only the mortgage lien holder (s) or alternatively Servicer acting on behalf of the lien holder, accepting less that the balance owed to facilitate the Short Sale purchase transaction of above said property as an alternative to foreclosure. Bank of America is in no way responsible for Listing or Buyer Realtor / Broker sales commissions, since that is the sole responsibility of the property seller under the terms of the listing agreement.

2. Brokers hereby acknowledge and agree that Brokers are actively licensed and in good standing by the appropriate authority within the State that the property is listed for sale, or a licensed Attorney in good standing in the State where the property is listed for sale.

3. Seller's Broker acknowledge and agree that the subject property has been listed on the local Multiple Listing Service at fair market value to provide open market competitive bids to present to seller as per the terms of seller / agent listing agreement and that the marketing is in fact and "in spirit" seeking to maximize the selling price of the property.

4. Seller's Broker acknowledge that Seller has been presented with all offers to purchase home from this open market listing, and seller has selected the buyer of said transaction at the sales price terms disclosed and agreed to within the purchase contract.

5. Brokers' acknowledge and agree that there are no agreements, understandings of contracts relating to the current sale or subsequent sale that have not been disclosed to property seller and Bank of America as the mortgage lien holder or Servicer on behalf of the Lien holder.

6. Brokers' acknowledge and agree that Seller, Buyer or Brokers have not received, nor will receive directly or indirectly any form of compensation outside the official terms of closing as presented in the purchase contract and what will be presented in the preliminary and certified HUD-1 closing settlement statement.

7. Brokers' acknowledge and agree that they have disclosed to Bank of America any relationship to the buyer or ownership interest in the buyer's company, or represents that Listing Realtor/Broker has no existing business relationship with buyer.

8. Brokers' acknowledge and agree that there are no Dual Representation. Dual Representation is defined as a single agent representing both the Buyer and the Seller in the transaction giving rise to the underlying Purchase Contract.

9. Brokers acknowledge and agree that that any misrepresentation or omission may subject the responsible Party to civil and/or criminal liability.

Listing Broker/Realtor Agent: _____   Buyer('s')Broker/Realtor Agent: _____

State License Number: _____   State License Number: _____

Date _____   Date: _____

LMO-503 — SS Purchase Contract Addendum

Short Sale Purchase Contract Addendum

Dated _____ Bank of America 1st Loan# _____ Bank of America 2nd Loan# _____

Seller _____ Buyer _____

Seller _____ Buyer _____

Seller _____ Buyer _____

Seller _____ Buyer _____

This Addendum to Purchase Contract is entered into and is effective as of ___/___/___ by and between Seller(s) Buyer(s) Seller(s) Broker/Agent and Buyer(s) Broker/Agent(hereinafter referred to as "the Parties") and shall be deemed to amend, modify and supplement that certain Contract Dated ___/___/___ by and between Seller(s) and Buyer(s) (the "Purchase Contract")

NOW, THEREFORE, in consideration of the mutual benefits to be derived from this Short Sale Purchase Contract Addendum and of the representations, warranties, conditions and promises hereinafter acknowledged, Sellers, Buyers and Broker hereby agree as follows

1. The Parties acknowledge and agree that the Subject Property is being sold in "**as is**" condition
2. The parties acknowledge and agree that the seller may cancel this agreement prior to the ending date of the contract period without advanced notice to the broker, and without payment of a commission of any other consideration, if the property is conveyed via foreclosure to the mortgage insurer or the mortgage holder
3. The Parties acknowledge and agree that the Subject Property must be sold through an "Arm's Length" Transaction. Arm's Length means two unrelated parties characterized by a selling price and other terms and conditions that would prevail in a typical real estate sales transaction. No party to this contract is a family member related by blood or marriage, business associate, or shares a business interest with the mortgagor (Sellers)
4. The Parties acknowledge and agree that neither the Buyers, or Sellers, nor their respective Brokers/Agents have any agreements written or oral that will permit the Seller or the Seller's family member to remain in the property as renters or regain ownership of said property at any time after the execution of the Short Sale transaction. This includes if the seller is retaining a direct or indirect ownership or possessory interest in the property, and/or have a formal or informal option to obtain such as interest in the future
5. Seller agrees to vacate the subject property within _____ days PRIOR TO closing of the transaction OR Seller agrees to vacate the subject property within _____ days after closing subject to terms as shown on the purchase contract
6. The Parties acknowledge and agree that none of the parties shall receive any proceeds from this transaction except approved sales commissions
7. The Parties acknowledge and agree the purchase contract cannot have any provisions for Assignment / Assignee and / or Option to purchase. Bank of America will NOT approve any transactions with these sales contract provisions and any such provisions are expressly deemed unapproved
8. Buyer agrees that property cannot be sold or otherwise transferred within 30 days of closing. Or 90 days if transaction is approved under the Home Affordable Foreclosure Alternatives program (HAFA)
9. The Parties acknowledge and agree that upon Bank of America's request the Parties shall provide all material documents involved in the short payoff transaction, including but not limited to, the Buyer(s) and Seller(s) HUD-1 Settlement Statements
10. The Parties acknowledge and agree that this Short Sale transaction will not constitute appraisal fraud, flipping, identity theft and/or straw buying
11. The Parties acknowledge and agree that any misrepresentation or deliberate omission of fact that would induce the Bank of America, Investor or a Mortgage Insurer to agree to the terms of a short payoff which would not have been approved had all facts been known, constitutes Short Sale Fraud and may subject the responsible Party to civil and/or criminal liability
12. The Parties acknowledge and agree that this Addendum together with the **Sales Contract** shall constitute the entire and sole agreement between the Parties with respect to the Sale of the Subject property and supersede any prior agreements, negotiations, understandings, optional contracts, or other matters whether oral or written with respect to the subject matter hereof. To the extent that any term or condition contained within the Short Sale Contract is contradictory or inconsistent with this Addendum, the Parties agree that this Addendum shall supersede. No alternations, modifications, or waiver of any provision hereof shall be valid unless in writing and signed by Parties, FHA, VA, government agencies, any Investor, and/or mortgage holder, hereto

IN WITNESS WHEREOF, the parties hereby have acknowledged the terms and conditions contained in this Addendum as evidenced by the signatures appearing below

Seller _____ Buyer _____

Seller _____ Buyer _____

Seller _____ Buyer _____

Seller _____ Buyer _____

When signing Bank of America's Short Sale Purchase Contract Addendum, pay special attention to Paragraphs 7, 8, 10, and 11. These paragraphs point out the specific requirements pertaining to assigning or selling the property. If the requirements in this addendum are not adhered to, Bank of America will constitute the transaction as short sale fraud!

Bank of America also has a Realtor®/Broker Listing Agent Certification that must be signed. A copy of this document is below:

Realtor / Broker Listing Agent Certification

Subject to and including the terms and condition contained in the attached Short Sale Purchase Contract Addendum Seller(s) Broker/Real Estate Agent_____ and Buyer ('s') Broker/Real Estate Agent _____ (hereinafter referred to as "Brokers") further acknowledge and agree as follows:

1. Brokers' hereby acknowledged and agree that Bank of America is not the property seller, but only the mortgage lien holder (s) or alternatively Servicer acting on behalf of the lien holder, accepting less that the balance owed to facilitate the Short Sale purchase transaction of above said property as an alternative to foreclosure. Bank of America is in no way responsible for Listing or Buyer Realtor / Broker sales commissions, since that is the sole responsibility of the property seller under the terms of the listing agreement.

2. Brokers hereby acknowledge and agree that Brokers are actively licensed and in good standing by the appropriate authority within the State that the property is listed for sale, or a licensed Attorney in good standing in the State where the property is listed for sale.

3. Seller's Broker acknowledge and agree that the subject property has been listed on the local Multiple Listing Service at fair market value to provide open market competitive bids to present to seller as per the terms of seller / agent listing agreement and that the marketing is in fact and "in spirit" seeking to maximize the selling price of the property.

4. Seller's Broker acknowledge that Seller has been presented with all offers to purchase home from this open market listing, and seller has selected the buyer of said transaction at the sales price terms disclosed and agreed to within the purchase contract.

5. Brokers' acknowledge and agree that there are no agreements, understandings or contracts relating to the current sale or subsequent sale that have not been disclosed to property seller and Bank of America as the mortgage lien holder or Servicer on behalf of the Lien holder.

6. Brokers' acknowledge and agree that Seller, Buyer or Brokers have not received, nor will receive directly or indirectly any form of compensation outside the official terms of closing as presented in the purchase contract and what will be presented in the preliminary and certified HUD-1 closing settlement statement.

7. Brokers' acknowledge and agree that they have disclosed to Bank of America any relationship to the buyer or ownership interest in the buyer's company, or represents that Listing Realtor/Broker has no existing business relationship with buyer.

8. Brokers' acknowledge and agree that there are no Dual Representation. Dual Representation is defined as a single agent representing both the Buyer and the Seller in the transaction giving rise to the underlying Purchase Contract.

9. Brokers acknowledge and agree that that any misrepresentation or omission may subject the responsible Party to civil and/or criminal liability.

Listing Broker/Realtor Agent _____   Buyer('s)Broker/Realtor Agent _____

State License Number _____   State License Number _____

Date _____   Date _____

In addition to GMAC and Bank of America, Wells Fargo also has a Short Sale Contract and Short Sale Listing Addendums. Much of the verbiage in their Short Sale Contract Addendum is similar to the same requirements as Bank of America. Once again, please pay special attention to all the verbiage in these addendums. Full disclosure must be made. You do not want to be accused of fraud.

Funding Resources

If you have a great deal, you will be able to get money easily. If you have a difficult time obtaining money, you probably don't have a great deal. There are several funding sources nationally that will provide transactional funding in between the A-B and B-C closing. These national companies will fund even the high-dollar deals—for example, the million-dollar-plus transactions. Just Google "short sale transactional funding," and you will find many lenders who will fund.

If you are doing a fix and flip, there are hard money lenders just about everywhere. Go to your local investment club meetings; they usually have brochures for money lenders there. Or if you network, you will find many people attending the meetings who are small hard money lenders, or you may find individuals who want to become private lenders or partners. Always attend as many meetings in your state as you can. This is a big resource for finding money, birddogs, partners, etc.

Monica Adams

March 24, 2011

RE: Loan Commitment

To whom it may concern:

This letter is a commitment to finance Pink Real Estate. I have reviewed the borrower's credit and they are approved for a loan, this is a private money loan in the amount of $105,250 and the money is available quickly. We agree to supply the financing on the subject property located at 4994 Umatilla St Denver, CO 80221 as long as the following requirements are met:

    1. All pre-conditions of contract are met prior to close.

    2. Appraised value of subject property meets minimum criteria.

    3. Verification of assets.

    This commitment is void if the above requirements are not met.

    Please feel free to contact me with any questions regarding this commitment.

Sincerely,

John Doe
Mortgage Advisor

Pine Financial Group, LLC
10200 W 44th Ave #220
Wheat Ridge CO 80033(
303) 835-4445 | (303) 600-9688 fax
www.pinefinancialgroup.com

Chapter 15
Build Your Short Sale Business
and Make It Done for You

Building Your Short Sale Business and Your Short Sale Team

You should plan on starting small and working your way up. When I first started, I did everything myself. There are opportunities you can do without money and some that require money. Find a "birddog" whose job is to find you deals. They can be out knocking on doors every day for you, and maybe they can become a partner on a deal. You can tell them that if they find you a deal, they will get a certain percentage of the deal when it closes.

You can hire a short sale negotiator and pay them on commission. For example, you can offer them a commission of $750 if there is one lien on the property and $1,000 if there are two liens on the property, and they will be paid when the deal closes. The fees are paid by the listing or buyer's agent commissions. I pay them an extra $100 bonus if they get the bank to pay the short sale fee. You can also pay your negotiators an hourly amount plus a bonus for every approval letter received.

We also have a "birddog" who works off and on who goes door knocking for us to find deals. We pay them in one of four different ways:

- $100 up front and $1,000 when we buy the house
- $250 up front and $500 when we buy the house
- $500 now and nothing later (we prefer not to do this method)
- Or nothing up front and 15% of the profit when we sell

If you are actively marketing, you need someone to answer your phones or you need to be available to answer the calls yourself. Currently, we have a receptionist who answers all of our calls for both our brokerage company and investment company. We pay her an hourly wage, plus a bonus.

If you don't have the money to hire a receptionist, you can always use an answering service to answer your calls. Companies such as Voice Connect are good choices; however, live operators are expensive. They generally charge $1 per minute when they are on the phone with someone. These companies will send you an email that contains all the information you request them to ask for. Having this information allows you to do some research so you know what to sell them before you call them back. Once you get really good, you will instantly know what your exit strategy will be.

Building Credibility and Recognition

You should begin building credibility immediately when you start your business. Always do business in an ethical manner. The last thing you want to do is make a bad name for yourself and ruin your reputation. The first thing you should do is contact your local BBB. Get accredited with them right away. When you are working in the foreclosure business you will find that you compete with people who are not very ethical. You want to make sure these homeowners can do some research on you before they work with you. If they are able to check you out through your local Better Business Bureau, it will make you stand out from the others. Make sure you maintain an A rating and don't get any complaints from homeowners. Do everything you can to resolve any complaints right away.

The next thing you should do to make yourself stand out is sponsor a local charity. If you become a sponsor, you can use their logo on all your marketing pieces. This makes you look like a caring person who supports a good cause or the community. If someone has the choice to choose your business or another business like yours, they will choose your business because of your BBB affiliation and your support for a local charity because both of these will make a statement about your character and the nature of how you do business.

I sponsor the local Susan G. Komen for the Cure. With every closing, I donate $100 to the charity. I have a minimum contribution of $10,000 to them, but I get to use their logo on all my marketing. It has definitely made a substantial impact on my business.

When you finally make it to the closing table, have the homeowners write a testimonial for you and have your picture taken with them. These photos and testimonials help give you credibility and can be used in your marketing and on your website.

Another thing you can do is contact the local radio stations, newspapers, and news stations. Tell them what you do and how you help homeowners avoid foreclosure. See if they would be willing to write an article on your business. Use this article to your advantage. Put the article in your marketing and on your website to build your credibility.

Done for You Short Sale System

If you are looking for a short sale system that is actually done for you and is very simple, it is out there. You can actually run this business and not do anything but sign a contract, look at a house when the bank counters and show up for closing. It is really that simple.

Phase 1: Acquiring Deals

• Use real estate agents, birddogs or scouts to find the deals for you. If you choose to find a birddog or scout who wants to learn the business and is willing to find you deals, you can either pay them an upfront fee, or you can offer them a nicer profit when the deal closes.

• Train your bird dog to hunt deals for you and teach them the basics of short sales so they can more easily sell the deal. They can hunt for deals for you by door knocking, building relationships with attorneys who know people who need help or by working with real estate agents to find deals.

• Or, your birddog can meet with the homeowners to collect all documents and get the house under contract for a fee. This means no real estate agents will be involved.

• Or, you can have your buyer's agent go to the meetings with homeowners for you to collect all the short sale documents and get the house under contract.

• Or, if the property needs to be listed, have the agent be a transaction broker representing nobody—they are simply the paper shuffler for you to get the deal done.

• The real estate agent's job is to get all the paperwork together for the short sale and to negotiate the short sale for you. This is how they earn their 3% commission.

Phase 2: Negotiating

• Option 1: Your real estate agent negotiates the short sale for you.

• Option 2: You hire a negotiator to negotiate for you, paying them a bonus per deal when the deal closes. You don't need to pay anything up front. You can offer, for example, $750 for one lien and $1,000 for two or more liens, payable at closing. Or, if you have money and can afford to pay your negotiator an hourly rate plus a bonus, you can consider $12 an hour, plus a bonus of $150 for one lien and $250 for two liens.

• Option 3: You can partner with us on a deal and let my short sale team negotiate your short sales. We split the profit 50%-50% (see requirement for deal partnering).

• Option 4: Use a short sale negotiation company to negotiate your short sales. They usually charge a non-refundable fee of $250 and then $750 at closing.

• Option 5: You negotiate the short sale yourself for free (I must warn you this is very time consuming and not worth the effort).

Once you get short sale approval and get to closing, you now have a nice property you can either wholesale, fix and flip, hold, etc.

The only thing you have to do in this system is train ur birddogs to find you deals and possibly interview some agents who know how to negotiate short sales. You may need to provide additional training to the agents regarding list price, meeting with the BPO agent, etc. The better the agent does, the better success rate you have for getting your offer accepted and getting to closing. With this process, once you have your team in place and trained, you are out absolutely zero money, you do absolutely zero work, you collect a check and you are in a position to build your short sale business and manage your own short sales in-house. I highly suggest this because it gives you a better success rate.

Phase 3: Selling

- Use your buyer's agent to resell the property for you once the property has been fixed up.
- Or sell the house yourself as a FSBO.
- Blast an email out to buyer's agents and offer them a 4% commission if they bring you a buyer before the house is listed.

Investor Duties with Your "Done for You Short Sale System"

As the investor, you need to be in full control of your system. You should be doing as little work as possible. The investor's only duties in the short sale business should include:

1. Getting the business set up
   a. Registering your company name
   b. Getting a tax ID from IRS
   c. Opening up your bank accounts
   d. Marketing, if any

e.Ordering business cards

2.Managing your business

a.Hiring employees, birddogs, real estate agents

b.Making sure everybody is doing their job

c.Making sure there are no hiccups with the bank negotiations

3. Assessing the deal to see if it makes sense for you to buy

4.Getting all the document from your buyers agent for the short sale

5.Giving all documents for the short sale to your short sale negotiator

6.Planning your exit strategy

a.If it's a fix and flip, getting contractors lined up

i.manage the contractors yourself (or)

ii.hire a project manager to manage the contractors

iii. check on your properties once a week to make sure there is progress and pay the contractors once a week (or)

iv.hand the deal off to your fix and flip partner

b.If it's a wholesale

i.sending out an email to your wholesale list to get a buyer lined up instantly (or)

ii.listing the property with your buyer's agent who is now the listing agent for the transaction to find your C buyer

c.If it's a buy and sell

i.getting your hard money lined up

ii.getting your buyers agent to list the property right after the BPO is done to find a retail buyer to sell the house to

iii. making sure the buyer has done their inspection

and appraisal and has full loan approval before you purchase the property with transactional funding

iv. calling the buyer's lender to make sure they don't have low seasoning requirements—tell them how long you will be on title, or have your buyer's agent do this

7. Showing up to closing for one hour, signing documents and getting your check.

Why Do Investors Fail?

- They try to do everything themselves.
- They don't outsource.
- They spend all their time on the phone.
- They spend all their time on appointments.
- They haven't figured out a system to outsource.
- They don't leverage their time.
- No confidence, scared, analysis paralysis.
- They don't take action.
- They don't adapt to changes in the market, laws.
- They try to invest in too many things at once (sub 2, fix and flip, short sale, rentals).

The Importance of Building a Pipeline

It is very important you build up your pipeline, meaning the number of deals you are working at any given time. My pipeline consists of 110 active short sales. It will take time to build up to this level. The reason you want to build up your pipeline is because the short sale process does take time. If you have a large pipeline, you should have several closings per month so you have a steady cash flow coming in. This way if one deal is a little thin and you end up wholesaling it and only make $5K, it's ok because you will have other deals closing very soon. Once you build up a pipeline like I have, you will have several closings per week. By March 15th of 2011 I had already closed on 20 short sale deals since Jan 1st. That is definitely where you will be soon.

If you only add one new deal to your system every month and each deal can take three months to close, you won't have any cash flow. This is why it is very important to build your pipeline.

Starting the Business

Before you start your short sale business, there are things you need to line up and put into place first.

- **Determine a Company Name:** Pick a catchy name that sounds friendly, like you are there to help homeowners, or pick a general name you can use for branding yourself and making your business unique. Check with your state business registration to see if your business name is available. For Colorado, the website where you can check the name availability is: www.sos.state.co.us/biz/BusinessEntityCriteriaExt.do.
- **Register Your Business name:** Once you have a business name, you need to register it with the state. You can do this yourself or you can hire an attorney to do it for you. You can also conceal yourself so no one knows you own the company. Use someone else to be your registered agent to ensure your privacy. The cost to register your company name in Colorado is $50. The cost may vary depending on the state.
- **Tax ID Number:** Once you have registered your business name, you need to get a tax ID number from

the IRS. You can get this by going to their website: www. irs.gov/businesses/small/article/0,,id=102767,00.html

• **Bank:** After your business is registered and you have your Tax ID number, you need to open a business bank account. Choose a bank where you can establish a good banking relationship. I have gone through several banks, such as Chase and Wells Fargo, and have been very disappointed with the service and the excess service charges. I prefer community banks or local credit unions that work well with small business and don't charge high fees. You need to track all expenses through your bank account. We like to charge everything to our debit card.

• **Order Business Cards:** When you first start out, order the cheapest business cards you can find. There are several online printing companies that offer standard, inexpensive cards or give you the option to design your own. I recommend www.Uprinting.com. If you already have a template for the business card. If you don't have a template, www.VistaPrint.com is inexpensive and has great templates for investors that you can choose from.

• **Setting up your office:** You can deduct on your taxes part of your house as your office. So dedicate a room or rooms in your house to run your business. You will need to speak with a qualified tax professional to find out how much you can write off. You can possibly write up a lease for your business to rent part of the space in your home. You can possibly write off your utilities, cleaning the house, lawn care, etc.

• **Keep track of all expenses:** You want to write off

as much as possible to save yourself the taxes. I write off all business expenses like computer, software systems, upgrades, office supplies, mileage on my car, advertising, business cards, etc. If you can't make a loan to your new business to start the business, you should dedicate one personal credit card to be your business credit card. This is what I did to start. I tracked all my expenses with this credit card. It is probably a good idea to either learn how to use QuickBooks to keep track of all your income and expenses or hire a bookkeeper.

Your Power Team

You should have a Power Team for each area you plan to invest in. Below is a list of the people you want on your Power Team:

• **Real estate agents:** Work with several real estate agents in your area whom you can trust and who have a good track record, are motivated, investor friendly and hungry and eager to work with you. Use your real estate agents to find deals for you. They are doing their own marketing but need buyers for their houses, so they will become your best friends if they find deals and bring them to you. Real estate agents can also go door knocking for you as well for more deals.

• **Birddogs:** Find a group of "newbie" investors who are eager to learn the business and willing to go deal hunting for you. You want to get several birddogs lined up, and they need to agree to work for free or to partner with you so you don't have to pay them any money upfront. These people will need to have time to work for you.

- **Door knockers:** If you do not want to go door knocking yourself, you can use your real estate agents, birddogs or other people willing to door knock and find deals for you. You can pay them a fee for each deal you sign. If you do this yourself, it is absolutely free and very effective.

- **Short sale negotiator:** You need to find someone to negotiate your short sales for you. Short sales are time consuming, and you should not do them yourself. You can possibly use your buyer's agent to negotiate for you if they are experienced with the process. There are agents willing to negotiate for you for a higher commission. You can hire a negotiator and pay them hourly or on commission. I used to pay my negotiators on commission ($500 for one lien and $750 for two or more liens), and they were not paid until the deal closed. Currently, I pay my negotiators $12 an hour, plus a bonus of $150 for one lien and $250 for two or more liens. If you hire a negotiator but don't have enough business yet to keep them busy, you can also double them up as a personal assistant until your portfolio grows enough. You can also hire a negotiating company. There are negotiating companies and title companies that negotiate short sales; however, I personally do not think they do a good job. They charge you a deposit fee upfront and a fee at closing, and they are not consistent or persistent with their calls to the bank or their efforts to get foreclosure sale dates postponed. Or, you can partner with Pink and let my experienced short sale team negotiate your short sales for you and we can split the profit 50-50.

• **Personal Assistant:** You should hire a qualified personal assistant who can professionally handle your phone calls and marketing campaigns and be willing to run errands for you.

• **Answering Service:** You can use an answering service to answer your calls for you. I suggest using Answer Connect. They are affordable and answer the phone very professionally. If you let them know Monica Adams referred you, you will get a $50 discount on your first bill (and I will get a $50 credit)! The contact information for Answer Connect is below, and a sample call script is at the end of this chapter. You can use this script to create your own that is specific to your business.

---

www.AnswerConnect.com

Phone: Sales: (800) 525-1315

Client Services: (800) 531-5828

Fax: (800) 803-8486

Address: PO Box 80040, Portland, OR 97280

Email: Sales – sales@answerconnect.com

Email: Client Services –

clientservicesanswerconnect.com

• **Real Estate Attorney:** This attorney will represent you. You want a real estate attorney who is very familiar with the foreclosure process, short sale laws and sales contracts in the state you are working in. You want this attorney to understand and be familiar with the investor short sale double closing transaction. If you will be investing in more than one state, you need to find an attorney in each state you plan to invest in.

Be sure they clearly understand the nature of your business and what you plan to do, so you know that what you are doing is legal. If you ever do get sued, it is best to already have a retainer with an attorney.

• **CPA/Bookkeeper:** You should find a bookkeeper and CPA right away. Find one you like and think you will click well with. Don't use someone who will intimidate you or doesn't understand your business. This person will be doing your taxes and keeping your company books straight, so you will need a good working relationship. My bookkeeper is also my CPA. We have a lot in common, she understands my business and we refer new business to each other all the time.

• **Title Company:** Introduce yourself to several title companies and escrow closers to find out which one you want to work with. You want to work with a reputable one and be very loyal to them. Establish a close relationship with an Escrow Closer you like to work with. You will find this relationship very rewarding when it comes to needing HUD-1 statements, short notice closing dates or help with liens and property information.

• **Cleaning Service:** Find a reliable cleaning crew to clean the houses you plan to resell. Whether you are doing a fix and flip or you plan to do a buy and sell, you should have a reliable cleaning service clean your houses.

• **Plumber:** During the winter cold months, you will need a plumber who can winterize properties cheaply. While we try to get the banks to do this first, there are times when we need our own plumber to ensure the pipes won't freeze. Our plumber charges about $75 per house. This is very important because you don't want to experience the mess or the cost of damages if the pipes freeze and burst. We have had this happen to several homeowners' properties. The damages could amount to as much as $50K.

• **Staging Service:** Find a good real estate stager to stage your houses for faster resale. If you plan to do a fix and flip or a buy and sell again, you should stage your houses to get them sold faster. You can do prop staging on a fix and flip and lower end houses. If you are doing a luxury home you should do full house staging. You can Google "home stagers" in your area to find one. The cheapest route to go is to prop staging. Once you get more money, I recommend buying your own staging materials and having your assistant stage the houses for you.

• **Handyman:** Find a handyman capable of fixing minor repairs that are needed in order to get your houses sold. This is very important if you plan to do buy and sell transactions. You want to have one lined up if the buyers ask for minor fixes to pass their VA or FHA appraisals.

• **Locksmith:** You may run across times when you will have to have the locks changed on a house. Again, we try to get the banks to do this first, but that doesn't always happen. If your handyman can do this, great. But if not, having a locksmith as a friend will do you justice.

• **Sign Guy:** Hire a good sign guy to put together and put out your Bandit signs. You can usually get them to do this for $1 per sign. This is the rate in Colorado, and you can easily find someone to do this by posting a local ad on Craigslist.org. You may need to adjust your price for other areas where the cost of living is higher.

- **Inspector:** Find a home inspector who is inexpensive but does a good job at finding everything that might be wrong with a house. This is especially important if you plan to do fix and flip transactions. You want to know what you are getting into. They are also beneficial if you need to dispute the BPO or appraised value of a house. They must be able to provide you with a PDF color version report with pictures.

- **Appraiser:** Find an appraiser you can trust and who understands your business and knows values need to come in as low as possible. They need to be willing to work with you if you need to dispute a value on a BPO or prior appraisal that was done. They also need to be willing to appraise properties in "as-is" condition and as a distressed sale.

- **Bankruptcy Attorney:** You need to build a good relationship with a bankruptcy attorney to whom you can refer your deals and clients. They must be willing to do Orders of Abandonment on properties so you can close short sale deals if the client is in active bankruptcy.

In addition to all the people you need to make a successful power team, you also need to have a list of reference sources that you can easily access when you need information. Over the years that I have been investing and doing short sales, I compiled a list of websites that I frequently refer to for information and updates. Below is a chart that contains many of these websites. As you come across more reference sites, add them to this list so they are always at your fingertips!

Pink Short Sale Mentor	www.PinkShortSaleMentor.com
Pink Short Sale Mentor Forms	www.PinkShortSaleMentor.com/FreeForms
Making Home Affordable	www.makinghomeaffordable.com
Loan Look Up—Fannie Mae Investors	www.fanniemae.com/loanlookup/
Loan Look Up—Freddie Mac Investors	ww3.freddiemac.com/corporate/
Freddie Mac HAFA Program	www.freddiemac.com/singlefamily/service/hafa.html
Fannie Mae HAFA Program	www.efanniemae.com/sf/servicing/hafa/
Bank of America Short Sales	homeloanhelp.bankofamerica.com/en/foreclosure.html
Reporting Lenders—complaints and staying up to date on new laws and Regulations	www.HelpWithMyBank.gov www.occ.gov/customer.htm www.ftc.gov/bcp/edu/pubs/consumer/homes/rea04.shtm www.federalreserve.gov/pubs/foreclosurescamtips/defa www.hopenow.com
Skip Tracing Service	www.merlindata.com
No-cost Resources for Skip Tracing	www.theultimates.com www.Phonenumber.com www.switchboard.com www.anywho.com/ www.reversephonedirectory.com/ www.whitepages.com/ people.yahoo.com/ www.yellowpages.com
Mailing Lists	www.MelissaData.com
Fax Service	www.RingCentral.com
Answering Service	www.Answerconnect.com
Signs	www.SuperCheapSigns.com www.signstapler.com www.supercheapsigns.com www.webuyhousessigns.com www.banditsigns.com
Staging Homes to Sell	www.stagedhomes.com
Business Cards	www.Uprinting.com www.tasteofinkstudios.com www.vistaprint.com
Get a Tax ID #	www.irs.gov/businesses/small/article/0,,id=102767,00.ht
Running Comparables	www.dataquick.com www.Renav.com (Colorado only) www.homegain.com www.real-comp.com www.homeradar.com www.domania.com www.trulia.com
Construction Cost Calculator	www.get-a-quote.net www.constructionworkcenter.com www.nt.receptive.com/rsmeans/calculator
Foreclosure Reporting Services	www.equisystems.com www.public-record.com/market/foreclose.htm www.foreclosureaccess.com www.foreclosures.com www.mddailyrecord.com www.propertytrac.com www.foreclosure-report.com www.foreclosuretrac.com www.foreclosurereport.com www.foreclosuredisclosure.com
Public Property Records Info	www.publicrecordfinder.com/property.html www.publicrecordsources.com www.access-central.com www.real-estate-public-records.com www.searchsystems.net
Foreclosure laws search	www.realtytrac.com www.usfn.org
RENAV—Colorado's source for distressed property leads. Use discount code "Pink" for 10% off 1st month.	www.Renav.com
Short Sale Commander—Short Sale Software. Use this link to get your $49	https://sscommander.infusionsoft.com/go/sschp/pink

How to Partner with Others

You should find a partner who has something you don't have or has something you need. For example, a person with money but no time should partner with somebody who has time but no money.

Scenario 1: Person with Money (should be a 50-50 partnership)

Partner—They are in charge of providing the funding for your deal.

You—You provide the partner with time and leads.

Scenario 2: Person with Time (should not be a 50-50 partnership; they should get 10–15% for providing deals)

Partner—They are in charge of finding deals.

You—You provide the partner with finishing up the deal.

Scenario 3: Person with Time (50-50 partnership)

Partner—They can be in charge of managing the fix and flip.

You—You provide the partner with the leads and both split the money costs with a hard money lender.

Scenario 4: Person with Money and Time but No Deals (50-50 partnership)

Partner—They can fund the fix and flip and manage the fix and flip.

You—You provide the partner with the leads and keep feeding them to him to keep him happy.

Scenario 4 is my favorite person to partner with. My system is already set up so I don't do any work with my short sales. No answering phone calls, no meeting with homeowners, no negotiating. Once I have my deal, if partner #4 is available, I send my fix and flips over to him for a 50-50 partnership. This really is my favorite scenario because I have put absolutely no work and no money into this deal. I just get half of the profit after we sell the deal. We love this method, and our partner loves the partnership because he gets 3 times more deals this way and he doesn't have to go deal hunting. He used to get his deals by making offers on the MLS and going to the auction. But deals are so thin now that he isn't getting the deals he used to. This is a great partnership because the fix and flipper is getting deals he never got before, and the short sale person can just focus on bringing the good deals to him.

Warning: Make sure this person is a seasoned fix and flip investor who has done over 30 of these types of deals. You want to work with someone who has experience and knows what they are doing!

How to Partner with PINK

If you are interested in partnering with us on a short sale, please let us know. We are always happy to accept the following types of deals on a partnership:

1. Any fix and flip: If you plan on doing a fix and flip transaction, you must have a fix and flip system in place to go this route with us or, if you plan on wholesaling the property, we can do a partnership.

    a. House that needs work

    b. House that won't pass FHA or VA financing

c. Any ugly or outdated house

d. Any price range

2. If you plan to keep the house as a rental, any pretty house or a slight fixer-upper would qualify, as long as you can buy it at a price where the market rent will bring a positive cash flow. In order for us to partner on a deal of this type, you must qualify for a loan to buy the house and have a partner in place who can get a loan, or we can short the second mortgage and bring the loan current on the first. You must have the cash to bring the first current and pay off the second.

If you want to partner with us and you have found a deal you think will work, you can submit a completed Deal Partnership Checklist along with the required short sale package documents.

NOTE:

The most important criteria required to partner with Pink is Integrity! We do NOT partner with investors who are unethical, commit fraud or take advantage of homeowners!

See a sample of our Deal Partnership Checklist and the complete Short Sale Package Checklist for Agents and Investors on the next pages.

Create your own *'Done for you'* Short Sale System

DEAL PARTNERSHIP CHECKLIST

Please fill out this form and send us all the items on the checklist. You can submit the information to:

Fax: (888) 533-4917

Emai: Team@PinkShortSales.com

Main Office Number: (719) 471-PINK (7465)

Downloadable Form

Date:_____   Student Name:_____
Seller Names: _____ Marital Status:_____
SS Number:_____ SS Number: _____
Date of Birth:_____ Spouse Date of Birth:_____
Address:_____ LOW comps: _____
City: ST:_____ Zip:_____HIGH comps:_____
Mailing Address:_____Repairs:_____
Phone: (H)_____(W)_____BPO Target:_____
(Cell)_____ (Fax)_____SS Offer:_____
Email:_____MAX Buy Price._____
Is home (circle one)   VACANT   OWNER OCCUPIED RENTED
Type of Loan: (FHA, VA, Conv):_____
Who do we contact for BPO:
Name:_____Phone:_____
Actual/Estimated (Circle One)   SALE DATE: _____

1st Lender:_____ HOA Name: _____
Contact:_____ HOA Phone:_____
Loan #: _____ HOA Fax: _____
Phone: _____ Listing Agent's Name (if there is one):_____
Fax: _____Listing Agent's Company:_____
2nd Lender:_____ Listing Agent's Phone #:_____
Contact:_____Buyers Agent's Name:_____
Loan #: _____Buyers Agent's Company:_____
Phone:_____Buyers Agent's Phone#: _____
Fax: _____

293

Complete SS Package Checklist for Agents and Investors:

☐ Last two years of Tax Returns—must be signed
☐ Last two years of W2s (if you don't have, don't worry)
☐ Hardship letter—must be signed and dated
☐ Bank statements—last two months
☐ Pay stubs—last two months
☐ Mortgage statement from all mortgage companies
☐ Financial worksheet from lender—must be filled out
☐ Other proof of income (disability, SSI, retirement)
☐ If self-employed, business bank statements—last two months
☐ If self-employed, profit and loss statement—last two years
☐ Current utility bill
☐ Death certificate (if applicable)
☐ Personal representative info—Estate info (if applicable)
☐ 4506T
☐ Listing agreement or FSBO disclosure
☐ Authorization
☐ Confidentiality agreement
☐ Contract
☐ HUD
☐ O&E (title search, name and property search from title company)
☐ HAFA agreement (conventional only)
☐ Application to Participate (FHA short sales)
☐ Proof of Funds
☐ Low comps
☐ Contractor estimate
☐ Copies of any liens or judgments against the property
☐ Pictures (ugly and pretty)
☐ FTC disclosures

www.AnswerConnect.com – Sample Call Script

Below is a sample call script used by my company. You can use this script as a guideline and personalize your own script to meet your company's needs.

When somebody calls, please try to obtain the reason for the call and their name and number, and tell them we will call them right back. We are experiencing a high volume of calls.

Company Info

Company website for Pink Realty is: www.Pinkrealty.com

Company website for Pink Real Estate is: www.PinkRealEstate.com

Our company address is 2760 N. Academy Blvd., Suite 201, Colorado Springs, CO 80917.

Office hours are Monday–Friday 8–6. If they call after hours, we will call them back.

We are members of the BBB and proud local sponsors for Susan G. Komen Breast Cancer Foundation.

Phone number for Pink Real Estate is (719) 471-PINK (7465)

Fax number for Pink Real Estate is 888-630-9087

Email address for Pink Real Estate is Info@pinkrealestate.com

Phone number for Pink Realty (719) 393-PINK (7465)

Fax number for Pink Realty is 888-256-0766

Email address for Pink Realty is info@pinkrealty.com

If the caller asks for the following people:

1. If the caller asks for (first and last name here), transfer call to (phone number here), email is (email address here).
2. If the caller asks for (first and last name here), transfer call to (phone number here), email is (email address here).
3. If the caller asks for (first and last name here), transfer call to (phone number here), email is (email address here).

If the caller asks for the following people, please do not transfer the phone calls; please tell them we are not available and you will leave a message for us. Here is our contact info:

Emails for us: Monica is Monica@pinkrealestate.com and her phone # is (phone number here)

(Person's name here) is (email here) and (his/her) phone # is (phone number here)

Please tell them, "I'm sorry, (person's name) is not available at the moment. Can I please leave (him/her) a message and have (him/her) call you right back?"

Please transfer calls to the above three people only if it is an emergency situation.

Information to get:

1. Name
2. Number
3. Email
4. Reason for call

Caller got a letter or saw an advertisement TO AVOID

FORECLOSURE:

If the caller is calling to discuss a letter they received in the mail or to avoid foreclosure, please tell them, "Ok, let me take down your information and I'll have a representative who can help you call you right back." Ask the following questions:

1. Name
2. List all phone numbers where they can be reached
3. Address
4. Email
5. Are you currently in foreclosure? If yes, when is the scheduled foreclosure sale date? If no, how many months behind are you?
6. Who are your mortgage lenders? If there are two, list both.
7. What type of loan do you have? (VA, conventional, or FHA)
8. How much do you owe on each loan?

Again, tell them, "I will give the information to a representative who can help you, and they will call you right back."

If the caller asks to be removed from the mailing list:

Please get the exact spelling of their name and the address of the house that is in foreclosure. Kindly ask the reason they would like to be removed. Also tell them to allow two weeks for the mailings to stop because some of the mail may have been processed already for the following week. Tell them we apologize for the inconvenience.

If the caller is interested in a property:

Please tell them, "I will have the buyer's agent call you right back with the information." Get the following customer information:

1. Name
2. Phone number
3. Address interested in

If the caller would like to schedule a showing on a property:

First, ask if they are an agent. If so, ask to check the appointment contact on MLS. It should say Centralized Showings. If it does, tell them you will transfer the call to them. The number is 888-229-2208.

If it says to contact the agent directly, please transfer the call to the agent.

If the person is not an agent, please tell them you will have an agent call them back to schedule a showing. Get the same info above for callers interested in a property.

If the caller is a real estate agent wanting more info on a property:

Ask them who's listing the property and transfer the call to the listing agent.

Chapter 16
Putting It All Together

Congratulations! You made it through my "Done for You Short Sale" system. Let's take a look at what you have learned and where you go from here. First things first! We talked about the importance of changing your state of mind. Remember that in any aspect of your life, believing in yourself is the primary key to achieving your desired outcome. Thoughts do manifest reality, so believe in yourself and your success. Proceed with this challenge with confidence and a positive attitude and don't give up and you will achieve the success you deserve.

In this book, we took you on a detailed tour of every aspect of short sales investing. We provided the necessary information about short sales, foreclosures and foreclosure laws so you can help homeowners make the right decision for their situation. We taught you how to work with all types of homeowners and the benefits of partnering with real estate agents.

Step-by-step, you learned about the different types of short sales; how to prepare and submit short sale packages, successfully negotiate short sales and other property liens, work with lenders and deal with counter offers. We provided cost-effective marketing techniques to promote your business and showed you the best ways to build your business. You know how to find leads, screen leads and properly determine the right exit strategies. You have reference resources at your fingertips and the knowledge to build your own "Done for You Short Sale System."

Now that you have the tools and information, you are ready to start investing and negotiating short sales. Be sure to use this book as your reference guide to refer back to when you have questions or need to review a particular topic.

Remember: Laws and regulations change frequently, so stay updated on the laws and regulations in the state where you do business. You want to be an ethical investor, so follow the laws! When in doubt, always contact a good real estate attorney in your state. You don't want to get caught committing fraud.

While some of you may be ready to dig right in and get started, others may be feeling a little overwhelmed about exactly where to start and how to proceed. Facing a new challenge is a scary endeavor for anyone. When I was getting started I needed more help, so I took advantage of every opportunity available to learn more. If you are like me and need more help getting started or need to gain a bit of confidence, don't worry. Mentorship help is available.

Whether you are ready to get started or you want that extra advantage before you roll your sleeves up, I recommend taking advantage of one of my mentorship programs. Whether you take advantage of one of these programs now or later, they will enhance your knowledge and give you more experience.

We offer an in-class, three-day Boot Camp Mentorship Program several times a year in Colorado Springs. This class not only teaches you everything you need to know about investing and successfully negotiating short sales, it also provides real-life experience with live lender negotiations. Participating in an instructor-led program provides many benefits. The class size is small, so everyone has the opportunity to get their questions answered. There is the opportunity to discuss real-life scenarios from personal experience, and you get to meet peers embarking on the same career as you.

An added benefit to attending this three-day mentorship program is the personal help and mentoring you get after the class is over. Students get the opportunity to meet once a month for additional training and to discuss updates and changes in the industry, laws and regulations. Students can call, email or make an appointment to see me for any additional help they need or to get questions answered. They can also sign up for my newsletter updates to help stay abreast of the changing market. Taking this three-day Boot Camp Mentorship Program greatly enhances what this book teaches you and will give you that extra information and education edge you need to gain full confidence in yourself.

If traveling to Colorado Springs for the three-day Boot Camp is not practical for you, don't worry. There is a home study course available as well. This program provides the same great education and experience as the in-class, three-day Boot Camp program and offers the same benefits once you have completed the program. Students can call or email me for any additional help needed or to get questions answered. They can also sign up for my newsletter updates to help stay abreast of the ever-changing market.

These programs come with a 100% money-back

guarantee so there is absolutely no risk to you. You will be refunded your money if you are not completely satisfied with the program!

In addition to these programs, always take responsibility for your career and continue educating yourself on a regular basis. You can do this by attending any local investment meetings in your area and networking with other real estate agents and investors. Build a strong network of people in the industry. The more you learn and the more you get yourself and your name out there, the more referrals and leads you will get.

Additionally, Pink Real Estate and Pink Realty are now being offered as franchise businesses for investors who want to take advantage of my proven "Pink" marketing, branding and investing strategies. While both franchises are offered separately, having both a Pink Realty Franchise and a Pink Real Estate Franchise allows a higher level of cash flow. This is because you will always earn income from your agent's closings.

If you would like more information about the franchise opportunities that are available, please visit our website: www.PinkShortSaleMentor.com/PinkBusiness

Or you can call us directly at (719)-471-PINK or email me at Monica@pinkshortsalementor.com. We are here for you because we want you to achieve the success you want and deserve!

To receive your free downloadable forms, go to:
www.PinkShortSaleMentor.com/FreeForms

Go to www.PinkShortSaleMentor.com to get six free training videos. Stay connected with my blog and industry updates. You can also check upcoming classes and Boot Camp programs.

Monica's Home Study Course

With my home study course, I teach you everything you need to know about the short sale business from A–Z. Below is everything that is included.
Go to www.PinkShortSaleMentor.com to order your home study course!

Done for You Short Sale System – 6-Book Manual, DVD, and CDs (Value: $3,000 for only $997)

This six-book manual contains over 1,000 pages of the most comprehensive and straightforward short sale information ever compiled. Nothing compares to the incredible money-making strategies contained in this program, which includes REAL details to make REAL profits right now! Everything in the program is step-by-step, and no detail has been missed.

Done for You Short Sales Forms CD (Value: $500)

- All Short Sale Documents
- All Bank Docs
- All HAFA Docs
- All FHA Docs
- All Double Closing Documents and Disclosures
- Birddog Training

- HUD 1
- Contractor Forms
- Marketing Material
- And Many, Many More!

Done for You Short Sales Audio CDs (Value $300)
- This includes the whole Boot Camp in audio CD so you can listen in your car
- Live phone calls to the banks
- Live phone calls signing up deals

Done for You Short Sale DVD from 3-Day Boot Camp (Value $500)

The whole three-day Boot Camp on 9 DVDs

If you are ready to have the most comprehensive short sale home study course ever assembled in your hand right now, listen up!

If sold individually, the three components included in my Done for You Short Sales Home Study Course would total $3,000. But together we are offering an extraordinary discount: ALL of these components in one complete package for just $997!

That's Right—ONLY $997—You SAVE $2,303!!!

Monica's recommended services, and services she personally uses:

RENAVwww.Renav.com

(Use discount code "Pink" to get 10% off your first month.)

Renav.com is Colorado's source for distressed property leads.

• Search for REOs, Pre-Foreclosure, and PT Auctions

• Pulls data from all public trustee websites as soon as a house hits the foreclosure list

• Automatically notifies you of a new lead

• Search Pre-Foreclosures with your search criteria

• Look up houses sold at the Public Trustee auction in a given area

• Run MLS comps—this is awesome for those of you who don't have access to the MLS

• Notifies you whenever the foreclosure sale date has been postponed or a house has bid figures for the auction

• Ability to track the houses you want to track

• Auction Buyers—pulls up the list of houses going to auction with all the bid figures, assessor data, ability to order O&Es for $4, plus get a title commitment for the auction

Use this link to get $49 setup fee for free:
sscommander.infusionsoft.com/go/sschp/pink
Phone (800) 658-3420

- HAFA Simplified Wizard
- 100% web based
- Mortgage company database
- Mortgage forms library
- Auto-populated lender documents
- Document & photo storage
- Detailed task manager
- Full email & e-fax capability
- Automatic package generation
- Guest access ability
- BPO Builder to give to the BPO agents
- HUD-1 Generator
- Notify homeowners and agents instantly of updates

www.AnswerConnect.com

- **Answer your phone calls for you**
- **Send you text and email transcript of the calls**

Tell them Monica Adams referred you to get $50 off your first month!

Phone: Sales: (800) 525-1315

Client Services: (800) 531-5828

Fax: (800) 803-8486

Address: PO Box 80040, Portland, OR 97280

Email: Sales – sales@answerconnect.com

Email: Client Services – clientservices@ answerconnect.com

Index

A

B